Ripped Hearts Book 2

A Dark Why Choose Vampire Romance

Sasha RC

Independently Published

Ripped Hearts
Copyright © 2023 by Sasha R.C.
All rights reserved.

No part of this publication may be reproduced, stored in or introduced into a retrieval system, or transmitted in any form or by any means (electronic, mechanical, photocopying, recording, or otherwise) without written permission from the publisher or author, except for the use of quotations in a review, and as permitted by U.S. Copyright Law.

The unauthorized reproduction or distribution of copyrighted work is illegal. Criminal copyright infringement, including infringement without monetary gain, is investigated by the FBI and is punishable by fines and federal imprisonment.

Please purchase only authorized electronic editions and do not participate in or encourage the electronic piracy of copyrighted materials. Your support of the author's rights is appreciated.

This is a work of fiction. Names, characters, places, brands, media, and incidents are either the product of the author's imagination or are used fictitiously. Any resemblance to actual events, locales, or persons, living or dead, is entirely coincidental.

Formatting/Development/Editor: Melony Staab
Author Assistant/Development/Alpha Reader: Kaylea Fink
Illustrator: Bretnie Shepherd
Cover by: The Author Buddy

Author Note

Hello, My Fellow Readers,

This is a Dark Why Choose Vampire Romance. This book dives right in from the start. Some things within this book might trigger and be uncomfortable for some readers.

Please remember that this book does not follow the rules. This book is heavy on smut, which happens very early in these pages, the fated mate's trope, and breeding kink.

This book brings forth a different point of view on vampires and fated mates. Please know that this book does contain the breeding kink. The MFC does a dance, and it is sexual and can trigger some readers.

This book contains some themes and topics that may be hard for some to handle. Please make sure that you read **all** the warnings at the beginning of this book. Your mental health matters.

Please remember that this book is a work of fiction, and no true events occur inside these pages.

Please read the Trigger/Content Warnings.

Please do not use this book as a guide for BDSM. The acts in this book can be dangerous. Do not attempt these sexual behaviors without education and proper guidance.

Trigger/Content Warnings

This is a 'Why Choose' Dark Vampire Romance. This book has dark elements and themes, including psychological and mental abuse flashbacks.

Please be aware that chapters within this book are told from the Villian's POV.

Sexual scenes include Heavy BDSM. Bondage play. Knife Play. Blood Play. Impact Play. Chain Play. Candle Wax play. Breathe Play. Breeding Kink. Anal play, Water Breath Play, Gun Play. Group sex, Branding, Dominant Sexual Behavior, and Submissive Sexual Behavior.

Other dark themes and elements include Extreme violence, unaliving, and torture.

Criminal Behavior includes drug use, alcohol use, and distribution of drugs. Very obsessive, possessive, and jealous MMCs. Sexual Assault (not by MMCs) by ex-love interest. There is **NO** Rape.

Gas lighting, foul language, stalking, and offering of daughters (not sex trafficking) fated mates.

Mental and physical abuse in the present and flashbacks of the past.

Please remember that all sexual behaviors between the main female character (FMC) and the multiple main male characters (MMCs) are consensual, even if it does not look that way.

This is an MMFMM(male, male, female, male, male) type of romance. Please remember that it is 'why-choose,' meaning the MFC has multiple consensual love interests.

This book is **fiction**. There are no real events or people depicted in this book. This book is all **fantasy**.

I want to make it clear. I **do not condone** anything that happens in this book.

Please use caution. You know yourself best.

It is advised that this book is for mature adults over 18.

Please do not use this book as a guide for BDSM. The acts in this book can be dangerous. Do not attempt these sexual behaviors without education and proper guidance.

Lastly, I wanted to mention that my writing style is different. I do not focus on the outside world from the characters. I write from their POV, and a lot of what happens is from their perspective and written in their internal monologues. Please be aware that this is on purpose. Remember that you are reading about possessive, controlling, and jealous MMCs and a MFC that have been through trauma. Sometimes, their thoughts will be repetitive and may sound crazy or not make sense.

I do not write perfect characters. I write them as I see them in my head, including how they think, behave, and what they say internally.

These characters' love is **TABOO**, which means that it might not make sense to the reader. Things happen quickly, and sometimes, you may feel that there is no interaction between the characters. Please remember that this is all on purpose. This **BOOK** is based on the sexual connection and desire between the characters and **not focused on the world around them or senseless dialogue**.

You Have Been Warned

Special Dedication

Kay-Author Assistant/Development/Alpha Reader: Where to begin. You have been such an amazing, strong foundation for me. Thank you for being my North Star and walking side by side with me through this crazy madness called life. I appreciate you for all the hard work you put into being my AA and taking the time to read my books. Thank you so much for all of your suggestions. I want you to know that you are appreciated. Thank you for being you.

My ARC/Street Team: You are all so amazing. Thank you for signing up, promoting, reviewing, and always being willing to read my crazy stories.

To all my readers: Thank you so much for taking a chance and reading my books and diving into my crazy, dark, smutty romance world. I appreciate all of you and could not have made my dream a reality without you.

Mel-Formatting/Development/Editor: Thank you so much for everything that you do. Thank you for going through this crazy process with me. I appreciate you for all the long hours, hard work, and phone calls and for falling in love with my stories as much as I have.

Bretnie Shepherd: Thank you for being you, for staying up until 4 a.m. with me on the phone, listening to my craziness, and helping me come up with more crazy-ass ideas. Thank you for creating the chapter image and map for this book; you are absolutely amazing. I appreciate you so much.

The Author Buddy: Thank you for the 3-D graphics, all of the new covers, and for going on this crazy ride with me.

Acknowledgments

Jeff Christophersen: For being such an amazing husband. Thank you for always being willing to listen to my new ideas for books and helping me plot. You are my rock. Thank you for always cheering me on, believing in me, and pushing me to follow my dreams. I love you always and forever.

Karen Prosser: For being my best friend, my soundboard. Thank you for always being willing to listen to all of my new ideas for my books, giving me new ideas for more books, and helping me with the character names. I couldn't have done this without you. Thank you for being you.

Sunflower Downer: For always being there for me, making me laugh, and encouraging me to follow my dreams. Thank you for believing in me and always being there when I need you.

W.S.: You know who you are. Thank you for being one of my biggest fans. For helping me with cover ideas, book title ideas, character names, and plots and for keeping me on track. Thank you for encouraging me to continue to follow my dreams.

Jamie Williams: For being so inspirational. You are so amazing. Thank you for all of your support. Thank you for believing in me. Thank you for being my friend.

"*Middle of the Night*" by Elley Duhe
"*Nightmares*" by Two Feet
"*Bad Drugs*" by King Kavalier & ChrisLee
"*Play with Fire*" by Sam Tinnesz (feat. Yacht Money
"*Cravin*" by Stileto, Kendyle Paige
"*Body*" by Rosenfeld
"*Gimme Love*" by Rosenfeld
"*Make Me Feel*" by Elvis Drew
"*Desire*" by PCX Thousand
"*Do it for me*" by Rosenfeld
"*Gangsta*" by Kahlani
"*Say my name*" by Nello
"*I feel like I'm Drowning*" by Two Feet
"*The Devil and I*" by Nikki Idol
"*Watch me Burn*" by Michele Morrone
"*Ghost Town*" by Layto, Neoni

"Crazy in Love" by Sofia Karlberg
"The Best I Ever Had" by Limi
"Like u" by Rosenfeld

Welcome to The Born Kingdom

This Kingdom is ruled by the Guardians, also known as vampires in the human world.

This Kingdom covers the following States (and everything between them) in the United States: Arkansas, North Carolina, Louisiana, and Florida.

Kingdom Capitol is known in the human world as New Orleans.

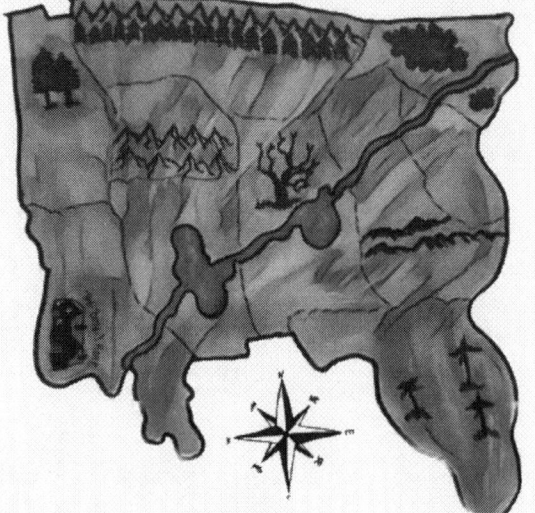

The Born Kingdom Guide

The Born – The Vampire world within the human world

Guardians – Vampires

The connection – The mating bond

The dance – The way the "Chosen Women" find their vampire mates

Dope – Drugs

Booze – Alcohol

Chosen Human Family – Families that have been chosen for their daughters to be mated to the vampires

Guards – The male humans that have been chosen to protect and serve certain vampire families

The Delucas – The main Mafia Vampire Family

The Rosettis – The rival Mafia Vampire Family

The Falcos – The enemy Mafia Vampire Family of both the Delucas and the Rosetties

Ace – Beta Wolf from the Blood Beast MC

Ashton – Cousin of the Deluca brothers

Enforcer – The character that protects, serves, and keeps things in line.

Night Walker – Werewolf

Starlight – Witch

Shadow – Fae

Touches – Gifts

Delicate – Empath

The Meeting – A neutral area where the different Paranormal Kingdoms and their inhabitants come together to discuss potential disagreements where peace is strictly enforced.

Please Read

Hello, my smutty dark romance lovers,

This is for those who love the sexy, tattooed, possessive, no-boundaries kind of men.

Inside these pages, I use the words *Fuck* and *Fucking* **A LOT**. They are, in fact, two of my favorite words.

I want to inform you that the words *Fuck*, *Fucking*, and any other lovely cuss words I use are not used for **dramatic effect.** This is the way me and my characters talk.

Have fun getting lost in this smutty fucking goodness :)

Lastly, I wanted to mention that my writing style is different. I do not focus on the outside world from the characters. I write from their POV, and a lot of what happens is from their perspective and written in their internal monologues. Please be aware that this is on purpose. Remember that you are reading about possessive, controlling, and jealous MMCs and MFC that have been through trauma. Sometimes, their thoughts will be repetitive and may sound crazy or not make sense. **I do not write perfect characters.** I write them as I see them in my head, including how they think, behave, and what they say internally.

These characters' love is **TABOO**, which means that it might not make sense to the reader. Things happen quickly, and sometimes, you may feel that there is no interaction between the characters. Please remember that this is all on purpose. This **BOOK** is based on the sexual connection and desire between the characters and **not focused on the world around them or senseless dialogue.**

P.S. I am not responsible for destroyed panties!!

1

Darius

Present Day

The fronts of our bodies connect for the first time since the connection started, and a jumbled mess of emotions and sensations hit me all at once. The heat from her body starts to seep into my chilled skin as I slowly start to thrust my hips driving my cock deeper into her tight wet pussy. Our fingers are entwined while we explore each other's mouths for the first time. Her back arched into me, pushing her breasts against my chest, and her hard nipples graze across me with each forward motion. Her pussy wraps tighter around my cock as I feel my balls starting to tighten from the wetness, the sound of our skin slapping together, her pussy muscles pulsing against my hardness, all of it driving me higher and higher. I have never felt anything like this before. The connection between us is getting stronger with each motion and moan. The pieces are slowly slotting together inside me.

I can feel the approval from the others as well as their happiness, anger, and extreme desire coursing through my body. Knowing their eyes are on Nellie and me as I allow myself to let go is the craziest feeling in the world. The feeling of being in control and completely out of control simultaneously. This woman is going to fucking kill me.

I pull back to look at Nellie, who continues to look into my eyes as she tightens her legs around my waist. She is giving me herself as much as I am giving her me. I can feel her, her heart, her soul. Our bodies are moving as one. I have dreamed of this moment a million times since my knees hit the club floor, but I never thought I would let myself be like this with her. Honestly, it wasn't her; I was trying to protect her from the monster inside me. Our kind is cruel, but I am different. I have always been different.

The thought of harming her or forcing her to do things killed me inside, but it was the only thing I could think of to keep my distance. It was easier for me to try and make her hate me than allow her to love me because I was afraid that when she found out who I was, I was fucking scared, scared that she would never look at me like this again. But Nellie is not like that; I know it. I have known it since what happened with Zayden at the club. The way her emotions went wild trying to find us, the way she felt pain rushing through her body from being away from us. I knew then that she would never judge me, not in how my mind was making it out to be inside my fucked up head.

My heart is racing so fast that it might jump out of my chest. Once again, everything is moving so fucking fast, my thoughts are trying to catch up. Nellie has consumed all of us, brought us together, and made us a family. A family I never wanted but have always needed. What a crazy fucking thought.

Zayden needs to die for what he has done and tried to do. He will not escape, but we will let him believe he is safe. We will even let him get comfortable with the thought that he has won and broken her, but in reality, he hasn't won shit. Instead, he has pushed us all closer together, and we are about to all go over the fucking edge.

But right now, it is all about her, and it is time for all of us to worship her together, just like it should have been from the beginning. I never should have acted the way I have to her. She didn't deserve for me to treat her like she didn't matter, to treat her like some whore I didn't care about.

I thought it would be easier for me and her and everyone else if I just fucking kept my distance and did my obligation, continued my bloodline, and moved on, but now I realize I was a fucking fool. It would have never happened that way, I fucking tried to force it to, and it almost fucking ripped us all apart. I felt the way it was affecting Nellie, Loyal, Neo, and Christos. They were trying to be patient with me, but finally, Neo broke and broke me. It had to be done; I know this.

I feel her hand cup my cheek, bringing me out of my impending thoughts that I would stay in forever because I can never fucking seem to get out of them myself, and pulling my attention back to where it needs to be. I press into her and stop for a moment. My new young heart stops as I close my eyes and take a deep breath. She isn't my ex. She isn't my ex. I feel an overwhelming urge to pull away from her and put some distance between us, but I don't. I stay still, trying to calm myself down as my ex's words come crashing into my head.

"Darius, look at me," Nellie whispers.

I slowly open my eyes and am met by her glistening green eyes staring back at me with desire, love, and understanding. Three things I never thought I would ever feel from another person, let alone feel towards someone. I never believed that I was worthy of a mate or someone loving me, not after what happened to me, but Nellie has started to put my pieces back together. She has crashed down my defenses and has such a tight hold on my heart and soul that I know I would fucking die without her.

"I'm looking, Nel," I whisper, sweat rolling down my back.

She doesn't shy away from me and doesn't look at me with disgust. Where the fuck did she come from? How can she act like this after what that fucker has done to her? How can she look at me like this, touching me like this after what I have done to her and what I made her believe I wanted from her?

I am so in love with this woman it fucking hurts. "Stay with me, Darius," she begs.

"I am right here, angel," I whisper back, shaky.

I can do this for her and stay here with her. I slowly start to move in and out of her again, feeling her wet pussy quiver around my cock, pulling me in further. She lets go of my hand, wraps her arms around my neck, and pulls my head down. I lower down to my elbows on either side of her head and curl my fingers into the covers beneath us, even though I want to touch her everywhere. This time, I will let her lead; this time, I will submit to her. I can hear the others behind me, but right now, all of my focus is on Nellie and Nellie alone. Since the beginning of being mated to her, I have treated her like a piece of trash, no fucking more.

Our lips come together once again, and she opens her mouth, allowing our tongues to dance as I pick up my pace, our bodies moving together. I need to feel her, to hear her scream and moan my name. I pull back, breaking the kiss, and she exposes her neck to me. I run my nose from her jaw down her neck, nipping and kissing my way until I get to the sweet spot where I can see her pulse beating in her neck. I lick the area before I bite down, and at the same time, I start thrusting into her like the wild animal that I am. She screams out my name as her pussy gushes around my cock.

Her blood enters my mouth, making me groan. Her blood tastes like fucking sweet honey. I have never tasted blood like hers before. Her emotions crash into me, all of it anger, rage, desire, longing, love, fear, all of it hits my fast-beating heart. My heart matches her beats, reminding me that she belongs to us, and we belong to her. We have always belonged to her, even me, even when I fought against it, and her. She had me from the moment my knees hit the ground at the club.

I slowly open my eyes and feel Nellie in my arms, I don't know how long we were fucking for, but I know it was long enough that Nellie passed out. Once I started, I just couldn't stop. I think it is partly because I was trying to make up for lost time, but we have the rest of our lives. I have the rest of my life to get lost in her and her tight pussy.

I just fucking can't get enough of her. I was so fucking foolish and stubborn. Holy fuck, the entire time could have been the way it was last night. Now that I have had her like this, I will never be able to get enough.

I look down, Nellie's head and hand are resting on my chest, and her legs are intertwined with mine. I lean down and gently kiss her forehead, a gesture I have never done before, but I have a feeling this woman will make me want to do many things I have never done before.

I slowly and gently move her off my chest and onto the pillow, which she snuggles into as I pull the blanket over her and tuck it around her. She is so fucking beautiful. I feel like I am seeing her for the first time since my knees landed on the floor in the club. I was hers, and she was mine, and from that moment on, I have felt a pain in my chest, a pain that was pushing me towards her.

The wounds from my ex are so fucking deep, but slowly Nellie is helping to heal them, and soon they will be nothing but a scar, a scar I can move on from. Knowing my ex, she forgot about me the moment she walked out of the door. Even without a beating heart and soul, she ripped me completely apart. Then Nellie came into my life, and she got the anger, rage, and violence from me, which she never deserved, but she took it anyways. She took it because she didn't have a choice. After all, I didn't fucking give her one.

Just like Zayden didn't give her a choice, knowing that he and I were monsters to her in different ways makes me want to throw up. This whole feeling emotions thing is going to be a struggle. I have never been able to express myself in healthy ways; none of us have. I think it is another curse of being what we are.

I pull my eyes off her and get out of bed. I can hear the rain pelting against the windows; it is really coming down hard today. The weather outside feels like the storm that is brewing inside me right now; wild and out of control.

I walk into the bathroom and step into the shower, turning the water on and letting it rush down my back while I press my hands against the wall with my head down. My heart is finally fucking steady and stable.

I feel arms wrap around my stomach and lips against my back. I know who it is.

Neo.

I take a deep, shaky breath as I close my eyes and allow myself to feel his touch, his lips against my skin.

"You did good, Dar. You did real good," Neo praises me, making my dick move. He knows me without knowing me. How the fuck is that possible?

I lift my head, drop my hands, and turn around in his arms. He is as tall as I am, and when I turn, our eyes lock, and I lean against the wall. I grab onto his naked hips. His eyes search mine.

"What do you see when you look at me?" I ask. My heart stops waiting for his response.

A small smile forms across his gorgeous fucking lips, "I see you," he whispers back.

I feel a rush go through me as I tighten my grip on his hips and pull him against me. He plants his hands on the wall next to my head as we both lean in, and our mouths crash together, exploring each other.

I was not ready for Nellie, and I was certainly not prepared for Neo.

But both of them complete me in every single fucking way I am missing.

2

Loyal

I make my way down the hallway into the front room, where Ashton watches things. Since what happened with Zayden yesterday, Ash has been on guard. He is annoyed, enraged, and concerned about how far this human will go to get Nellie. I share his concern, I want to go hunt down Zayden and rip out his fucking heart, but until Nellie gives me permission, I will not fucking touch him. She has had so many choices taken away that I refuse to take any more from her. When she is ready, she will give us the go-ahead, and once that happens, Zayden will fucking suffer. But until then, we will do our best to keep her safe and protected and remind her that we are all fucking in.

"Hey Ash, how are things going out here?" I ask.

"Everything seems quiet. The men are in constant rotation around the perimeter and watching the cameras for anything out of the normal," Ash replies.

"Perfect. How are things on the business end? Anything that I need to know about?" I inquire.

"I'm staying on top of everything. Profits are up from last month. It seems the combining of families has made a positive impact all around the board. I haven't heard of any unrest on the streets either, so that is a good sign," he reports.

I nod. "Hey, thank you for taking all this on for us while we are...well, you know," I laugh.

"No need to thank me, Loyal. I am happy you guys found your mate, and I know that if the shoe were on the other foot, you would also have my back. I will let you know if anything unexpected comes up," he says with a smile.

"Alright, well, I will leave you to it," I say as I turn to head to the bedroom.

This started as a responsibility to continue our bloodlines, but it is something completely different. It has taken us all by surprise, but I guess that is what is supposed to happen with love, or at least that is what I have heard over the years. Our love for Nellie is not the same as humans feel. It is more profound, intense, and unhinged, making us possessive and dominant. We take everything to an extreme level. She will be consumed by us as much as she consumes us.

There is no escaping each other, not now, and I will not let some fucking human take her away from us. He has tried to break her, convince her that he loves her, but he has no fucking idea what that word means. We will show her what true love feels like, and we will replace every fucking memory she has of that disgusting human. He will not win, and he will not get what he fucking wants. He will have to kill all of us to fucking have her, and I will not let that happen, either.

We took the first step last night, bringing her to the pool house. This is where all of our deepest, darkest sexual kinks will be exposed to her. This is the one place where we do not have to hide our true nature, a place where we can take off all of the masks we have to wear on the outside, and we will become fucking naked in every sense of the word. She will be able to explore what she likes and dislikes sexually as we bring her own desires to the surface, ones that she doesn't even realize she has.

I walk into the bedroom just as Neo and Darius come out of the bathroom together, wearing a towel, and I can't help but shake my head and smile. I have never seen Darius like this. He has been guarded from the beginning with all of us, even his brother, but we all saw something change in him yesterday. I can't put my finger on it just yet, but he has changed. My brother has that effect on people, though. Neo has something about him that draws both humans and Guardians in, like heat from a flame.

Neither of us knows the whole story regarding Darius' ex, but I can tell that that woman destroyed him in a way that I didn't know was even possible with our kind before receiving a soul and a beating heart. That woman was a fucking bitch. What she did to him, I don't know if it will ever be able to be undone, but I can see that Nellie and Neo are both helping him heal in their own way. Darius is letting them in slowly, but he is, and at the end of the day, that is all that matters. He is finally allowing himself to feel the connection that brought us, Nellie, and the connection that will bring us all together as one.

I understand why he is the way he is. We all have things that have happened to us in the past that cause us to be guarded, but if he continues to let his past keep him from Nellie, it could eventually cost us her, and I know he doesn't want that. I know that he loves her; we have all seen it now. He can't take it back, and it doesn't look like he wants to. We are making progress, and we are going in the right direction.

Last night was both amazing and completely out of fucking control. Zayden took things too fucking far, but the night ended with us watching both Darius and Nellie giving in to each other. It was beautiful to watch, and it was just the beginning. The door has now been opened, and we can't fucking let it close.

I make my way over to Nellie, sitting on the end of the bed with her legs crossed and wearing one of my t-shirts. This is the first time I have seen her carefree, smiling, even laughing. Christos is kneeling in front of her with his hand on her knee. They stop and look at me as I walk towards them with coffee. I pass one to each of them, and Neo and Darius come to my side and grab theirs.

Yes, we do love coffee and many human foods; people just don't know it. The normal human world has this weird conception of who we are, but almost all of their visions of us can't be farther from the truth, and it makes us laugh when we see movies or books trying to explain who we are. I don't know where they got their facts about our kind, but it is all wrong. We stopped correcting humans a long ass time ago, so if they want to see us as bats, can't go out in the sunlight, hate garlic, and whatever other shit they have come up with, that is fine by us.

I sit next to Nellie, lean in, pressing a kiss on the neck, and she moans into her cup, making all of us stop what we are doing and focus our attention on her. Blood rushes to my dick, holy fuck, all she has to do is let out a noise, and I am fucking melting inside. All she has to do is allow me to see her like this, open, vulnerable, and it is the most beautiful fucking thing I have ever seen. There are no words to explain what I see when I look at her fully, but I can say I see our future in her.

I pull back and take a sip of my coffee, keeping my eyes on Nellie. She will always be the center of our attention. I know that it makes her feel out of place, knowing that she is the most important thing to all of us, but she better get used to it because, if anything, it will only get fucking worse, in a good way. The more time we spend with her, the harder we will fall; it is just how it works. What we have shown her so far is just the fucking beginning, and in the end, she will be consumed by all of us, just like how we are already fucking consumed by her.

"What happens now?" She asks, looking at each of us.

I want to answer her entirely, but I don't know if she is ready to hear what we want to do to her and what we want her to experience. It is not something I know how to put into words; plus, it will be more fun to show her than to tell her. Letting her experience our love for her will always be more exciting than using words. Our kind has never been good at fucking words, it is something we need to work on so we are able to explain how we are feeling, but it will take time.

"It is time we show you what it means to be ours, sweetness," I say softly.

She has no idea, and I don't think any of us know how fucking crazy this is about to become. There is one big thing that we keep from the Chosen Humans about the connection; we keep it our secret until we find our mate. When the mate is ready and has entirely given in to her Guardian or Guardians, there is a period of a week or weeks, depending on how many mates she has, where the Guardian or Guardians show their mate their sexual kinks and bring out the women's sexual kinks and desires.

Nellie will spend the next five weeks experiencing each of our kinks, but it doesn't stop with just Nellie. Each week, one of us will take the lead in our designated rooms, and once he shows her his kinks, the other three will also participate and explore with Nellie in that room. This will continue until the fifth week, which will be used for Nellie to show us what kinks and desires she has discovered in herself, and we will all experience it all together as one.

This part of the connection is vital, and usually, the woman will become pregnant with her first child during this time. This stage we are about to enter will change our relationships even more, if you can believe that shit. This part of the connection will also finalize the bond. Once the bond is completed, more secrets will come out and be shared with Nellie, knowledge that will help her understand us a little better. Like I said before, this is when we will take off our masks and show her who we really are. We can only hope that she will not turn us away, but from what I have observed with Nellie, she doesn't seem like the type of woman who would turn away from us, not after what we have been through this far.

"I thought you had already shown me that," she says with amusement. Oh, this woman.

I love her innocence, and we all crave and need her, and we are ready to show her everything. She thinks we have already shown her, but we haven't. We have been holding back, and soon, we won't be able to, and she will see what being our mate really means. Fuck, I can't wait. It is going to be fucking magical.

I slowly shake my head and smile. "Nope, that was just the tip of it. We have so much to teach you," I confess to her. My voice filled with desire and need.

She nods and takes a sip of her coffee. I hear her heart rate increase when I wrap my arm around her and pull her into me. I don't like her feeling anxious or nervous with us. I have a sinking feeling, though, that her negative emotions have nothing to do with us, which stirs up my own fucking unhinged emotions.

The fucking human is becoming a fucking thorn in our damn sides, and it is almost time to fucking remove him permanently.

"What's wrong?" I ask calmly.

"Zayden," she whispers, lowering her cup into her lap.

I take a deep breath and look at my brother. He is standing next to Darius, and they are all looking at me now. Fuck man, I wish I had the answers, but I don't. What we want to do and what the right thing is are probably entirely different things.

"Don't worry about him, sweetness. We will not let anything happen to you," I confirm.

"I know. I trust you guys," she says confidently.

Her words warm my heart, warm my entire fucking body. I pull her against me more, and she gently lays her head against my shoulder and takes another sip of her coffee. The sooner we complete the connection, the sooner we can deal with Zayden and ensure he can never hurt us or Nellie again.

3

Neo

I push the club doors open with Darius right at my side as we make our way back to the office. The club does not open for a few hours, but the employees are busy getting things ready. I take a minute and look at the stage that brought all of us to our knees. I will never forget that moment.

Since then, so many things have changed, and as time goes by, more and more things continue to change. Things continue to get more unhinged and out of control in good ways and bad ways. Honestly, we are just trying to keep up with everything. There are so many moving parts it is insanity, but I know as long as we all have each other and work together and not against each other, everything will work out and be fine.

The whole Zayden situation is always in the back of our minds, but we will deal with him in due time. There are other things we need to make sure we take care of first to be ready to fucking deal with him and whatever fucking mess he is trying to make for us. I don't know why he thinks or believes that what he is doing will get him Nellie, but he is fucking nuts. I have been trying to understand his logic, but I still don't get it. You would think he would want to win her over from us, not fucking scare and force himself on her, but I guess he is one of those humans that make no logical sense. If he thinks he is going to take her from us, he has another thing coming.

The following five weeks are going to be absolutely insane. We will not leave the pool house until we complete the connection. All of our kinks will be experienced together, and at the end of the five weeks, the goal is that Nellie will be pregnant with one of our children.

This time will be one of the most important moments for all of us who are involved. Our father will be controlling everything in the clubs and on the streets while we are locked away in the pool house. We don't need any distractions, so the goal is to make sure that everything is set up because, come Monday, we will all be busy with Nellie, and it is crucial that we are not disturbed.

Keeping that fucking human away is at the top of our list. Ashton will be keeping watch at our house, and our father and other

Guardians will be watching at the clubs and on the streets. The goal was to find Zayden and lock him up until we figured out what the fuck to do with him or, better yet, what we decided to do to him, but so far, he has gone into hiding, and we haven't been able to find him. It is making us all nervous that the fucker is hiding. He is more intelligent than I thought he was. We don't know what he has planned next, but so far, all of his attempts at Nellie have failed, and we are going to make damn sure that it fucking stays that way.

We were supposed to meet my father sooner, but everything with the fucking human has made things a little more complicated than we planned. Our kind prides ourselves in being prepared, and fuck, man, we never fucking saw Zayden coming. We have heard of humans standing up to Guardians for a woman before, but nothing like this, and even though no one is saying it to our faces, we know there is talk going around. Talk that we need to make sure it doesn't fucking spread further.

The Falco brothers are just waiting for us to become weak, and this human is showing everyone just how vulnerable we are when it comes to Nellie. We need to ensure that all of us are protected and prepared for the Falco brothers to try and take what belongs to us. They are patient fuckers, and they have been waiting for centuries to see our family fall. But in order to make sure that my brother and I take things over, I know I need to meet with my father to go over a few things. It was hard leaving Nellie; neither I nor Darius wanted to leave her, but I know she will be safe with Ashton there, and she is spending time with

Loyal and Christos, which is needed. We all want to spend time with her and have her attention, but we also need to find a balance, and my being selfish with her will not help anything or anyone.

I make my way into the office and see Father standing and looking out the window with his hands behind his back. Our Father has always been observant, and that is how he built and maintained our Kingdom the way it is right now. But most of the time, he looks lonely, except for when he is with our mother. He doesn't let her out in public that often because if our enemies wanted to take us down, they would just have to go after her. She is the one thing that will bring our father to his knees. Our mother is one of the most important mates to our kind, and I know my Father will not take any fucking chances with her getting killed or taken.

He slowly turns around and looks at me. Darius stops at my side, making my heart race. The relationship between Darius and Nellie has changed, but things have also changed between him and me. We are drawn to each other, which is normal when you have a sexual connection with someone. Darius was the one thing I didn't see coming, but I am grateful for him and excited to see how things proceed from here. With our kind, I know it will be fun and crazy, just like everything else.

"It is nice to see you two are getting along," my father says calmly. He has always wanted to combine families. Combined families mean more power and control, but most do not know the other side of my father. Since his heart started to beat for my mother, he has changed.

He is not as cold and ruthless as he was before, or that is what others tell me. But he can still have his moments when he has to.

My father has had to deal with a lot over the years, ensuring that everything is going how it should with everyone. He would never say it out loud, but I know he is getting tired. I can see it in his eyes.

"Yes, you can say that," I say with amusement.

"This human thing is becoming dangerous, Neo," my Father says with disapproval. My father has always feared that the humans would try and stand against us again, but this time, it won't get that far; we won't let it.

We would be stupid to act as if Zayden is not dangerous. The things that he has been doing to Nellie, to all of us, will spread to the rest of our kind that we have a problem. And that type of information will only create more problems. Zayden has proven to be dangerous, but so are we. Once the connection is fully made, it is us that he will fear. He has been running, which honestly is the smartest thing he has done thus far.

"I know, Father. We will handle him after the connection is fully bound," I confirm. I know he needs assurance that we have a plan. We might not have a complete plan, but we will deal with it. Zayden will not be able to hurt our family.

"I will watch the clubs and streets until the five weeks is up, but after that, you and Loyal need to take charge and find this fucking human before he does something stupid that will affect all of us," my father says, keeping his eyes on me.

I nod. "We will, Father. I promise."

A smile forms across his lips. "Very well, son, I will leave you to it then. The paperwork is on the desk, and everything you need to know is on the laptop," he says calmly.

I nod and give him a small smile.

"I am proud of you and your brother. To see you working alongside the Rosettis for your mate brings me much joy," he says with pride.

"Thank you, Father," I say softly.

"Remember, the most important thing is your mate and each other. Everything else comes second, even the business," he warns me.

"Understood." That is the only word I can say.

I can tell by my father's tone he is serious, and I believe him. He needs to say it more for himself than for me, though. He says that a lot. I think it is his way of reminding himself of his own words. He looks at Darius and nods as he walks across the room, resting his hand on my shoulder for a moment before leaving and shutting the office door behind him.

I slowly make my way over to the desk and lean against it. My heart races with my father's words, but he is right. The most important things are Nellie and each other. Darius makes his way in front of me, standing still, keeping his eyes on me.

"What do you want, Neo," Darius asks darkly.

I stand up and walk into him, our chests touching. I run my fingertips up his arms, leaving behind goosebumps. I love the way he feels and responds to my touch. He doesn't know what I see when I look at him, but I see my future. He and Nellie complete me, bringing out something different in me, and I am craving them both.

"I want you to be a good boy and get on your knees," I say through gritted teeth. My heart races with my command.

Darius nods as I sit back on the edge of the desk. I grab tightly onto the edge as I watch him slowly kneel in front of me.

"And now," he asks in almost a whisper.

"Unbutton my pants," I demand, trying to control my desire and need for him.

He lifts his hands and does as he's told, making my dick throb in my jeans. He unbuttons them and looks at me, waiting for his next command.

"Pull them down with my boxers," I whisper to him, hearing the craving in my voice.

He slowly pushes my clothes to my knees and grabs onto my hips. I let my head fall back and close my eyes as he gently kisses my lower stomach and makes his way to my dick. I open my eyes, look down at him, and watch him take my hardness into his hand. He looks up at me as he licks the bead of cum from the head before he wraps his lips around me, sucking and running his tongue along the length. He takes me fully down his throat and swallows, making my balls tighten and a moan fall from my lips. I tighten my grip on the desk with one hand and grab his hair with the other guiding him as he starts to suck me harder, sliding up and down my length. He has one hand gripping my hip and the other palms my balls.

He groans as I growl.

Holy fucking shit.

There is something about getting someone to submit that gives me an all-time fucking high. I know Darius; he needs to be dominated, and I need submission. We are a perfect mixture of darkness and fucking madness.

4

Christos

Neo and Darius have been gone for a few hours but should return soon. At least we know that Neo and Darius are fine. We would all feel it if they weren't. There are a lot of things we need to talk to Nellie about, but we won't do it until we are all together.

Some things need to be taken care of before we sit down and help prepare Nellie for what will be happening for the next several weeks. But honestly, nothing we say to her will prepare her for what is going to happen inside these walls.

One of the first things we need to talk to her about is establishing a safe word for her to use over the next five weeks. It is extremely important that she understands that she is in control and can say it whenever she needs to. Nellie is our mate, and how she feels fucking matters to us. The safe word is to make her feel safe. She needs to know that the word is for her, not us. We have no boundaries with the sexual things we are willing to do. But we know she will probably come across some, but she doesn't know what they are just yet.

These next few weeks are all about her, us, and everyone officially becoming one. In the end, we want her to be pregnant. That is the whole reason our father and the others started the rules and laws surrounding mates in the first place. By doing it this way, Nellie will get to experience what it is we like sexually. Then we get to experience what she likes sexually, and by all of us coming together and sharing our deepest, darkest sexual desires, it will complete the connection. Her body will give in and become pregnant.

Don't ask me all the ins and outs of how it works because I don't know, but I do know that we will be giving away many of our Guardian secrets over the next five weeks. Ultimately, the goal is for her not only to become pregnant with one of our children but also to completely understand her part in our world. She will have a significant role in everything we do from here on out, and we will not keep anything from her. Our relationship with her and with each other needs to be built on pure fucking trust, and the only way that will happen is if we are honest at all times.

She will be our Queen and have as much power as we all do over the humans and others of our kind. What she says will go, and there will be no questions about it. If she doesn't like a law or rule, we will change it for her. We will fucking change everything if it is what she wants. She will understand that not only do we not have boundaries sexually, but we also have no boundaries of what we will do for her.

She will rule beside us as an equal because behind every powerful king is a strong-ass fucking queen, and that is exactly what she is. Without her, we have no direction, and we are nothing but fucking monsters. Because of her, we want to be more than that, and we will have the ability to be more.

I take a deep, shaky breath as I try to control my thoughts and emotions. It is crazy feeling everyone all the time, and from what I can feel from Neo and Darius right now, they are having fun and giving in to each other, which is good. It is good for both of them. There are no lines with who we will fuck within our group, and now that we have beating hearts and a soul, we, like humans, will make choices based on our emotions; it is just part of it.

My brother has been so guarded because of his ex whore, that I never thought anything would help him get over it and move on and be put back together again. I am grateful that somehow Neo and Nellie are finding a way to help him do all those things. As his brother, there is only so much I can do to help him, but they can help him differently, in a way that he really needs.

Watching my brother fuck Nellie the way he did, looking her in the eyes and not backing away from her touch, tells me he has finally given in to her. I have been feeling his guilt and shame in waves on how he has been treating her, but Nellie doesn't hold grudges. She loves all of us; we all can feel it, and we all need that from her.

Since finding her and Darius giving in, I am feeling more and more human, which is the craziest fucking shit ever to say. Still, they warned us that the longer we are with our mate, the deeper the connection gets, and the more we will change. I never thought it meant feeling human, but it is exactly that. I don't know how to explain it, but I do know that we are all feeling it.

I strip off the rest of my clothes and enter the bathroom. Loyal has his back against the wall, holding Nellie against his front. Her eyes meet mine as Loyal grabs and pulls her wrists behind her back. Nellie's eyes stay on me as her breathing starts to increase. Loyal wraps his arms around her, keeping her pinned against him. She lays her head against his chest as the water runs over them. Her nipples are hard, and her chest rises and falls with each breath as the steam from the water escapes the shower.

I don't think we will ever get sick of claiming her, having her like this, open and vulnerable. We will always fucking protect her, love her, need her. She is our reason for living now. Without her, we are nothing but monsters, but with her, we are able to become men. What a crazy ass fucking thought. We will always be Guardians, but different. I am learning with Nellie that different is good and should happen when you find your true mate, the person who is able to change you in the best possible ways. She is doing that for us, and we are hoping to do the same for her.

We don't know everything she has been through, but the parts we do know she has been through hell. She doesn't need fucking heroes, she needs the villains that will burn everything fucking down for her, and that is what we will be for her.

My dick hardens as I walk into the shower and stop in front of her. Her eyes follow me as I lean in and gently nip at her lower lip. Her taste is already taking me over, her smell consuming my nose. She is becoming more and more intoxicating.

"It is time to pleasure you, love," I whisper as I pull back. Her breathing continues to increase.

She doesn't respond as I lean in and start kissing her neck, over her collarbone, and down to her left breast. I cup her breast and bring it to my mouth so I can take her nipple into my mouth, where I roll and flick it between my teeth with my tongue before gently biting down. She lets out a moan as I move to her right breast and do the same thing sucking and nipping at her nipple. I slowly lower myself to my knees and place my hands on either side of her body against the wall.

I look up at Nellie and watch Loyal wrap his hand around her throat, pulling her into him so he can take her lips as he tightens his arm around her stomach, making sure she can't move. We both need to taste her, to claim her. This is the only way to distract her and ourselves from what is happening outside this pool house.

Zayden is out there somewhere, just waiting and probably watching. At least inside these walls, he can't see shit, we made it that way on purpose. No one needs to know what is happening within these walls. This is a time for us to let Nellie know who we are without our masks, and this is also a time for her to let us in fully.

We need her trust, and we want her trust. Hopefully, she will feel comfortable enough to open up about Zayden more. The more we know about him and what he is like, the more likely we will find him. We will not rest until we find him because while he is free there, there is still a possibility that he can hurt us and Nellie again.

We have our people looking fucking everywhere, but so far, no fucking luck. The human is better at hiding than I thought he would be. He has more connections with other people who hate us than we would like. The time will come for us to go hunting for all of the fuckers that are against us, and if we are not careful, they will all come together, and they are stronger together than they are apart. We need to watch our backs, or everything we love and care about can be taken from us.

I smile as I look at her wet pussy. I lean forward and press my mouth to her, pressing my tongue through her slick folds. Her body starts to shake as another moan leaves her. I could listen to that fucking sound every day for the rest of my life, and I plan on doing just that. Pleasing her pleases us; it is just the way it is.

I press my tongue inside her and slowly fuck her with my tongue. I groan against her pussy as she starts to rock against my face needing more. I smile against her as I continue to devour her. Her moans fill the shower, and she continues to move against my face, taking what she needs. She is the worst type of fucking drug.

She is our good girl.

I pull my tongue out of her pussy and gently push one and then another finger inside her as I look up at her. She is leaning against Loyal's chest, her head tilted. He bends down and bites down hard on her neck while I continue to move my fingers in and out of her, making sure that I rub that spot deep inside her. I watch her blood roll down her neck, breasts, and stomach until it reaches her pussy. I lean in and lick the blood away, and a groan escapes me as suck her bloody clit into my mouth and gently swirl my tongue around the bundle of nerves. I feel her pussy clench around my fingers as she lets out a scream. I lean in, licking her pussy, tasting her, stretching out her release until she is a quivering mess.

One orgasm down, a hundred more to go.

A smile forms across my lips as I pull my fingers out of her pussy and stand up. She lowers her head and watches as I suck her juices off of my fingers before I lean in and smash my lips to hers, forcing her to open her mouth. My tongue enters, her juices mixing in our mouth, and our tongues start to dance as I feel Loyal's hand move down her front to her pussy.

I place my hands on either side of her head, boxing her between me and Loyal.

I feel his fingers move into her wet pussy.

We are not done yet; far fucking from it.

5

Nellie

I stand still as I look myself over. Sometimes, I still don't recognize the person looking back at me in the mirror. I am trying to figure out who I am now that I am mated to my Guardians. Everything with Zayden is making it harder for me to find myself. I feel like I am drowning in the fear of what Zayden might do next. My Guardians are trying to keep me distracted, and they are trying to replace Zayden the best they can. There are times I am able to forget what Zayden has done and escape the dark thoughts of what he might try and do to me in the future, but just like with everything else in this life; the escape doesn't last forever. That is when the thoughts and images take hold again, weighing me down even more than they were before.

Even my dreams were consumed with Zayden and the horror of what he would have done to me in that car. I hate being afraid, and Zayden has made me a scared person. I didn't know how much I was affected by what he had done and is doing to me until I was mated. They have given me a way out, and I fucking want to take it. I feel myself screaming for what they are offering me, but deep down inside, I have a sick, sinking feeling that Zayden is far from being done with them or me.

I pull on one of their shirts and walk out of the bedroom and down the long hallway. This place is just as breathtaking as the mansion. The walls and floors are done in matching red marble, and everything appears to be brand new, which, honestly, I am not surprised. They are all wealthy and like nice things. I can smell the pool even though it is in its own area off to the side of the house somewhere. I haven't been able to explore much since they all have kept me busy with other activities, but I plan to explore. Maybe it will help take my mind off Zayden and everything that has happened.

The way Darius came in and saved me, held me, then made love to me still has me trying to catch my breath. Darius has been on guard with me since the beginning, but something changed in him when he saw what Zayden almost did in the car. If Darius were only a few minutes later, Zayden would have gotten what he wanted.

Zayden has made it clear that he wants all of me, and now that I have been mated, it seems to have made him completely lose his mind. He is acting worse than he did before I walked away from him. He was going to claim me in front of my Guardians house. He has lost his mind, and he scares the living shit out of me. He believes I am his, but now I know that I was never his, and what we shared was never love. What I have with Loyal, Neo, Darius, and Christos is love. This is what it should be like. A part of me is still scared of them, only because my future is still uncertain, and I don't know what will happen after we leave the pool house. I feel safe here with them for the first time in a long time.

We have all felt Neo and Darius' emotions since they left to meet with Loyal and Neo's father. I know they are giving themselves to each other; their feelings are coming through clearly, even without being there. A normal person might be jealous, but I am not normal, and I am not jealous. If Neo can give Darius something I can't, something that helps him heal from his past and what he has been through, I will not stand in their way.

I never thought I would feel like this once mated. Honestly, I didn't know what it would feel like, but with them, it seemed different. They seem different from other Guardians I have seen once they are mated. We are family, that much I can see, and instead of my Guardians remaining enemies like they were before me, they seem to have been able to move past it for me.

It is going to take me some time to get used to being the center of their lives. I feel selfish, but they don't seem to mind; they encourage it.

It doesn't change that all of this is weird to me. It reminds me of how I have been the center of Zayden's life, and we have all seen how that is turning out.

Neo, Darius, Christos, and Loyal are not like Zayden, I know that. They have proven to me time and time again that I am more than just the woman that they will breed with, and I think Zayden is starting to see that as well, which is what is causing him to lose more and more control of himself.

There are a lot of things I don't know yet, but I know that if I want them to open up to me, I will have to do the same for them, which also fucking scares me. If I open up to them, I will have to feel and relive everything I have buried deep down for the last year. Everything that I have been trying to fucking forget. I know we all need to let each other in and open up if we are really going to do this together.

I enter the kitchen and stop momentarily as I watch Christos and Loyal laughing and pushing each other as they cook. It is nice to see them like this because they are usually so serious. I know they are powerful Guardians, considering the families they are from, but at this moment, they look like two guys. Two sexy tattooed-covered guys in a kitchen shirtless making breakfast. Holy fucking shit.

I sit at the bar, and as soon as I do, Christos turns around with a cup of coffee in his hand. He comes over to me, leans in, and gives me a gentle kiss on the lips as he sets the cup down in front of me.

"Here ya go, Love," he says as he pulls away. I smile at him in thanks as I take the cup in my hands and watch him walk behind Loyal. He places his hands on the counter, boxing Loyal in as he rests his chin on his shoulder, making my heart race.

It appears that Neo and Darius are not the only ones falling for each other. I never thought I would be a part of something like this, but then again, I really did not know what to expect once I was mated, and anything that happened should not surprise me with the world we live in. Guardians have never been shy about sex and showing affection. They are the ones who have taught us, the Chosen Human Families, that it is okay to give in to our desires. The normal human world would say what we have and are doing is wrong, but there is nothing wrong with this.

I sit at the bar in the kitchen while Loyal and Christos work together to make me something to eat. This is so strange, yet I have never felt more at home. We have not left the pool house since what went down with Zayden, and from what I have overheard the guys saying, I will not be leaving anytime soon, which excites me and makes me nervous.

I can feel the nerves, excitement, and desire from all of them, and it is building up to something, but Loyal and Christos want to wait to explain until Neo and Darius return. Whatever they want to tell me, they want to make sure that we are all together.

I hear the back door open and close. It looks like the wait is over, and my heart races with what will happen next. Darius and Neo's emotions crash into me. All of us can feel them as Neo wraps his arms around me and leans in, resting his lips against my ear. "Hello, baby girl," he whispers in a low, dark voice. Fuck, that voice of his does funny things to my body.

They all affect me differently, but I am still trying to sort out exactly what they each make me feel. They all make me feel worshipped, loved, and free.

"Hey," I whisper back. I want to say more, but feeling his warm breath on my skin has sent all my thoughts to the tingling sensation he has elicited in my core. He slowly moves his hand to the hem of my shirt and finds that I am already wet as he circles his finger around my clit, making me moan as he pushes his finger into my awaiting pussy.

Neo chuckles in my ear. "You ready for me, baby girl?" Neo asks into my ear.

"Always," I say softly. I don't know when I got so damn bold, but these Guardians are bringing out a different side of me, that is for damn sure.

Neo slowly pulls his finger from my wetness and pulls back. I look back at Christos and Loyal, who are still standing in the same position but quiet. I know they feel all of my emotions right now, and I can't hide the fact that I am turned the fuck on. I can smell my own arousal.

"It looks like I am not the only one that is having fun, huh," Neo asks in an amused voice.

"Shut up, Neo," Loyal says back, trying to sound serious, but he is not fooling anyone.

Neo laughs as he lets me go and sits in the chair next to me. I smile when Darius comes up behind me next and kisses my neck. "Hey, angel." His voice is soft and sweet, which I am still not used to.

I had gotten used to how Darius was with me when we first mated, so it will take some time to adjust to him being like this. Don't get me wrong, I love this Darius; it just catches me off guard, is all.

"Everything okay?" I ask, wanting to know where they have been, but I still don't feel like it is my place to ask. I am their mate, but that doesn't give me the right to question them.

"Yeah," he whispers against my skin, causing my stomach to flutter.

"Ashton is on his way. He just texted saying he has something important to talk to all of us about," Neo says calmly.

Christos backs away so Loyal can turn around with my plate. He crosses the kitchen and places the plate loaded with breakfast foods in front of me. He leans against the bar with a gorgeous-ass smile on his face as Christos comes up behind him and rests his hands on his shoulders. I have a feeling that things are about to get exciting and much more fun.

I look at each one of my Guardians, and their eyes are all on me as I pick up the fork. I smile and look down at my plate. Their eyes stay on me as I begin to eat. Once again, I am the center of their attention. Hopefully, one of these days, it will not make me feel so anxious and nervous.

I just hope I live up to the mate they are meant to have.

6

Ashton

I wanted to be able to bring back good news and tell my family that they have nothing to worry about, but that is not the fucking case. I don't do good with failing; right now, I feel like I have failed my family. They were counting on me, and this is the first time I will not be able to say that I have been able to deliver.

I might have found my fucking match, but they didn't make me the enforcer because I give up. They made me the enforcer because I get shit done. I need to stop looking at Zayden as one of us and remember that he has turned his back on our kind, on his own people. What is driving him is not fucking sane but pure fucking obsession with Nellie.

Maybe if I can get inside his head, like he has found his way to get into ours, I can fucking find him and make him suffer. He better fucking pray his luck doesn't run out because once I get my fucking hands on him, he is going to wish for death. Death would be too fucking easy for what he has done, I will keep him alive, but he will wish that he could fucking die. I will make sure he sees how happy Nellie is, how she doesn't fucking need him.

I make my way up to the pool house door and slowly turn and look out at the forest. I have felt like I am being watched all fucking day today, and for the life of me, I can never find whoever or whatever the fuck has been following me. I have a sinking feeling it is Zayden, and if it is, he is a lot better at this stalker shit than I thought.

I have a fucking stomach-twisting feeling that he is not at all who Nellie thought he was and that what he has done so far to my family is just the fucking beginning. I have seen men like Zayden, but never up this close and personally. I have seen how far obsession can go and what lengths some human men will go to claim what they believe is theirs. Zayden thinks he has a claim and is determined to prove it.

I should have fucking known that he was going to try and go after Nellie's family, but he was already fucking ahead of me in his thinking, which makes me think he has someone or something feeding him fucking information. If I can find out who or what they are, it will lead me to him, hopefully in time.

I have been out trying to find him, but so far, I have not found the little fucker. There are many places he can be hiding, and I know he has other fucking humans helping him. It is the only way he can disappear like he has. He also must have some of our kind working with him, which means he went to one of our fucking enemies. I have a hunch of who the fuck is helping him, but without proof, it won't fucking matter. Just like in the normal human world, we need evidence in order for us to make a claim.

We can't just go around accusing someone of doing something; with our kind, you better have fucking proof before you start running your mouth. I need to find the fucking proof, but it always takes fucking time, time that I don't think we have. Zayden is moving too fast and has taken us by surprise. No fucking more. I am over his childish little shit. He doesn't have the balls to go head-to-head with us yet because he knows what he will fucking lose.

I thought maybe Nellie's father would know where Zayden might be hiding. Perhaps because he is faithful to us, I thought he has been keeping his eyes and ears open, and I heard her father has never been a big fan of Zayden. He was the reason she finally walked away from Zayden, so that is why I chose to go to Nellie's house. But when I arrived, her father was dead in his bedroom, holding a picture of Nellie and her mother, I assume, and her sister was gone. I found footprints and tire marks on the ground. The blood from her father was still wet on the walls, which means that Zayden had just fucking been there. I probably only missed him by a few hours, if that.

I have been trying to fucking find her little sister, and the information I found out, I know, is going to fucking destroy Nellie. And in return, it will destroy my cousins, Darius and Christos, because they will feel all her pain. I tried to hunt her sister down, but she is fucking gone, sold to the highest bidder.

Even in our world, Guardians and the humans are not all on the same page as our families are, and they dabble in shit that they shouldn't. They treat women wrong, and they pride themselves in trying to make their own fucking rules. We have been trying to keep certain things out of our territory, but I have also failed at that. If I had done my job correctly, then her sister would not have been able to be sold to the highest bidder, and she would be safe in my arms about to see Nellie. But the reality is the news I am about to tell all of them is going to unravel them, and Nellie is going to fucking break. This is horrible fucking timing. I know this, but I also know that Nellie has the right to know about her father and her sister. It would be wrong to keep it from her.

We need her to trust us, and I need her to trust me, and the only way that will happen is if I tell her the truth. Fuck I don't want to tell her all of this. I don't want to tell any of them this shit because they go on lockdown for five weeks on Monday to complete the connection. They don't need any fucking distractions, and this is a big fucking distraction.

I will not stop until I fucking find Zayden and Nellie's sister. I just hope I find her in time. I take a deep breath as I turn the doorknob, walk inside, and close the door behind me. I walk towards the kitchen, and Nellie's laughs fill my ears, fuck man. Fuck.

I enter the kitchen, and as soon as I do, everyone stops talking, turns, and looks at me. All I can do is shake my head, and all four guys look at Nellie. I go to Nellie's side, and she turns and looks up at me, her eyes searching mine, and I watch the smile on her face disappear.

"What's wrong?" She asks me concerned.

She may not be my mate, but I care about her and would give my life for her. The same I would do for any of the guys; it is what you do for your family, blood or not. Nellie will find out pretty damn fast how loyal our kind is to family. She became my family the moment Neo, Christos, Loyal, and Darius fell to their knees for her. She is important to our kind, to them, and me.

"Nellie," I say softly, resting my hand on her lower back. I wish I could do something to make what I am about to tell her less painful, but I know there is nothing I can say to her that will make this hurt any less.

"Ashton, what is wrong?" Nellie asks again.

I take a deep breath, fuck. "I was looking for Zayden, and I went to your dad's house to ask if he might know where he might be hiding," I confess as calmly as I can. If I had a beating heart, it would be racing.

"What did my dad say?" She asks.

She wants me to find Zayden as much as the rest of us, and I wish I fucking wish I could tell her that I found him, that he is locked up and can't hurt her, but that would be a lie. He is still out there and has done something that will make her put back up her walls and change her forever.

"He didn't say anything, Nel. Your father is dead," I say softly, her eyes rapidly searching mine. If I had a beating heart, this would be the moment it would stop and sink, but I don't. Still, I can imagine what it will feel like once I do.

She does not say anything for a minute as she processes what I just told her. "What?" She asks, but I know she heard me. I can see it in her eyes. She just doesn't want to believe it.

"I'm sorry," I whisper. I know I should say more than those two words, but I can't. I wish I could, but for the first time in a long time, I don't know what to say, and I know that nothing I say to her right now will do shit. She is in shock, and my trying to make excuses will not help her or anyone else.

She stands up and backs away from me. I drop my hand to my side, and Neo, Christos, Darius, and Loyal all stand. Christos and Loyal make their way around the bar, and all four of them take a step toward her. She shakes her head and takes another step back. All the guys come to my side, all of us looking at her. I don't need to feel her emotions to know what she probably feels right now. Nellie feels everything so fucking deeply, and I can see everything she's feeling in her eyes and on her face.

"Nellie," Darius says softly.

"No," she says, shaking her head. She wraps her arms around herself, and the tears in her eyes start to build as she looks at me. "Where is my sister?" She asks in a fearful voice.

Fuck.

"She has been taken," I confess.

Her breathing increases as she keeps her eyes on me. "What the fuck does that mean?" She snaps.

"It means she has been sold, Nellie," I explain. This is the hardest news I have ever had to deliver, and I have had to deliver some horrible fucking news; it just comes with being the enforcer.

The tears escape her eyes and roll down her face. Darius and Neo step towards her, but she turns around and takes off, running out of the kitchen towards the bedroom. All of them take off after her.

I sit at the bar and lower my head into my hands. This is a fucking mess. She has already been through enough, she doesn't need this too, fuck. Fuck. Fuck.

I can hear all of them yell her name, chasing her down the hallway and into their room. She is never going to be the same after this, and this wound will never be able to heal for her entirely.

All I can do is find that motherfucker, and get her sister back, that is the only thing that will help her, and I will fucking not fail again.

7

Loyal

We chase her down the hall into her room, fuck she is fast. I should have fucking made my way to her before Ashton came into the pool house. I should have already had my arms around her. Fuck, man. Her emotions are loud and fucking painful, and all we want to do is take them away, make her feel better. But I don't think it matters what we are trying to do right now, and it will not change the fact that her father is dead and her sister has been sold.

"Nellie," I yell at her, but she doesn't stop. She doesn't say anything as she runs into the bathroom and slams the door. We all hear her lock it as we rush to the door and stop in front of it.

Ashton has been trying to find Zayden since what happened outside our house. He has never let us down, and even now, it is not his fault. Zayden is a lot smarter than we ever gave him credit for. He has always been a few steps ahead of us and is playing a dangerous fucking game. Ashton is doing his best, and even though he doesn't have a soul or a beating heart, I saw it in his eyes as he told Nellie he was sorry. He feels for and cares about her, and right now, outside of us, he is the only one I trust to keep her safe.

I know my cousin, and he won't stop until he finds Zayden; he doesn't know how to fail. He is very good at what he does, and Zayden will run out of the little luck he seems to be having right now.

Zayden isn't afraid of us. He has nothing to lose, which makes him so much more dangerous. He knows we love Nellie and will do anything to protect her. For all we know, he is out there right now, watching this place. He is very fucking patient, which we are not. That gives him the upper hand. We need to learn patience if we are going to win this game.

He might not have anything to lose, but we fucking do, and he knows that. He knows we can't just fucking react to what he is doing without thinking it through. He can do whatever he fucking wants because he is no longer playing by the laws and rules. The laws and regulations still bind us, but that is about to fucking change. He doesn't know how to care about anyone but himself, and he puts our selfishness to fucking shame. I have never seen a human so determined and heartless at the same time. It scares me to think about what he has planned for Nellie. It scares me because we never seem to see him coming. We need to be smarter, and in order to do that, we must think long and fucking hard about what our next move is.

Zayden decided to take it a step further by killing Nellie's father. He could have stopped there, but he didn't. He wanted to make sure that Nellie suffered further, so he chose to take her sister. No matter how hard we try, sex trafficking is a big business in the human world. We have outlawed it in ours, but that doesn't mean the Chosen Humans or all of our kind follow the rules and laws. There are too many blind spots, and we can't watch the entire territory simultaneously.

I place my hands on the door, rest my forehead against the wood, and take several deep breaths. Her emotions are crashing into all of us, and I feel my heart cracking inside my chest from her pain and grief. All of us are feeling each other, and we are all on edge. I have dreamt of chasing after Nellie a million times, but not like this, not because she wants to be away from us.

I want so fucking badly to take this from her. If we could take on all of her pain ourselves, we would, but the connection doesn't work that way. We can help her work through it, and we can try and calm her, but right now, I know it wouldn't work because none of us are fucking calm. None of us know what to do. We just want to hold her, and we don't want any fucking space between us and her.

Pain and grief can either make someone stronger or they can destroy them, and we will not let this destroy her. We need her, and she needs us. We are one now, and if she suffers, we all fucking suffer. We will help her get revenge, and I can fucking promise her that. It will take some time, though, we can't fight someone we can't fucking find.

"Nellie, please, sweetness, open the door," I plead with her. Fuck, she doesn't need this right now, she has been dealing with so fucking much. Of course, fucking Zayden had to go after her family. We should have put them under protection. We should have done more than what we have done. We have been selfish and wanted her so badly that we forgot to watch over the others she loves and cares about.

I don't know what it feels like to lose a parent or sibling, but I do understand what it feels like to be powerless, to want to take back something. I have felt powerless since she came into my life because we asked a lot of her. I know she was scared at first, and still, we had to make sure to secure the connection only a few hours after mating with her.

I want to take back how all of this started. If I could go back and take things slower with her, we all fucking would. I can feel it. We would all do things a little differently because even though we fell for her the moment our knees hit the club floor, she didn't know that. She only knew what she had heard of us, and we fucking fed right into what she had been told.

We can't change the past, and we can't change what Zayden has done to her or her family, but we can make sure that we help her get revenge.

We can make sure that we show her how much we love and care about her every single moment of every day so she never has to guess how we feel. That is how we make up for what has happened, and it is the only way we can fucking make up for it.

I am getting sick and fucking tired of this human being ten steps ahead of us. We need to figure out who the fuck is helping him. They will all die. I don't fucking care if they were directly in on it or not. Everyone that is assisting him in torturing our mate will fucking suffer in the worst ways.

She doesn't respond. The bathroom is quiet, too fucking quiet.

"Please, Nellie, let us help you. Please, don't shut us out," I plead with her again. She had finally let down her guard with us and was letting us in. Please, please, Nellie, don't fucking shut us out now.

The thought of her shutting us out fucking kills and scares me; it fucking terrifies me. I don't want to scare her, but I don't want to lose her to herself, either. Our minds can become a very dangerous place, and I fucking refuse to lose her now, not now, not after finally fucking getting her. My chest tightens, and my heart sinks as I feel the pain spreading across my skin, the same pain I felt when Zayden tried to force her to leave the club.

"Nellie," I scream and bang on the door. I pull back and grab onto the handle.

"If you don't open this fucking door right now, Sweetness, I will fucking break it down," I scream at the door. No, no, no.

Still no answer, the pain starts to get worse and worse. My heart is racing as I rip on the door handle, breaking it. I push open the door and walk in, and I feel Neo, Christos, and Darius behind me as I stand in the middle of the empty bathroom.

Empty. Fucking empty.

I turn and look at the open window, and my heart stops. She left, she fucking left.

A surge of pain goes through my body, forcing all of us to scream and fall to our knees. Her rage and sadness is fucking drowning me, mixing in with the physical pain from the separation. Fuck. FUCK.

"Ashton," I scream as I hold my chest.

I feel his hand on my shoulder. "Get the car. I know where she is going," I say in a shaky, low voice. I can barely breathe in from the pain I am feeling right now.

He does not say a word as he runs out of the bathroom.

Another surge of pain goes through me, causing me to scream again. I have never felt anything like this before. She has already gotten far enough away from us that it feels like my heart is being ripped from my chest. Like there is an actual fucking hand inside my chest squeezing my young beating heart in a vise.

There are consequences, consequences for us being apart. If we are feeling this way, then she is too. I can feel her emotions, and they are unhinged and fucking crazy. She is filled with sadness and pure fucking rage.

I grab onto the sink, forcing myself to my feet. My legs are shaking as I take in several shallow breaths, trying to get enough oxygen into my lungs. I slowly turn and look at Christos, Neo, and Darius, and for the first time in my life, I see tears building in their eyes. Tears are also forming in mine, partly because of the physical pain, but it mostly comes from the psychological and emotional pain we are feeling from Nellie.

Our mate, the love of our life. I am beyond fucking pissed that she crawled out of the fucking window, but at the same time, I am not surprised, she has fire in her, and right now, she doesn't know what emotions belong to her and which ones belong to us. Honestly, I don't either. Everything is so fucking mixed and jumbled inside all of us.

All I know is that we need to get to her, or the consequences will be more severe than just physical pain. She doesn't understand what will start to happen when we are separated, yet another secret we planned on telling her over the next several weeks. We are going to have to tell her much fucking sooner. Our kind holds many secrets, secrets that are only supposed to come out at certain times, but now we are the fucking Kings, and we can make whatever fucking laws and rules we want to, which means we can also fucking break them, and we will fucking break them all for her. It is only going to get worse until she is with us again.

She is going to the place where Zayden took part of her heart, a part that none of us will be able to give back. The thought of us not being able to make this right inside her fucking breaks me all over again and makes me want to scream out in a different kind of pain.

That motherfucker is going to die, and I will look into his eyes as he finally sees that he never had a fucking chance against us. We might have something to lose, but I will die for Nellie if I have to. We all will.

Can Zayden fucking say the same?

8

Neo

I lean my forehead against the cold window as I struggle to take a deep breath. I don't know why the first fucking reaction is to take deep breaths, but it is, it doesn't do shit through, but I guess it is better than doing fucking nothing. But even deep breaths are not going to make this pain go away. My chest tightens with each passing second, and my stomach is in knots, tight fucking knots that make me want to throw up. My thoughts are racing on a never-ending negative fucking loop, and my emotions are a mixture of a deadly fucking storm of all five of us together.

I keep my hand over my chest as if it being there will take away this pain, but it won't. Nothing is going to take it away until we have Nellie back in our arms. We have all been taught about the pain and even experienced a little of it when Zayden tried to take Nellie away, but it is nothing compared to what we are all feeling right now. All the teachings in the world could not have prepared us for this shit.

I am worried about all of us. If we don't get to her soon, the whole fucking kingdom is going to know. We can't fucking hide this pain, the suffering creeping towards our souls, the ripping feeling in our hearts. Fuck.

Ashton is driving like a mad fucking man towards Nellie's father's house; of course, that is where she went. She wants to see where Zayden took her father's life and where her sister was taken against her will. She needs to see the source of her pain and suffering, which makes sense; all of this makes sense.

One thing about Nellie is that not only does she feel us so fucking deeply, but she needs to feel everything deeply and experience it for herself. It is what makes her so fucking special. She needs to feel the source of the pain and suffering. For her, it will become a craving and overwhelming need, and the need and desire will not go away until she gives in.

She doesn't know it, but she has a gift, a very special gift in our world, a gift that many would fucking kill to have. In the normal human world, what she has would be called a gift; in our world, it is called Touches.

This is why we need to protect her. The connection not only connects us for sex and breeding but is also meant to give our mate special Touches. She had it before the connection, but now the Touches will increase and become very powerful. In the normal human world, she would be known as an empath; in our world, she is known as a Delicate.

We planned on telling her; we all felt it the moment our knees hit the ground for her. We felt her power. We should of fucking told her, but she wasn't ready. She wasn't prepared to let us love her and take care of her. But now she is, or was, before she found out about her sister and father. I am hoping we are not too fucking late and we haven't fucking lost her to herself.

She has no idea, and it will change everything for her again, but not only having Touches but her being a Delicate makes her status that much more powerful, and it is our job to keep her safe and her Touches a secret. If our enemies knew what she was, they would take and use her. The thought of someone using her for her Touches makes my skin crawl. Touches are very secret and protected for a fucking reason. The mate and the Guardians within that family are the only ones who normally know what the Touches are.

We have all seen what happens when Touches get out in the open for the rest of our kind to see. They will kidnap Nellie, do unspeakable things to her, and they won't fucking care that she is already mated. They won't even care that she won't be able to give them children and continue their bloodline; the lust for power will overpower everything else in our kind. It is like a virus that runs through them, and it can fucking spread, and once it spreads, it is almost impossible to get everything back under control.

People like Nellie are very special. Having the ability to feel the way she does makes her very powerful in our world. She can feel people's weaknesses, including our kind, once they are mated. That is why they would want her; our kind does not want anyone to know their weaknesses. Nellie is the only type of Touches that can. It was stupid of us to keep this from her; keeping her in the dark has put her in more danger. As long as Zayden doesn't find out what she is, then we will be okay. But the only way for him to know what she is is if he has one of our kind working with him.

It has crossed our minds, but we have not said the words out loud. I would hope that none of our kind would help him, but there is one fucking family that I know would do anything to destroy us, and I have a sinking feeling, the same sinking feeling we all have, that the Falcos are the ones that are feeding Zayden information. He is not this fucking smart, he can't be. No fucking human can be this good at fucking with us.

There are many different kinds of Touches. Our father told us about some, but not all. We don't even know what our mother's Touches are, which is another reason why he keeps her hidden. Is this starting to make sense?

Our mother has, like Nellie, special Touches, and one day, we might find out what hers is, but right now, it doesn't matter; none of this fucking matters. What the fuck is wrong with my thoughts right now. I am fucking spiraling out of control while fucking sitting here in a damn fucking car.

The car is filled with all of our screams off and on, and I can tell it is affecting Ashton, but he will not tell us that it is. He will stay strong because right now, we can't be. He will be our rock because right now, we are all fucking feeling like we are breaking inside.

I suck in a short breath as Ashton comes to a stop right in front of Nellie's father's house. One more big surge of pain goes through me, and I let out a scream as the tears fall and roll down my face.

Zayden thinks he is just trying to take his ex-girlfriend, someone he says he loves, but he doesn't understand what she is or how important she is to all of us. He doesn't understand the kind of pain that is forcing me to cry right now or the pain I feel in my chest. He doesn't fucking understand anything.

She is our future, and the children that come from her womb and her genes will also have Touches. Everything in our world is about to change because of her, and if I have to die to make sure that she lives, then I will fucking do it. Part of her heart might become fucking hollow and never beat again, but at least she would be alive, and the others could give her a fucking good life.

I am prepared to fucking give my life for hers because that is what you fucking do for those you love. I might be new to emotions, but I am not fucking stupid. I know how to show love, and I know how because Nellie has taught me. She has taught all of us in a short amount of time. She has allowed us to see what love is, and we will help her get revenge. We will help her heal and be able to move forward. We all know she will never get over something like this, but instead of freezing and taking her from us, we will teach her how to use her pain and suffering to get revenge.

Would Zayden give his life for hers? Fuck no, he wouldn't because he doesn't really love her. What he feels for her is obsession and ownership, nothing more. He thinks that he claimed her long before we did, but she was fucking made for us. There are things no one knows that only the oldest of our kind does, and they pass down their knowledge to a select few, like my father.

Zayden has no idea what the fuck he is messing with, but it doesn't matter if he kidnaps her, kills us, and tries to build a life with her; that is not how it fucking works. We were made for her, and she was made for us. All five of us fit together like a fucked up perfect puzzle. You can try and take the pieces away and put in new ones, but the puzzle would never fit perfectly together like it once did.

I suck in a breath as the pain courses through my veins like acid. I scream out against the window, feeling all of us at the same time surge with pain. It is so much worse feeling the pain from all of us at once, and I can't tell where my pain starts and anyone else's ends. It is so fucking intertwined inside me, and the only way to take it away is to be near her. The pain will decrease and leave with time, and the only thing left behind will be the internal scars that no one else can see but we will all remember. We will all feel it in each other.

Christos, Loyal, and Darius stumble out of the car, all of them holding their chests. I open the door and fall out onto the cold, wet ground. My heart is racing so fast I can hear it in my ears. My body is shaking from the pain. I want to get up and fucking move, but I can't. Talk about feeling fucking hopeless and helpless at the same fucking time.

I feel strong arms wrap around me and force me to stand on shaky legs. I see Darius, whose face is only inches away from mine. Tears roll down his face as he tries to keep me and him from falling. My heart starts to slow down a little, partly because Nellie is near and the other because of Darius. I need him, just like he needs me. Fuck man.

"It will decrease, I promise," he whispers. He leans in and gently connects his tears-covered lips against mine.

Before I can lean into him, he pulls back. "Let's go get our mate," he says, trying to give me a small smile, but behind the smile is nothing but pain and sorrow. I know once we get our hands on her, we are never ever going to fucking let her go. Our eyes will be on her at all fucking times because the fear of her disappearing again is the worse fucking fear imaginable.

I nod because I don't know what else to do.

I look towards the house and see Ashton helping Christos and Loyal through the broken-down door.

I can feel her. She is here, our mate, our love is here.

9

Christos

My chest is so fucking tight it is hard to breathe. Even though I can feel the pain starting to decrease, it will take time for all of us to get over the effects of being separated. Ashton keeps a tight hold on me and Loyal as we walk down the hallway toward Nellie's father's room.

I can feel the pain decrease as Ashton stops us outside the room. I lean against the wall for a moment as I take a deep breath. I can hear Neo and Darius behind me. I should have known she was going to run; we all should have fucking known. I will be putting fucking bars on those windows as soon as we fucking get back to the pool house. The thought of her running again makes me weak in the knees.

We are more connected together than we have since this all started; we can't be separated. We can't.

The sound of all of our screams will be something I will never forget. It will haunt me; everything that has happened will fucking haunt me. None of this shit should have happened. We should have fucking killed this human guy at the club when he first tried to take Nellie. If I could do things over again, there are a lot of things I would do differently, starting with that fucker.

I understand why we didn't, but now I am fucking regretting it. We wanted to make sure that Nellie gave her permission, we wanted to make sure we didn't fucking hurt her, and now look at what has happened. I am a selfish motherfucker, and I am beyond pissed that Zayden has taken over our lives like this. I am beyond fucking pissed that he is taking up space in her head, and I am pissed that his obsession with her has grown to whatever the fuck it is now.

This is why we have the laws and rules we do because of human men like Zayden. He wants something he will never have, and even though she will never be his, he will not stop until she is. I have a sinking feeling that none of this is going to end fucking well.

I take a deep breath as I push off the wall and walk into the room. My legs are still shaky as I rest my hand over my young, beating, pained heart. Nellie is standing behind the chair, with her left hand on the bloody wall. Her legs and body shake as she holds her right hand over her chest, and her hair is damp from sweat. All evidence that she has felt all that we have felt since she ran. I don't know how she was able to fight through it and make it here so fast. We will look into that as soon as we get her back to the pool house. We will sit down and figure out what the fuck is happening once we lock the doors shut and we are all safe.

We should have fucking told her that she is a Delicate. She is confused, hurt, and overwhelmed, and part of it is our fault, our fucking fault for keeping her in the dark. We need to tell her everything, but not all at once; right now, she wouldn't be able to handle it. We don't want to hurt her even more, and we sure as shit don't want to overwhelm or scare her more than she already is.

I know that if we felt that surge of pain, she did too, and it pains me and pisses me off that we weren't here to hold her through the screams. It is hard knowing that it took us longer to get to her. We should have broken down that fucking door as soon as she slammed it. Fuck man, she makes us all lose rational thought.

I just want to take her in my arms, never let her go, and protect her from everything and everyone. I just want to keep her locked up in the pool house for the rest of our lives; that way, I will know that she is always safe and protected. I want those things so fucking badly, but I know, I fucking know it would not go over well.

Nellie is not the type of woman who would do well being locked up; we know that, but that doesn't change my powerful urge to do it anyway. I will fuck and claim her, reminding her not to ever fucking run from us again. She scared the living shit out of me, out of all of us.

Zayden could be watching us right now, watching her, we could have fucking lost her. He could have been waiting here for her. I close my eyes and take a deep breath as I try and calm down my negative thoughts, but the breathing is not fucking working. Nothing is going to take it away until I wrap my fucking hands around that little fuckers throat and watch the life leave his eyes. His death is the only thing that will make these thoughts go silent.

I understand why she ran and why she needs to be here, but I don't understand why she felt the need to do this on her own. It pisses me off that she is shutting us out, and I am pissed off that I am afraid. What a fucking weird ass fucking cycle. I am fucking confusing myself with my own thoughts and emotions.

These fucking emotions make us weak, but they are also why we can love her the way we do. We need the emotions just like we need her. You can't have one without the other. There is no way around it; we all need to get a handle on our fucking emotions. She already feels enough pain and sorrow and doesn't need us adding to it. We need to be her foundation, and we need to be the ones that are strong for her right now. That is what mates do, and she needs us more now than she ever has before.

I slowly make my way across the room and stop close enough behind her that I can feel her body heat. I want so badly to fucking touch her, but I can tell she doesn't want to be touched. She is feeling this room and everything Zayden did to her father. She is reliving it, and we can feel all of it radiating off of her. Her emotions are drowning her, and if we don't find a way to help her through this, we are going to fucking lose her.

After all, that is what Zayden wants, isn't it?

He took her family because he wanted a reaction. He wanted to make sure she hurt, and he knew this would fucking crush her, which is why he did it. If he thinks this will bring her back to him, he doesn't know shit, and he isn't as bright as we all think he is. If anything, he is making her hate him even more, not love him. He is not going to get the reaction from her that he wants.

We are never going to let her go; there is no fucking way. If anything, now we are going to hold onto her even fucking tighter. The fear of her disappearing is now drowning all of us.

"Nellie," I whisper behind her. Her sobs fill the room, and I wrap my arms around her stomach and pull her against me. She drops her hand from the wall, allowing me to hold her tighter. Her body continues to shake, her emotions hurting my heart like fucking knives.

"This is my fault," she confesses.

My heart stops at her confession. "What?" I ask, but I hear her. I hear the lie come out of her mouth.

"Zayden did this because of me," she says, holding back her tears.

I release my hold on her, turn her around, and walk into her, forcing her back against the bloody wall. Her eyes are cast to the floor, but she never has to fucking be ashamed of her feelings. Her feelings are valid, but the lie she is currently telling herself right now is fucking not. We will not just sit back and let her blame herself for something she had no control over. We will not let her lose herself in the lies she is telling herself.

Zayden does not get to fucking take her from us, not physically or mentally. She is ours, and she will always be ours.

I grab onto her throat, forcing her to look up at me. She opens her eyes, and the tears escape her eyes and roll down her face. She keeps her hands at her sides.

"That is not fucking true, you hear me," I say through gritted teeth.

My heart is racing with her words. That fucker is actually making her believe that all of this is her fault. It is not her fucking fault; it is his.

I lean in as I tighten my grip on her throat. I stop when my lips almost touch hers. "This is his fault, not yours, love," I say softly, pleading with her to hear my words.

Zayden has already taken so much from her, and he doesn't deserve to take anymore. He wants her to break and give in to him, but that is not going to fucking happen.

"I should have just given him what he wanted from me, and none of this would be happening," she says, looking me in the eyes.

Over my fucking dead body, is he ever going to touch her again. Neo, Darius, and Loyal stop at my sides, all of us boxing her in. All of us needing to be close to her.

"You are not his to take Nellie Ocean. You are ours, and we are yours," I say, looking over her beautiful, teared-covered face.

She takes in a shaky breath as her emotions become increasingly unhinged. The physical pain is leaving all of us, but the mental and emotional pain is still very intense and overwhelming right now. "I'm scared."

"Baby girl, we won't let him hurt you," Neo whispers.

"I know that, and that is why I am scared," she says, looking at Neo and then back at me.

"What do you mean, angel?" Darius asks in a pained voice. I hear the softness in my brother's voice, a softness I never thought I would hear from him. I feel more tears build in my eyes.

"What if he hurts you guys to get to me?" She asks in a scared tone. I hate that she is afraid, and I hate that we can't fucking take the fear from her.

"Sweetness, you must give us more credit than that. It is not us that will hurt; it is him," Loyal replies softly.

"I can't lose you guys. You guys are all that I have left," she says as more tears escape her eyes and roll down her face.

"Love, we aren't going anywhere, we promise," I say with as much confidence as possible.

She nods and leans her head back against the wall. I lean in and press my lips to her. I will not fuck her right now, but I at least need to fucking taste and touch her and know that she is actually fucking here with us.

The moment we saw the bathroom was empty, I felt overwhelmed with a feeling of loss and fear, and I never ever want to fucking feel that way again.

I need assurance that she is real and not going anywhere, just like she needs validation from us right now.

10

Darius

Christos pulls back and releases his grip on her throat; as he backs away, I move in front of her. My breathing increases as I lock eyes with hers for a moment. I hate that she is going through any of this, and I fucking hate that a fucking human has brought us to our knees. This hasn't happened in fucking centuries; a human having the balls to act like Zayden is.

I can see it in Nellie's eyes and feel it in her; she is struggling. She is drowning, and she needs us to keep her above water, and that is exactly what we plan on doing. That is exactly what I plan on doing. I have failed her since we have mated, and I will never fucking fail her again. She needs me; she needs all of us to replace what she is feeling now before it fucking destroys her.

"Let us help you, angel," I whisper, keeping my eyes on hers.

"Darius," she whispers. Fuck the way she says my name. No drug in the world can compare to how she makes me feel.

I reach down and grab onto her legs, lifting her off of the ground. She wraps her arms around my neck, her legs around my waist, and she shoves her face into my neck. I never thought she would act like this with me, not after what I have done. But Nellie is a good person, and I can feel her love and desire. It might be underneath the grief at this moment, but I can feel it; it is still there.

I turn around and look at Christos, Loyal, and Neo. All three of them move aside as I quickly make my way across the room and out into the hallway. I need to get her the fuck out of here. Her staying here will not help her heal or begin to heal. Staying here will keep her frozen, unable to process what has happened. Living in the pain and sorrow of what has happened here will not give her what she needs.

She needs to be able to feel safe and cared for. She needs to be able to let go, and she can't fucking do that here.

I can hear the guys walking behind me as I walk through the house and out of the broken front door. Ashton is leaning against the car, smoking a cigarette, and when his eyes lock with mine, he pushes off the car and gets inside. Loyal goes to the passenger side and gets in, and Christos and Neo open the back doors and get inside.

I can feel her tears against my skin as I get into the car and shut the door. She tightens her grip around me as I sit back in the seat, and Ashton starts the car and backs up.

I have this distinct feeling of being watched, but right now, that doesn't fucking matter. The only thing that matters is Nellie and getting her back to the pool house, and once inside, we will lock the doors and stay inside for the next five weeks. At least her being in the pool house, we know for a fact that Zayden will not be able to get inside. He will be forced to watch from a distance.

From what we have learned about him, I would not be surprised if he watches us with her. I hope he is watching because he needs to see Nellie when she really loves. He needs to see how she deserves to be treated. The connection may have forced us together, but now, it is our love for each other that is making us stronger and keeping us together.

Zayden can't fight fucking fate. Nellie was ours before she was even born; it was already written. He had already lost the moment he fell for her.

What Zayden has done doesn't change what is going to happen over these next five weeks, but it does mean that we need to give her a few more days before we explain to her what will take place, and we need to explain to her what she is. Keeping it from her was not right, but what she is makes us all afraid, not of her, but of what our kind would try and use her for.

We must keep her Touches a secret, and Zayden can not find out. Even though I don't think he would understand what it means, we will not risk it. He already knows a lot of things about us that he fucking shouldn't. We have to assume that he knows about Touches and will be watching all of us closely, waiting for his opportunity to take her from us.

I knew what she was, which is partly why I was trying to keep my distance. All she has to do is touch us, and she will be able to feel our pain and suffering on a different level than she has thus far. I didn't want her to know exactly what I was feeling, even though she was feeling my emotions anyway. So far, I have been able to keep my barriers up to most of my past. I will have to share eventually; over the next five weeks, she will discover what has happened to me. But I want it to be in my time and not because my emotions fucking gave it away.

So far, I have been able to keep my past trauma under control, which is why she isn't feeling it right now. I know I won't be able to keep the barriers up for long, and when they come crashing down, she will finally understand what my ex has done to me and why I was the way I was with her at the beginning. I know it is not a fucking excuse, but at least she will have a better understanding.

We will all need to fucking open up to her, just like she will need to open up to us about what exactly went on between her and Zayden. As far as we know, everything he feels and believes about her appears to be in his head, which means his head is filled with nothing but lies. We need to know the whole truth from her.

We all need to be fucking honest with each other. It is the only way this is going to work, which I know sounds fucking nuts coming from me, but I am all fucking in now. No more half in and half out, and no more acting like this is just an obligation. She has never been just an obligation to any of us, even when I was trying to act like she was.

I know it will take time for me to help her heal from what I have made her believe, but right now, with her face in my neck and her allowing me to hold her tightly against me, it confirms that things have already changed between us for the better.

The way I have acted since knowing her will be something I regret for the rest of my life. I have wasted so much time being a fucking asshole. I have to make up for how I have treated her and what I have done, and over the next five weeks, I fucking will. She will never ever second guess my love for her again. I have given in to her; she is my Queen, and I will never let things go back to how they were.

I tighten my hold on Nellie as Ashton drives us back to our house. It's the only place I feel like is safe for her right now.

When we return, I head straight to the pool house and go to our room. Crossing the room, I take her into the bathroom so I can wash the blood from her body. The others are going throughout the house and ensuring that all the doors and windows are locked up tight while Ashton is outside, watching the pool house.

We will have bars on the windows and chains on all the doors to ensure that none of us can leave and that no one is coming in. The next five weeks will be fucking intense, and no matter what, we all have to fucking stay and face it together.

I walk over to the counter and try to place Nellie on top of it, but she still has a tight grip around my waist and neck.

"Angel, please, let me undress you," I ask softly.

She releases her hold on my neck and waist, and I pull back and force her to stand. I grab the bottom of her t-shirt and pull it over her head. I look over her naked body, and a surge of rage goes through me. I didn't even fucking realize that the only thing she was wearing when she left the pool house was one of our fucking shirts.

I inhale deeply and wrap my fingers around her throat, forcing her to look into my eyes. "No one will ever fucking see you with only our shirt on again, angel. You understand me," I say through gritted teeth.

The thought of anyone seeing her like this makes me want to rip all of their eyes out. Whoever fucking looked at her, I will fucking hunt down and make them suffer. No one will see her vulnerable like this, no one but us. She is our mate, only ours, which means no one has the right to see her like this, ever.

"Yes," she answers back. I can hear the desire in her voice.

"I love you, Nellie. We all do. Please don't leave us," I beg her. I just got her like this, and I can't fucking lose her.

"I am right here," she confesses. She is trying to reassure me, but it won't work until I taste her fucking juices in my mouth.

I release my hold on her throat and quickly remove my clothes, throwing them to the side. I grab her wrist and lead her into the shower, pushing her against the wall.

The water automatically turns on and rushes over us as I look down at her naked body. She needs a distraction and to feel more than just the grief she is feeling right now. I can do that and make her forget, even if it's for a little bit.

I slowly sink to my knees in front of her, resting my hands on either side of her body on the wall as I lean in and slide my tongue through her folds. She grabs onto my hair, guiding me where she wants me. I follow her lead and kiss her mound before I explore her folds with my tongue. I groan when the first taste of her arousal touches my tongue, making me shove my face as far as I can between her sweet thighs.

I spread her lips and suck on her clit before I move to her dripping entrance, and I push my tongue into her tight hole. The walls of her pussy wrap tightly around my tongue as she moans out her pleasure. I lift her leg and rest it on my shoulder so that I can get a better angle as she rides my face while I fuck her with my tongue. I close my eyes as she starts to grind against my face, taking everything I have to offer her and getting lost for different reasons. I have never been good at talking, but I have always been good at this right here.

Nellie needs assurance, and she needs to know that we will love her no matter what state of mind she is in. This is the only way I know how to show her that I love and need her.

She needs to see what I am willing to do to help her forget Zayden and her pain, and he is about to see just how far I am willing to go.

11

Ashton

I lean against the side of the pool house and look out at the forest. I have the same fucking feeling I had when I first went to give Nellie the bad news; someone is watching me. I turn and nod at one of our guys. He nods back and starts to head toward the pool house. I turn and look at the forest, push off the house, and walk through the grass towards the trees.

There are too many things that are not adding up, and I need to figure it all out before the five weeks are up. My family is counting on me to find Zayden and Nellie's sister. I don't know if finding her is possible, but I am going to try.

I walk into the trees towards the swamp as the wind begins to pick up. The clouds are moving in, and it will not be long before it starts to rain again, washing away any evidence that someone or something is watching us.

I stop next to a tree when I see a grey wolf with white markings and black chains around his body. I slowly walk over to him and kneel in front of the wolf. Its eyes searching mine as I lift my hand and gently stroke his fur down his back. "Ace," I whisper.

I slowly stand and begin making my way deeper into the forest as Ace walks beside me. Even after all these centuries, I will never get used to seeing him in chains during the day. His kind has curses just like ours. I don't know much because they keep their secrets between their own just like we do, but I know enough.

I inhale sharply when I see a figure leaning against one of the trees. It starts raining on us right as Ace and I stop a few feet from Zayden. This fucking human, I swear he has no fucking fear, or at least he hides it well. Maybe he is just fucking stupid, or maybe his obsession with Nellie has completely made him stupid and not care about what happens to him. I will find out what his weaknesses are soon.

I want so fucking badly to wrap my hands around his neck and watch the life leave his eyes, but I can tell others are watching us. When I find out which one of our kind is helping him, I will fucking lock them away. That is worse than death for our kind because being locked away prohibits them from finding their mate, and that is so much worse than fucking death.

I will ensure that everyone that has gone against us will pay, maybe not today or even tomorrow, but I will get the upper hand on this fucking human. When I get my hands on him, there will be no mercy for him after what he has put my family through. I have never seen my cousins show fear before, not until this human. I need to take away the threat, and the only way to do that is to end his life or lock him away and force him to fucking watch my cousins and the others enjoy a life with Nellie, which might hurt him more.

I will not stop until he is suffering. He thinks he is obsessed and he can do whatever the fuck he wants without consequences because of who is helping him. He has no idea what obsession is, and he has no idea just how much of a nightmare I can fucking become for him, but he will.

I know he is not alone; he would be stupid to be out here alone. He has others with him, others that refuse to be seen. I can smell that he is getting help from our kind, but I can't tell who they are. Whoever it is has been smart enough to mask their complete smell, but they are clearly enemies. The only question is which ones?

"It took you long enough to finally come out here," Zayden says with amusement, continuing to lean against the tree with his arms crossed over his chest.

He thinks he is so fucking smart and has everything figured out, but he will find out that nothing in our world is certain, nothing but the connection. He wants to break it, and my family, but the only one that is going to break is him. He better fucking pray he always stays a step ahead of me.

"You have some balls on you, kid. I will give you that," I say through gritted teeth. Ace stops at my side, and I rest my hand on his back. I can feel his heart beating. I know he wants to rip Zayden apart, and I would let him if we were alone, but I won't risk my friend's life. Friends are hard to find, and you need to protect the ones you do find. Ace might be a Night Walker, but he is still family to me.

"I see you have a pet," Zayden says, looking down at Ace.

Ace growls and takes a few steps forward, ensuring he is between me and the human. I can't die, but Ace can. He knows that, but I can tell he doesn't care. Ace is fearless and will never back down from a human, not after what the humans did to his kind. We all have reasons why we are the way we are. Night Walkers haven't forgotten what humans do when they are afraid. Night Walkers used to live behind bars because of humans, and they hate humans more than they hate our kind, which is saying a lot.

We have all seen what humans are capable of when they fear something they don't understand. This human, however, has no idea about the other paranormal creatures that exist. He has no idea who the fuck he is baiting.

"Stupid for you to come alone, vampire," Zayden says, smiling.

I tilt my head to the side as I smile back at him. "You are the stupid one, human. I can't die, but you can," I warn him.

"Are we really going to play my dick is bigger than yours?" He asks, laughing.

"Stupid human, he is not alone," a voice says from behind me. I turn slightly and watch as he comes out of the shadows.

What the fuck is a Shadow doing here? It has been centuries since I have seen a Shadow. They usually stay in their own kingdom and don't get involved with our kind or the Night Walkers. The only ones they are close to are the Starlights. If this Shadow is here, then others have heard of what Zayden has done or at least what he is trying to do, which is not fucking good.

He stops at my side and leans against the tree, folding his arms over his chest, his eyes on the human.

"Who the fuck are you?" Zayden snaps at him. Bad fucking move, dude. One thing we have all learned is you don't fucking piss off a Shadow.

I look at Zayden, and he has his hands balled up into fists; he is such a stupid fucking man.

"Who I am is not your concern. Your concern should be are you willing to die today?" The Shadow asks in an amused voice, sending chills down my fucking spine.

"Give her to me, and all of this will be over," Zayden says calmly.

Zayden's voice might be calm, but his breathing and racing heart indicate that he is starting to lose control. "She doesn't belong to you, Zayden. She never did," I snap at him. I guess he is not the only one starting to lose control.

"Fine, I will trade her sister for her," Zayden confesses with a smile.

Her sister is gone. I have searched everywhere, and all the information indicates she has been fucking sold.

"You don't have her sister," I say with not as much confidence as I wanted to.

"Do I or do I not?" He taunts.

"I am not playing your fucking games," I snap at him, my hands forming into fists. This motherfucker is good, too fucking good.

"Oh, but you already are, and guess what, Ashton, I am winning," he whispers.

"For now," The Shadow answered.

"You have a month to decide. Bring her to me, or her sister dies," Zayden says, looking at each of us. I don't do good with fucking ultimatums.

Zayden doesn't give me time to respond before he turns around and walks deeper into the woods. I can hear whoever is with him following behind.

"What the fuck are you doing here, Ajax?" I ask, turning and looking at him.

"I have been watching. You seem to have a problem on your hands," Ajax says calmly.

I shake my head and look back in the direction Zayden just disappeared in. "We got it."

"Do you?" He asks.

His voice has no amusement, only concern, which makes me curious. His kind typically stays away from ours, so I am fucking curious as to why he cares if we have a human problem. Shadows have more of a connection with the humans than any of the rest of us. They even call some friends, as do we, but we are fucking selective. We only allow the Chosen Human Families in our circles, which right now appears to be a bad idea.

Zayden comes from one of those chosen, and look at the mess he is making. He really feels untouchable, which, I must say, narrows down my search for which our kind who is helping him. There is only a particular group of our enemies that would give him this much confidence and who would advise him to ask us to fucking choose.

They must not know my cousins that well, and I will be keeping this to my fucking self until after the five weeks are up. They must complete the connection, and this little encounter would stop that from happening. I will tell them about Zayden when it won't be a distraction from Nellie. She needs to be their primary focus, and right now, she is, and I will do whatever I have to do to keep it that way.

"Yes, now go before the others know that your kind is in our kingdom," I warn him.

The last thing we need right now is to start a fight with the Shadows, and from what I know of Ajax, he is the enforcer for them just like Ace is for the Night Walkers, and I am for the Guardians. We have that in common. He is distant and cold, just like the rest of us who haven't found our mate yet, but that is the only other thing we have in common with Ajax.

"I will stay close by. You know how to reach me if you need me," Ajax says softly.

I nod because right now, I am fucking confused, and I don't know what else to do. His kind makes all of us fucking nervous. He quickly turns around and disappears into the shadows of the forest.

I look down at Ace, and he is staring up at me. It won't be much longer before he will be able to take human form, which is what I need right now. Even though most of our kind would not agree with us working together, I need his help.

We need to find Zayden and Nellie's sister before the time is up. Even though I don't believe Zayden, he is not stupid, which means he plans on hurting my family even more than he already has. I will take my best friend's help if it means that my family stays safe and we finally can get rid of fucking Zayden.

12

Zayden

The rain is coming down harder, and the wind is picking up. My hair and clothes are soaked as I approach my parked car on the other side of the forest. I didn't think Ashton would come out, and I didn't think he would bring friends, but I shouldn't be surprised. He would be stupid to meet me alone.

I don't want to make any fucking deals with any of them, but if it means I will finally get my fucking hands on Nellie for good, then fucking fine, I will make a deal, even though I have no intentions of keeping it.

Ashton has to know that, but I know him and his kind; they will not take the risk. Not when it has to do with Nellie and her happiness. Her Guardians think they have all of this fucking figured out, but the truth is I am already ten steps ahead of them. They might be fucking her right now, but I will be able to fuck her for the rest of my life.

I am done playing games, even though I must say it has been fun, but the games have to end sometime. I am giving him four fucking weeks to bring her to me, and if he doesn't, he will have to face the consequences. Either way, they are all going to suffer. Either way, they are going to lose.

They have already lost; they just don't fucking know it yet. Other paranormal creatures being in the mix complicates things, but at the same time, it will make it so much more fun.

This started out as me wanting her, needing her, but now it is more than that. This is about revenge, and this is about saying and doing whatever I need to do to make them pay and to make sure that they don't have her. I will take them all down if I have to. I will even kill her and me if I have to.

I don't fucking care anymore. This has gone way too far as it is, and none of this should have happened. I should have taken her fucking years ago and ran, but I didn't, and now I have to pay for my mistake.

She did this. She is the reason that any of this is happening. If she would have just fucking given in to me and loved me the way I deserve, then she wouldn't be suffering right now. Her father would still be alive, and she would know where her sister was.

I know that all of this must be fucking killing her inside, and I would be lying if I said it didn't turn me on, knowing that I am the cause of her pain, and this is just the start. She hasn't felt pain yet, but she will once I get my fucking hands on her. She has made me look like a fool, and because of that, she will fucking pay. Her fuck boys will pay, and the world they have built will fucking burn.

I stop when I see two figures step out from behind a tree; their hands are in fists, and their eyes are dead-locked onto me. I knew that they were listening and watching, and I knew that they were close. Ashton has no idea who the fuck is helping me, but he is smart. I know it won't be long before he fucking figures out who is helping me, but until then, I will watch him try and keep up with me. I am surprised they haven't figured out that the Falco brothers are the ones feeding me information. They have kept up their end of the deal, and so far, their information has been helpful and it has allowed me to understand their kind better. But I can tell they are not happy with me. They think they own me or something because I am supposed to be their guard, but they don't. They think they do, but I am playing them as much as I am playing Nellie, Ashton, and her Guardians. All of them are just in my way, and I am using all of them until I get what I want.

The Rosseti brothers, the Falco brothers, and the Deluca brothers all will die and suffer. I will do as I am told with the Falcos until I don't need them anymore, then I will throw them away like trash, just like I know they will try and do with me. Right now, we need each other, but very fucking soon, we won't anymore. So, friends will once again become enemies, just like it should be.

"What the fuck was that Zayden?" Gain asks through gritted teeth. They hate that I didn't ask for permission, but I am not the permission-asking type; just ask Nellie.

I am fucking sick and tired of the Guardians acting as if they own me and my family. My family is gone because of these fuckers. These fuckers should have stayed wherever the fuck they are from. Why did they have to take over our world? Why the fuck did they have to bring their violence, rules, and laws to us?

We were doing just fine without them. We don't need the Guardians; they need us more than we need them. They need our women because, without them, they can't continue their bloodlines, so if anyone owns anyone, we own them. They fear the day we humans realize it and stand up for ourselves.

I will not just sit back and let them do whatever the fuck they want anymore. Nellie has changed everything for me, and because of her, we will start a war that will destroy everything these fucking monsters care about. They will soon discover that we are, in fact, the fucking monsters, and it is us who they should fear, not the other way around.

"I made a deal," I reply. I might hate these fuckers. I might want to destroy them and watch them suffer, but like I said, right now, we need each other, so I need to fucking act as if I will do as they say, or everything can go up in flames, and I could lose her forever. I am not willing to fucking risk that, not when I am so fucking close to getting her back.

"A deal without our permission," Salem says, calmer than his brother did. Salem is the reasonable one, and Gain is the one I have to fucking watch my back with. He is more unstable than most of the Guardians and so thirsty for power and control that he doesn't care who he has to destroy. He will do anything to get what he wants without a second thought.

"You want them, and I want her. This way, we both get what we want," I whisper back. I don't fucking care if, at the end of the day, they don't get shit. I don't care about the Falco brothers. I am using them, just like they are fucking using me.

Salem and Gain quickly close the distance between us and stop in front of me.

"Don't play games with us, human," Gain warns

If I could fucking kill them right here, right now, I would, but I can't, I just fucking can't.

I take a deep, shaky breath and shake my head. "No games."

"No deal," Gain snaps back.

He hates not being in control, and I know he doesn't trust me, which means I need to walk in a fucking straight line so my plan doesn't fucking blow up in my fucking face.

"No shit, but I had to say something. We want to fuck with them and make them suffer. Well, this is the way to do it," I snap back. My heart is racing so fast I can hear it, and I know they can too. These fuckers know how they affect me, and it pisses me the fuck off. We might be on the same side right now, but that will change, and when it does, it is going to be an all-out war.

"You better be right, Zayden," Salem warns me. His voice is low and stern.

They both quickly turn around and walk into the forest in the opposite direction that I am going. Thank the heavens. I allow myself to take another deep breath. I feel better when they stay out of sight; the less contact I have with them, the better. They think they have everything figured out but made a big mistake. They made the mistake of trusting me, and I will lie, steal, do, or say anything to get Nellie. They think because I am human, that I will keep my word. They have no idea just how dishonest and cruel I can be, but they will find out; everyone is going to find out.

I just need to get Nellie, and once I have her by my side, everything else will fall into place. I don't give a fuck if she has fallen in love with her fuck boys. She loved me first and still loves me; I know it. I know I have to make up for what I have done to her, and I will, but she will fall in line with me just like she has fallen in line with them.

I will become her king, and she will be my queen, and once we rid this world of Guardians all together, she and I will rule it all, side by side, just like it was always meant to be.

It fucking took longer to get to my car than I thought, stupid fucking weather. I swear the weather has no fucking idea what it wants. I can't relate; I know exactly what I fucking want.

I pull into the motel parking lot, and the whore has her door open waiting for me. I tried to fucking stay away from other women, but a man needs what a man needs. Until I have Nellie back, I have to get off somehow. Even if it is a whore sucking my dick, at least I will be able to find some release.

"Are you ready for this boys?" I ask Mal and Wes. Both of them nod without saying a word. As they open the car doors and get out, I sit back in my seat as they walk past the whore and into her room. We all need to get off some time.

Nellie will be my fucking whore. I tried, I fucking tried to be the nice guy for her, and even at one point, I really wanted to be the nice guy, but it is just not who I am.

I should have known that I would be just like my father when it came to women. I tried to fight it for Nellie, but ultimately, my genes won. I shouldn't be surprised I couldn't be the good guy forever. Good guys always come in fucking last, and with Nellie right now, she is choosing fucking Guardians over me. She wants a man that will force her, take charge, and not give her a choice; well, I can be that fucking man.

She thinks the Guardians can give her what she needs, but they don't know her like I do. They will never ever fucking know her the way I do. I will awaken so many things inside her. She will ask for forgiveness for what she has put me through, and when I am done with her, the girl her fuck boys have fallen in love with will be gone.

I open the door and get out of the car, closing the distance between me and the whore. I stop in front of her, and before she can say a fucking word, I grab onto her throat and push her against the wall, forcing the breath out of her lungs as I lean in and smash my lips to hers. She tries to fight, but I tighten my grip on her throat, and before long, I feel her body melt against mine.

No one tells me no.

13

Darius

5 Years Ago

I pull up in the same spot I have been parking in off and on for the last few years. This place, this spot, has become like my second home. I never saw her coming, but now that she is in my life, somehow, she has wiggled her way inside me. Even though my heart doesn't beat, and I have no soul, I have a soft spot for her that I can't really explain.

Obligations. Obligations, fuck Obligations. Nothing is set in stone until my heart starts to beat, and I am given a fucking soul.

Our kind typically doesn't fall for humans who are not our mates, but I am not normal. I never have been, which is why I am the unstable, out-of-control one. Most are uncomfortable around me, even my own kind, which is funny because we are all unstable and out of control. I just don't hide it like the others do.

There is no reason to hide who or what I am inside, plus it fucking keeps people away for the most part.

This woman who has taken over my life accepts me this way, and I have to say she amazes me every day. Most would turn away and fear me because of what I am, but it appears that she has accepted it all. She craves me and what only I can give her. I plan on giving her the world, even though one day I will be mated to another, and one day she will be mated to another; right now, that doesn't matter.

Even once we are mated, it won't matter. Many of us have women on the side once mated, and whoever she is mated to won't fucking tell me no, not with who I am, who my family is. I will be able to keep her even if it is her obligation to breed with another, even though she can never give me children; it doesn't fucking matter.

I don't know how she did it, and at first, I questioned her, questioned this, whatever this is we have together, but now after several years, I have just learned that what we might not make sense but nothing in our world fucking makes sense. My brother, our father, Ashton, everyone has tried to warn me, but I won't listen, I fucking can't. I am addicted to the feeling of her pussy wrapped tightly around my dick and the way she moans my name.

I might not love her, but love has nothing to do with needing someone, and I fucking need her, and she knows it.

I walk into her house the same way I have since we started seeing each other. She doesn't want others to know we are a thing, and I don't mind hiding. The less people know, the better; if others know about us, they keep it to themselves. They wouldn't fucking dare go against me. It is one of the good things about my kind and the humans fearing me.

I would rather be feared and respected than anything else. If people like you, they act differently around you, and I don't need to be liked. I don't fucking care about many things, but the things I do care about, I would die for. This woman is one of those things I would die for if I were able.

But lucky for her, I can't die, not until I find my mate, then a lot of things will change, but until that happens, I am a free Guardian, and I can do whatever the fuck I want with whoever I want, and right now, I choose her.

I don't understand it, but she knows I will do whatever she asks. I never thought I could feel this way about a human, but with her, it is so fucking easy. It doesn't make sense; I can't feel anything, not really. If I were to have to guess, what I feel for her is strong; it is love. No, Guardians like me can't love, I don't deserve love after what I have done, but it is pretty fucking close.

She stoled my non-beating heart the moment I laid eyes on her, and even though I know one day another will claim her, it is worth having her right now. Deep down inside, I know that when the time comes, neither of us will be able to walk away from the other. She has become addicted to me, and even though I shouldn't, I have become addicted to her.

I didn't know I could even feel the emotion of need, but she has changed everything for me. My brother thinks I am crazy for falling for a woman that is not my mate, but I can't fucking help it. She is so fucking intoxicating.

I walk through the living room and down the hallway. When I walk into her room and see her already bent over the bed with her ass in the air, my dick moves in my jeans as I unbutton and unzip my pants and make my way across the room. I stop behind her and drop my pants and boxers to my ankles as I grab her hair, pulling her face off of the bed as I align the tip of my cock with her dripping pussy. I rest my lips against her ear, and her breathing increases as she tightens her grip on the blanket. Fuck, she knows exactly what I need, when I need it, even before I fucking do. I don't need to ask; she already knows and does as she is told with no words spoken. She is fucking gorgeous.

"I have been craving you, Angie."

"I am right here, Darius," she whispers back.

I push myself into her tight fucking pussy, the pussy that no one else has touched but me. She moans as I pull her head back and kiss her jawline to her neck. I bite down hard, my teeth cutting through her skin, and her blood enters my mouth as I place my hand next to her head.

She screams out my name like she has done a thousand times before. Her pussy wraps tightly around my dick as I bite down harder on her neck. Right now, she is mine.

My fucking whore.

14

Loyal

Present Day

Week 1 – Day 1

Nellie has kept her distance for the past five days. She hasn't said much as she tries to process what has happened to her father and sister. I don't think time or distance will help her right now. I don't know if anything is truly going to help her right now. We all want to help and show her that we are right here and not going anywhere, but honestly, we don't know how to do that without sex.

I know it fucking sounds wrong, and maybe in the outside world it is, but for us, it is our way of assuring her, and right now she needs that. She is feeling ashamed and guilty about what happened, but it is not her fault; none of this is her fucking fault. We just need to prove it to her and show her that the only person responsible is Zayden, and we will, but for the next five weeks, she is fucking ours. We will make sure Zayden is the furthest thing from her fucking mind.

This is the time when we need to surround her, consume her, and make her fucking forget. This is not the time to give her space or leave her alone, and we need to remind her that she belongs to us, and we belong to her. This is the time to distract her and replace every fucking thought and emotion she has towards Zayden.

We are about to open her eyes to our real world. A world where we are able to remove our masks and allow her to see our deepest, darkest desires. She will learn with us that there is nothing we won't do for her. If she asks for it, it will be fucking hers. There will be no turning back after we give into our base desires, and she gives into hers. It will be completed, and no one, not even Zayden, can take her from us.

Darius, Christos, Neo, and I sit silently in the living room. We are not big on communication, and right now, all of our emotions are going fucking crazy. We will get a handle on them eventually, but it will take time. Lucky for us, we have the rest of our lives with Nellie to get a handle on them. We won't be the only ones teaching her shit. She will always be teaching us, teaching us how to use our humanity.

Nellie running and going to her father's house, needing to experience the pain and sorrow there, scared the shit out of us, but keeping her distance has worried us even more.

I never thought I would use that word. These feelings are new to all of us; fear, anxiety, all of these emotions are drowning us. We need to forget just as much as Nellie does. We need to distract ourselves so we don't do something fucking stupid, which is why we have locked all the windows and doors from the inside, and Ashton has locked all the windows and doors from the outside.

We will be forced to give in to each other for the next five weeks, and there will be no escaping. This is the only way to make sure that the connection is finally fucking completed. After this, nothing will be the same, and Zayden will be the one that is fucking afraid. After this, there will be nothing holding us back from ripping his heart from his chest and watching the light leave his eyes.

We have shown him mercy because of Nellie, but now, she will no longer want to show him mercy after what he has done to her family. She is wild and strong, and it is time we show her how to use that to get revenge. We will teach her and walk beside her through this because I am learning that is what you do for the people you love. Our kind has always been loyal to our families, but now it is time to be nothing but loyal to Nellie. She is the most important thing to all of us now, and everything, and I mean everything else, comes fucking second.

I inhale deeply while we all sit here in uncomfortable silence. But soon, it will be replaced with screams and moans of pain and pleasure.

We hear the bedroom door open and close, and Nellie's emotions slam into me like a storm. She is feeling overwhelmed, enraged, and fucking turned on with desire. Regardless of how we feel right now, she is our priority, and we need to make sure it stays that way.

I hold my breath as Nellie walks into the living room, wearing nothing but a t-shirt. Fuck, words have not been invented yet for how she looks wearing my shirt. She stops in front of me and looks over my naked chest before she slowly climbs into my lap and rests her head against my chest and her hand on my stomach, causing my heart to race.

I wrap my arm around her, press my nose into her hair, and inhale her calming scent, reassuring myself that everything is going to be okay. I rest my chin on her head as I look at my brother and the others, all leaning forward on their elbows while they keep a watchful eye on Nellie. It has been fucking hell for all of us over the last five days. We have all wanted to fuck her, hold her, and tell her we are sorry, but she needed her space, and we needed to be able to give it to her, no matter how fucking hard it was to do.

I slide my hand along the skin of her bare knee and up until my fingers gently brush against her core. Her skin is so fucking soft, and the heat radiating off her is sinking into the coldness of mine, warming me from the outside. Her chest rises and falls faster as I move my fingers over her clit, and down through her soaked folds. She is so wet and needy for us.

I close my eyes as my heart pounds in my chest. I slowly slide two fingers into her hot pussy, her walls wrapping tightly around them, and she sinks her nails into my stomach, making me growl in need.

"Before we do anything else, sweetness, we need to go over a few things with you," I say calmly, trying to hold myself back from devouring her.

"Hmmm," she replies. We have to make sure she understands how important her words are, especially while we are exploring our desires.

Fuck me, her pussy flutters around my fingers; I need to fucking focus. But I can't resist slowly moving my fingers in and out of her, winding her up.

"We need to start with a safe word," we all say simultaneously.

She slowly sits up, pushing my fingers into her deeper as she turns and looks at me while rocking her hips against me. She moans as she braces herself on my chest, and her eyes fall shut. I lean in and nip her bottom lip, drawing a drop of blood. "The safe word is for you to use if you feel uncomfortable and want any of us to stop what we are doing," I say, licking the drop of blood before it falls.

"The safe word is also to remind you that you are the one that is in control, love," Christos reassures.

Nellie opens her eyes, stares at me, and runs her tongue along her bottom lip, pulling it between her teeth as she starts to grind against my hand and my hard dick underneath her ass. Fuck, she is not the only one that is wet. I can feel my precum wetting my sweatpants. Fuck, she is gorgeous when she takes what she wants from us.

"If you want us to stop at any time, angel, you will use the word *'Black.'* As soon as that word leaves your lips, we will stop, no questions asked," Darius explains. His words are true; the safe word is an automatic stop button. It doesn't matter how turned on we are; what she wants is the only thing that matters. She will always come first.

"If you use the word *'Orange,'* baby girl, you are telling us to continue but to proceed with caution," Neo says in a low, dark, desired voice.

"If you say the word, *'White.'* You are giving us full permission to continue however we want," we all say at the same time, making me smile.

"Why would I say the word?" She asks with a moan.

I press my face against her neck, licking my way up to her ear, as I slide a third finger into her, increasing my pace. "Because our deepest darkest desires might be too much for you; a limit. The words are important, sweetness. Make sure you remember them," I growl against her ear.

"White," she moans out, making my heart skip a beat.

Fuck it, I can't hold back anymore.

I slide my fingers from her pussy, and I take her into my arms. She wraps her legs around my waist and her arms around my neck as I bite down on her neck. She screams out as I take long strides to a part of the pool house she hasn't been to yet.

Each of us has our own sex room, depending on our kink. We will each spend time in each other's rooms for one week, all of us giving into the other's kinks. It is our way of submitting to each other and to Nellie. In each room, we will all experiment and experience each other's kinks with Nellie, and she will learn who we really are. There will be no need for words, just pure fucking sex to show her. We have always been better with actions than we are with words, and this is no different.

I stop in front of the door to my room, and I swallow down my nerves as I open the door. I walk in and hear the guys come in and shut the door behind them as I lay Nellie down on the bed. My knife was already laid out waiting for me, making my dick throb. I push my sweats down and walk out of them before I lean over Nellie and waste no time stepping between her legs and pushing into her hot wet pussy. I groan against her neck as I pull back and slam into her again, making her cry out as her pussy pulses around me as I bottom out and still. I grab my knife and look down at her. She lifts her arms above her head and smiles at me as I hold onto the shirt and slice down the front of it, exposing her beautiful body to me.

Her full breasts with hard nipple call to me, and I start to thrust into her roughly, causing her luscious tits to bounce with every forward thrust. I press down on her lower stomach, and I can feel my hardness pushing up under my hand as I lean down, hovering just out of reach of her lips.

I place the knife against her chest. "I want to taste your blood, sweetness. I want to mark you," I whisper against her lips while I watch her face for her reaction to my request.

"White," she moans. FUCK. I push up, slowing my pace. Putting pressure on the knife, I start to carve the letters of my name across her chest. Blood lined each letter, making my dick harden further than it had before.

She arches her back off the bed, letting out a moaning scream. Our breathing increases as she moves her hips to meet mine thrust for thrust. Her pussy squeezes me in her iron grip with each slice into her skin. I watch the blood roll down her stomach as I carve the last letter of my name. I toss the knife to the side and bend down to lick the blood from her body. Her blood is so fucking sweet on my tongue, I pick up my pace. Our bodies slapping together, the wet sounds of my dick pushing in and out of her, has my balls tightening. Fuck, I am not going to last as long as I wanted, but having her like this, hearing her say *white* without needing to think, is better than anything I have experienced so far in my long life.

Her emotions hit me straight in my heart. Desire, passion, love, all the things I never thought I would feel towards or from a woman. She is intoxicating in all of the right fucking ways, and I know, I fucking know I will never get enough. She is my drug, my reason for living, and this is my way of showing her just that.

I press our bodies together, her blood coating my stomach as I continue to rut into her with wild abandon, bringing us both to climax. She screams out my name as her pussy milks my dick, and I paint her pussy with my release, her name a moan on my lips.

15

Neo

Day 2

I lean against the wall with my arms crossed over my chest as I watch Nellie sleep. She is so beautiful right now. Fuck, she is always fucking beautiful, but right now, it feels like I am seeing her for the first time. She gave Loyal permission, and she said the right word that allowed him to continue, which reassures me that she was fucking made for us, all four of us.

Having a mate would change things and who we are, but I didn't think it would change us this much. Nellie is the center of my life, but now I also have Darius, the Guardian whom so many have feared. I am not afraid when I look at him. I want to help and show him that he is not the monster he thinks he is.

He is changing, and he has changed. In a short time, I saw his walls crash down when he saved Nellie from Zayden, and now he is all in. We are all finally on the same page together, which only makes us stronger. We are so much stronger together than we will ever be apart, and our kind and the humans fear that. They fear us and the power that we have.

Our world is filled with more fear and violence than ever before, and I have a feeling it will only get worse. There will be an all-out fucking war for her if they learn about Nellie and her Touches. If anyone, and I mean anyone fucking tries to take her from us, it won't matter if they can die or not. We will make them feel nothing but pure fucking agony.

We will put Zayden's head on a fucking stake, showing everyone in our kingdom and the others what happens when someone chooses to go against us. Our kind has always been powerful, but Nellie has changed things more than she realizes right now, but she will. She will see that she is a fucking Queen, and it will be a beautiful day when she finally realizes that she can have whatever the fuck she wants.

She has lived her entire fucking life by the rules and laws, and now, with us, she will be the one to make up the laws and rules; what she says will fucking go. Everyone will kneel for her and see that she is their

Queen. The humans and the Guardians will either fall in line for her, or they will suffer the consequences for going against us. There is no more fucking mercy and gray areas. Those things have not proven to be effective for us recently, so no fucking more.

Memories of watching my brother finish inside her flood my mind. The front of her body is completely covered in blood. Loyal has a thing for blood and knives, but this was the first time I saw him let go and allow himself to feel what was happening. He couldn't hide his emotions, love, desire, and craving for her. She couldn't hide her need for him, for what only my brother could give her.

We will all feel what he felt last night—how she gave in, her moans, and screaming out our names. The sound of her voice when she lets go and allows herself to feel our desire for her is gorgeous and breathtaking.

I guess it will also be the first time for the rest of us. We have been trying so fucking hard to keep her safe that it has taken over everything else, and we are finally able to feel more than just rage and anxiety. We all know that Ashton is outside, keeping watch, and I know we can trust him with our lives. We all know that there is plenty going on outside of these walls, but our Father will keep everyone in line.

Ashton and our Father know how important completing the connection is. I hope that one day, Ashton can find his mate and experience what we are all about to experience with Nellie. Ashton has been waiting for centuries for his mate, and if we could help him find her, we would, but it doesn't fucking work that way, or all of our kind would be mated.

But one day, Ashton will find her, and when he does, he will never be the same again. He will change just like we have. It will be a good day. He deserves to be happy and feel what I and the others are feeling right now. Ashton is loyal and honest and will do anything to protect those he cares about. Even though he doesn't have a beating heart or soul, he is a good person, even if he doesn't see it. I do; we all do. My brother doesn't trust many Guardians or humans but trusts Ashton, which means something in our world.

He is patient and will do his duty for us until the day comes when his heart is jilted to life, and he is given a soul. When that day comes, his life will never be the same, and we will no longer be the most important thing in his life. But that is how it is meant to be. We have all been taught that way, our mate comes first before anything or anyone else. It is the only way the connection stays the way it should.

I take a deep breath as I look around the room. We are all spread out across the room, waiting for the right time to continue with Nellie. We might not need sleep, but she does, and we want to introduce her to things in the best possible way we can. We want to pleasure and love her, but we can't do those things if she is not taken care of first. I look at my brother sitting in the chair with his eyes closed and breathing steady.

He was able to find a balance between being rough and gentle, and I will try and do the same. Loyal and Nellie have been going at it for the last several hours. She fell asleep not long ago, and we have all just been watching her sleep. Just watching her stirs emotions in all of us. I can feel it, and we are all in awe of her; we are all addicted.

We need to be gentle, and at the same time, we need to be rough. It will be a battle for each of us in different ways. Loyal made it look so easy, but it is hard to keep control. We love her, and we don't want to hurt her, but at the same time, there is a euphoric balance between pain and pleasure, and if done correctly, it enhances the sexual experience to unimaginable heights.

Her moans and screams of pleasure filled the entire room, and we all got off by just watching her and my brother. This is the time when we all get to let go of who we are outside of this pool house and when we get to truly be ourselves with Nellie, but this is also when she gets to discover who she is, now that she is our mate.

Zayden has complicated things in ways I wish were not even a problem, but we can't change it right now, and we can't change what he has done to our mate. But what we can do is show her what it is like to actually be fucking loved. She deserves to be loved and worshipped and so much fucking more.

So many things have happened since we fell to our knees in the club, and a lot of it we never saw coming, but now none of that matters. It is in the past, or at least that is what I am trying to tell myself. Once we leave this pool house, there will be many things we need to take care of, but until then, it doesn't matter.

I push off the wall and grab the knife from the dresser as I approach the bed. I take a deep breath and look down at Nellie lying on her back. Her front is fully exposed to me, and I lick my lips as I pull down the sweatpants and step out of them.

I don't need to look at the guys to know their eyes are on Nellie and me. I crawl onto the bed, settle between her legs, and place my hands on either side of her as I lean down and gently start to kiss between her breasts. Slowly nipping and kissing my way down to her stomach and perfect fucking pussy. I prop myself up on my elbows to watch her face as I explore her while she sleeps. I lean in, slowly dragging my tongue from her entrance to her clit, paying extra attention to the small bundle of nerves with the tip of my tongue. She starts to rock her hips slightly, and a small gasp escapes her mouth as I taste her.

I sit up, sliding my body up her body until my cock nudges her entrance. I hover over her as she turns her head and slowly opens her eyes. She smiles at me, making my heart race. "White," she whispers.

I press my lips to hers and run my tongue along her lips. She opens for me, and I explore her mouth with my tongue. The taste of her still lingers on my tongue, and she moans at the taste of her on my lips as I push into her slowly. Once I have eased into her, I break the kiss, grab the knife, and slice across my pubic area. She watches as I cut myself, and I feel the blood flow down between us. Dropping the knife, I wrap my fingers around her throat, pull her towards me, and capture her lips again, deepening the kiss as I lift her by her ass, and she wraps her legs around my waist.

I never want any distance between us, and I want to feel her naked skin against mine. I need to feel her body shake as her pussy wraps tighter around me. I want to taste her. Fuck, intoxicating is not a strong enough fucking word for her.

She wraps her arms around me and digs her nails into my back as I bounce her up and down on my dick, controlling the pace and depth with each thrust into her. I pull back, breaking the kiss to look down at where we are connected. I watch as my blood coats my dick and slides into her, mixing my blood with her juices, making me fuck her harder. I close my eyes, enjoying the feeling of our bodies slick with blood and sweat racing towards our release.

Using knives and blood play has never been something that I have ever enjoyed, but right now, it is my kink, not just my brothers. Any sexual act that will allow me to have her like this; vulnerable, turned on, and wild, I am game for.

I look at Nellie; her eyes are closed, and her head has fallen back. I tighten my grip on her throat as I lean down and bite hard into the pulsing vein in her neck. My teeth sink into her skin, and her life force flows into my mouth as she moves her hips with mine. Her sweet pussy pulled me into her further, hitting her sweet spot every time I thrust into her.

Fuck me sideways.

I bite down harder as her scream fills the room, and my name leaves her lips. Fuck, baby girl, say it again. I have never craved to hear my name come out of a woman's mouth like I crave right now. I will never

ever get fucking sick of hearing her scream my name as she bounces on my dick, chasing her sweet release.

No wonder they tried to warn us that it would be different once we were mated. I can fucking feel the connection between Nellie and me completely. It is hard to explain, but it feels as if our hearts and souls are becoming one, intertwining us in a way that can never be undone.

16

Christos

Day 3

I have never felt so alive in my entire life, and I haven't even fucking touched her yet. But now it is my turn, three days in, and we all feel consumed by her. We all feel complete. What a strange and amazing feeling. If there were more words to explain it, I would fucking use them, but with Nellie, there are never enough fucking words or ways to describe what she does to us or how we feel when we are with her.

Just fucking watching her getting fucked by Loyal and Neo has made me lose myself twice already. The next five weeks are going to take a lot out of all of us, but with Nellie, a lot of things I never thought were possible are becoming fucking possible.

I look around the room; Neo and Darius are standing by the locked back door, looking out the window. It is amazing to see my brother like this, calmer and more stable. Neo took Darius off guard, that is for sure. I think he took us all off guard, but my brother hasn't been this much at peace in a very long time, and as long as he is happy, I am so glad, and from what I can feel from the both of them, they are happy.

I look over at Loyal, who sits in the chair, watching his brother and mine. Loyal is calm at this moment; I knew he would be. With each of us being able to share our kinks and experience them all together, it is all going to make us calmer and more understood. Being understood has never been important to us, but it is when it comes to Nellie. We want her to understand the real us, just like we want to understand the real her.

She is more than just a woman from the Chosen Families, more than just a Delicate, and more than just our mate. We want to know everything about her and don't want her to hold anything back, so we must be willing to do the same.

Most women would be unable to handle all four of us, and that is where Nellie is different. She was made for us, and we were made for her. We were all destined to be together long before we were even born, which is why Zayden makes no sense to me. He knew who she was when he laid his eyes on her, and still, he allowed himself to fall for her. He has pushed limits that no other human would have, and no matter how he tries to justify his love for her, his love is nothing compared to our love for her, and it never will be.

I am excited to see how giving in to each other again changes things for us all. I know for a fact it will make us more possessive and jealous. Still, there will be a lot of things that we are not prepared for that will happen once these five weeks are over, including Nellie being pregnant with one of our children. She will eventually give each of us a son or sons. That is all we know, though. We have no idea what it will be like to be a father, and we won't until it happens.

One time, I asked my father how it felt to have two sons, and all he could say was that he was proud of his sons. He is proud to have two sons who are strong and will be able to continue on the bloodline. I know there is more he wanted to say, but my father is one of the Guardians who has never gotten a handle on having a beating heart and a soul. He struggles with showing affection, even with our mother's help. The only person who gets to see his real side is our mother, which is how it is supposed to be.

I sometimes wish he would have opened up more than he has with us, but I understand why he hasn't. He takes the whole don't show our weakness thing to the extreme and will never do anything that will make our kind question his strength. He will make sure that most fear him because, in his eyes, that is the only way to protect himself and our mother.

We might be the same as well. I haven't figured out yet how we are all going to be with the outside world with Nellie. Luckily, I don't have to worry about that for a few more weeks. Once we leave this pool house, there will be so many obligations that our heads will spin, but it is what happens when you are King. I wouldn't change it, but at the same time, I wish we could stay inside these walls of the pool house forever and not have to worry about what is happening on the outside.

We have all been waiting to be fathers for so long that sometimes, this doesn't feel real. It will hit all of us in the face that this is real once we see her belly start to grow, and that is when we will all become unhinged and on edge. Our kind typically loses all sense of reality and control when their mate is pregnant; it is just how it is.

From what we have heard, fear takes hold, and the idea of something possibly happening to our mate intensifies. We will do whatever we need to protect her, even if that means putting our lives down for hers. We will die for her without a second thought; it is just what you do when you fucking love someone.

While we wait for Nellie to get out of the shower, the steam fills the bedroom. I walk into the bathroom, knowing that she has washed her body clean and it is time for us to mark her again. We all want our scents on her skin, our fingertips bruised into her skin, our cum filling her, reminding her that we belong to her and she belongs to us.

I couldn't fucking wait anymore. So, I enter the bathroom needing to fucking hold her, taste her, lick her, and mark her; all the fucking things. Just waiting in the fucking room for her to come out is fucking hard, and I know the others feel the same way. We take obsession, need, and want to a whole new fucking level, a dangerous fucking level.

I open the shower and see Nellie standing underneath the water. She turns around and leans against the wall, showing off her new carving on her chest from Loyal. Fuck, seeing his name on her chest is a total fucking turn-on.

It hurt all of us to feel what she felt when Darius saved her from Zayden. We all could feel her pure fucking paralyzing fear, but Darius took care of her. I trusted my brother, and he needed to be the one to save her that time. He needed to be the one to hold and comfort her. When he finally looked her in the eyes, it made me tear up; the tears were of joy. My brother needed that push, and Nellie needed him at that moment. Darius is strong and possessive, which she needs from him.

Nellie opens her eyes and looks at me, and my heart skips a beat as I take the knife out of my pocket before I remove my sweatpants, throwing them to the side. I walk into the shower and stop in front of her; her hands are now against the shower wall as her eyes search mine. She is going to be beyond tired and sore once we are all done with her, but she will never be able to fucking forget what happened within the walls of this pool house.

This will be our place with her, and this will be our place together. I step into her, and her eyes stay on me as I lift the knife and place it right underneath the carving of Loyal's name. Her breathing starts to increase as I lightly guide the blade over her body, leaving behind a red line but not hard enough to break the skin. I trace up one arm, across her collarbone, down and around one nipple, repeating the process on the other, causing them to pebble into stiff peaks. Her body is covered in goosebumps as I continue my exploration down her other arm. I slowly lower myself to my knees, keeping light pressure against the knife and her skin. Nellie drops her head back against the shower wall with a moan as I continue to outline her lower stomach.

I slowly bring the blade around her full hips and down to her thigh. Leaning in, I kiss her mound briefly before I lift her leg and rest it over my shoulder, opening her up for me to slide my fingers through her folds. Her pussy is glistening for me, and I can't resist burying my face into her sweet cunt, sliding my tongue from front to back. She pushes her body against my face as I flip the knife around, holding the blade as I place the tip of the handle against her tight, wet hole.

I want to watch her get off on the handle of the knife. I want to show her that everything can be used for both pleasure and pain, and with us, we can find a balance between the two for her.

I sit back on my heels and watch Nellie's face as I push the handle into her pussy. She moans out my name when I start to fuck her. I glance down at where the handle is disappearing into her and can't hold back my growl when I see her juices dripping down the handle and coating my hand each time I pull it out and push it back in.

Everyone will fucking know that she belongs to us, and we belong to her.

There are not many things in our world that are certain, things can change in a moment and destroy fucking everything, but now in our lives, there is one thing that is certain, one thing that we can fucking count on, and that is Nellie. She is our everything; she is our Queen, and I know she is going to teach us as much as we teach her.

We need to be more for her than what we have been and more than what others think we are. We need to be her everything, and if need be, we need to be willing to change for her, just like I know she is willing to change for us. I can feel it right now; she is opening herself up to us in ways she never has with anyone else. We need to fucking do the same for her, and we need to make sure that we are not treating her like all the other women we have fucked over the years because she is fucking different.

What happens in this pool house between us will show her who we are, and we will see who she is. And when we walk out of this pool house, we will all be one. We are no longer two separate families, and whatever we were before Nellie no longer fucking matters.

When we leave this pool house, she will be a Queen, and we will be her Kings.

I pull out the knife and push my tongue into her pussy. Her walls wrap tightly around it as she screams out my name and cums in my mouth.

Just like the good girl she is.

17

Darius

DAY 4

I sit on the edge of the bed, holding tightly onto the knife as I look towards the bathroom. Steam continues to come out, with her moans and screaming of my brother's name, causing my heart to race and stop simultaneously. Her screams, her moans, everything about her is ripping me apart and putting me back together again. Holy shit, what I feel for her shouldn't be possible, but it is. Our world allows it to be. I wasn't grateful for it before, but I am now. I am thankful that she hasn't turned away from me or us. I am grateful for her, so much so that my heart beats because of her, and I feel because of her.

She is the cause of everything we are all feeling and experiencing right now.

Things are fucking crazy inside my head right now, and honestly, I can't tell if it is coming from me or all of us. I don't think it matters anymore; we are no longer separate; we are now one or will be after the pool house. I thought things were insane before everything we had been trying to get through, but it will be nothing compared to the next few weeks.

Knowing she will be pregnant when we leave this building scares the fucking shit out of me because if anything ever happened to her because of us, because of me, or because of Zayden, I would never fucking forgive myself. I would die inside; we all would. Protecting her has never been more important than it is now.

She will be vulnerable, easy to kill, and break when she is carrying our children. Her Touches will become more intense and increase, and her emotions will become more unstable, as will her ability to control herself.

We need to ensure that no one figures out what she is or what she can do, or our kind and the humans will want her to use her against us. They don't care about her, not really. They will only care about what they can gain from having her.

Once I said that all I can give her is the fucking, that I have nothing else to give her, that was a lie. It was a lie when I thought it and a lie when I tried to make it true. I am the one that put us in these dangerous situations with Zayden. If I had just been all in from the start, what had happened to her would have never happened.

I can feel it; she doesn't blame us for her father or sister. Instead, she is blaming herself, which isn't fucking right. It is our fault. We are the ones that should have fucking protected her and her family. Zayden should have never been able to get as close to her as he did when she was waiting to be mated. Our people failed her, and when we leave this pool house, each and every one of our men that didn't do what they were supposed to will fucking suffer. I will make sure they will never be able to find their mate, and that for them will be worse than me fucking killing them. I have done a shitty fucking job protecting our mate, no fucking more. She will see and learn that she can count on me. She can count on all of us.

We will be strong when she is weak.

We will be her foundation when she feels unstable.

We will be the strong arms that keep her safe when she is scared.

Everything and anything she needs, we will fucking be. Our whole fucking lives, we have been all selfish and cruel and did whatever the fuck we wanted, but now we are mated. Now we finally have the women that brought us all to life, and the least we can fucking do is try and be better for her. No, we will fucking be better for her.

I saved her from Zayden. I wanted to rip his fucking head off, but I couldn't bring myself to let her go, so he got away again. We should have fucking killed him a long ass time ago. If we had just killed him and got it over with, what he tried to do to her would have never fucking happened.

I will never forget the emotions I felt when she was in the car, her shaking body in my arms, or her tears soaking my skin as she shoved her face into my neck, a gesture I am starting to crave from her. I need her to need us, to need me. I never thought I would want this, want her. The connection made sure we came together, and now it is our job to make sure that we stay this way.

It broke my fucking heart when I brought her into the pool house bedroom, and she put her face down on the bed. I trained her to feel like she was just an object for me to use, but now I will spend the rest of my life showing her that she is so much fucking more. It killed me inside to see her bent over, just waiting for me to get off and be done with her. That is why I had to turn her around and make her look me in the eyes as I claimed her to show her that it is different now, that I am different now.

Tonight will be no different; I will let her touch me and look her in the eyes as I claim her and try to make love to her. I need her to understand that she is more to me than just some fucking hole I am fucking. I was such a fucking prick for treating her the way I have, and the shame and guilt of my actions are eating me alive. I don't know how to convince myself that I can make up for what I have done. I can only hope she will help me with that because I can't do it on my own; I am drowning here.

I am the one that made the mistake of keeping her at a distance, treating her like a fucking whore that I was just going to fuck and not love because I didn't fucking believe I could. Not really, not after everything that has happened with my ex, but once again, Nellie has proven me wrong. I can love; I love her. I love her with all I am and need to remind her of that. I need to reassure her like the others have, that she has all of me, not just parts of me.

She is the reason I am put back together again; my pieces are sharp and don't fit all the way just yet, but with time, they will, and with her, they will.

I have never met a woman like Nellie before, and even after what Zayden has done, she hasn't let it change her sweetness, her gentleness. Zayden never fucking deserved her, and it pisses me off to even think that he has tasted her lips, touched her fucking perfect skin.

It makes my blood boil, knowing he has forced himself on her, trying to take what was always meant to be mine and the others. Soon, she will not even remember what his lips tasted like, what his touch felt like, or what it felt like when he pushed himself on her. We will fucking erase all of it and replace it with us, always us.

I look up and see Nellie come into the room. She crosses the room and stops in front of me as I slowly stand up, holding onto the knife. She smiles and nods as she walks around me and climbs onto the bed. I quickly turn around and remove my sweatpants as she lays down on the bed, but this time, she is not face down on the bed. This time, she is lying on her back, staring at me.

She has already forgiven me. I can feel it, and it fucking hurts that she is so sweet, so fucking forgiving, but it is who she is.

I crawl onto the bed and settle between her legs. She watches me when I lift the knife and cut across the palms of both my hands, and she doesn't flinch or make a sound when I repeat the process with her palms. I drop the knife to the ground and hover over her, searching her eyes. She does the same, making me wonder what she sees when she looks at me; maybe one day, I will have the guts to ask her.

I take a deep breath and lean down, my lips almost touching hers. I grab my cock with my left bloody hand and rub the tip through her wet pussy lips. I want so fucking badly to just fuck her, but like I said, I want to be more for her and to do that, I have to fucking try to be more.

Her chest rises and falls quickly when I slowly push myself into her sore pussy. I reach up and grab her hands, and she laces her finger with mine as I bring her arms over her head and press our bloody hands into the mattress. I can feel her blood mixing with mine, making my cock throb inside her tight, wet pussy. I keep my eyes locked with hers while slowly moving my hips in short, deep thrusts.

"Thank you," I whisper. She wraps her legs around my waist, pulling her lower body up and meeting my shallow thrusts. At this angle, I am able to thrust deeper into her. I growl out my pleasure, I can't fucking help it. Her pussy is fucking perfect, stretching to accommodate my girth and wrapping tightly around me. Fuck, I want to taste her.

"For what?" She whispers. She has been used and abused by me and Zayden, and now it is time for her to feel what it is supposed to feel like to be loved. We will all show her in our own ways, and this is mine, looking her in the eyes and allowing her to hear it in my voice and touch. This is my way of giving her me.

"For loving us," I whisper back. I see the tears forming in her eyes as I lean in the rest of the way and gently ghost my lips across hers. She will learn that we can be gentle and we can make love to her, not just fuck her.

She chases my mouth with hers, and when our lips finally connect, she opens for me, and our tongues twist and twirl around each other. I start to lengthen my thrusts, keeping a slow and steady pace, as I pull almost all the way out before sliding back in until our pelvises connect again and again. I want to stretch this out as long as I can to show her that I can be more than what I have shown her. I watch the tears escape and roll down her face, making my heart stop. I tighten my grip on her hands, and she squeezes back as I increase my rhythm, deepening the kiss. I need more; I will always fucking need more.

My heart is racing so fucking fast I can hear it in my ears. Our bodies are slick with sweat, and she matches my pace, bringing her hips up as our bodies slap together, making the most erotic sounds, not only with our bodies but the sounds she makes as I hit that spot that drives her crazy. Her emotions are intertwined with mine, and I can feel the guys' eyes on us, turning me on more. We all like to watch. No, actually, we all need to watch. This is for all of us to experience together; it is what completes the connection, us all seeing each other being vulnerable and opening up in ways we never have before.

It is scary as fuck, but at the same time it feels right.

Nellie makes me want to be gentle, and she makes me want to become more human if that is even possible for a Guardian like me.

We will see soon what kind of miracles can happen with her by our side, and I have a feeling it will take us all by surprise.

18

Nellie

Day 5

I scoot closer to the fire as the flames warm up the pool house. This house smells like sex everywhere. Honestly, it makes me smile, and butterflies flutter in my stomach when the memories of what we have done over the last few days wash over me. I know they are all thinking about it, too. I can feel it in them. They are just as turned on as I am. I never thought in a million years when I was finally mated that it would be like this.

It is not just the sex, but how in a short time, I am completely fucking in love with all four of them, and I know they feel the same.

I feel it in them.

I feel it in their touch.

I see it in their eyes.

I taste it when they kiss me.

I hear it in their voice.

They are not holding anything back, not even Darius. Something changed in him when he pulled me from the car, and now we are all so intertwined with each other that they consume me in every fucking way.

Today, I can hear the thunder, lightning, and rain coming down; it is another gloomy day out there. The weather is as upset as my Guardians about what has happened outside these walls.

I lost my shit when Ashton told me about my father and my sister, so much so that I made a fucking stupid choice and left my Guardians, and we all felt the consequences of that fucking decision. But I had to go to the place where Zayden took something that never fucking belonged to him again. I honestly don't know what he is thinking. The things he has done and whatever he plans to do will not make me want to be with him; quite the opposite.

The man I loved once is gone. I saw it in his eye in the car. The man I once knew was gone, or maybe he was never there, and I only saw what I wanted to see. I don't know anymore. I am confused and angry, and the only time I am able to forget about all the fucked up shit that has happened is when I am with my Guardians. Now that they are giving me space to rest, I feel everything I don't want to feel and remember crash into me, and it hurts so fucking much.

I am so fucking mad at him. I felt what my father felt when Zayden shot him in the head. I knew the Guardians were keeping secrets about mates and what happens, but I didn't think I was different. Now I know that I am different, way fucking different. I don't know what it all means yet, but I have a feeling it won't be long until I will have all my answers.

One thing I trust is my Guardians. They won't lie to me, but I also know they will keep information from me to protect me. I know they love me, which means they would never do anything to hurt me, and that includes giving me information that might cause me pain.

I lift the mug and take a small sip while I watch the flames dance in the hearth as the rain pelts against the windows. The thought of not leaving this house for another four weeks makes me nervous, but not for the reasons you may think. My relationship with my Guardians has changed; it has changed for all of us. I am worried because I know they have been with others, and I have only been with Zayden, but I never gave myself to him that way, no matter how hard he tried to take it.

I knew it was important to remain pure until I was mated. I have seen what happens when the mate is not pure and does not end well. So I made sure I was, which means everything they have been doing to me I have never experienced before, and honestly, I don't want to disappoint them, which I know sounds stupid. I know I sound fucking stupid, but after everything, this is what I am obsessing over right now. But I can't fucking help it. Being with them now will change my life even more than it already has, and I don't want to mess up, and I don't want to disappoint them. I want to please them and pleasure them in the same ways they have me, but I have no fucking idea what I am doing. I have learned to let them lead and just follow, and so far, it has been working.

They don't seem to care that I have no experience, and honestly, I have never worried about it either. I learned the basics of how to please my mate when we were taught the dance and what was expected of us when we became mated. Still, them showing me their kinks and what gets them off is starting to make me think about what types of things I would like to try and might enjoy. Even though I have no experience and it has only been a few days of us sharing with each other, I already know what I want from them.

I want all of them at the same time. If that I possible, I fucking want it.

Why?

Because I want to be loved and pleasured by all of them simultaneously. They affect me in different ways and complete me in ways I never knew I was missing. I wrap the blanket tighter around me, bringing the mug to my lips and taking another small drink. Things have been calm today. The guys said that we would all rest for the next few days. I know they don't need to rest, and I also know they are just doing it because they know I need it.

I don't feel like I need rest, though. My entire body feels alive and full of energy, and my pussy is a little sore, along with the new carving on my chest, but except for that, I feel fine. They won't hear it, though. They say that I need to take time to process and allow my body to rest. So, I plan to sit by the fire for the next few days and maybe read. I also want to check out that dang pool.

They have opened not only my eyes to new sexual experiences but also to a new life. I wasn't poor by any means, but my Guardians are very wealthy, and I can tell they all like new and shiny things. I want to experience their world with them. It is the only way this will work, which means me getting used to all the new shiny things they enjoy having, like an inside pool, which honestly makes no sense because there is also an outdoor pool right outside this house.

I have a feeling that these Guardians are going to open my eyes to a lot of things. I was so nervous the first night I was with them, but even though we haven't been together long, I feel comfortable with them.

I take a deep breath as I continue to watch the flames dance. There are a lot of things running through my head and a lot of emotions hitting me all at once. I feel guilty for being happy in this pool house and ashamed that I am experiencing what I am when my father is dead and my sister has been taken.

I hear footsteps behind me, pulling me away from my dark, twisted thoughts.

I can tell it is Loyal; his emotions give him away. I am starting to be able to figure out what each of them feels like inside my head. It gets pretty twisted inside my head, but it seems clearer and calmer tonight.

I feel his hand on my lower back as he sits behind me. He wraps his arms around my stomach and pulls me back against his chest. Loyal is strong and stable. I have felt that from him since the moment I laid eyes on him, and with each encounter we have, he becomes more strong and stable.

He leans in, resting his lips against my ear, making my heart race. His smell calms me, and I can feel his cold skin against my back, sending a shiver through my body.

"What are you thinking about, sweetness?" He whispers into my ear. "Are you cold?"

In moments like this, I am glad they can only feel my emotions and not hear my thoughts. I shake my head. "No, the fire is plenty warm. And as far as what I am thinking about…there are a lot of things," I whisper back.

"Like," he whispers again, making my heart race even more. I can feel his steady heartbeat against my back, reminding me that I am the one who made it beat for the first time. It is crazy to think that they weren't like this before me. Their heart never beat before, and they didn't have the humanity they were trying to figure out.

"All of you," I reply, feeling the wetness between my legs. These Guardians are going to be the death of me. They don't even have to do anything but speak, and my body reacts.

I wonder if it will always be like this; part of me hopes so.

"I can feel more, sweetness," he warns me.

"Zayden, my dad, my sister, all of it, I guess," I confess to him.

I don't want to destroy the moments I have with them by talking about things that I know they can't control, things that I know are also eating them up inside.

"You know we will never let anything happen to you," he confesses into my ear.

I believe him. I believe all of them when they tell me that they will not let anything happen to me, but it scares me. It scares me because I know they would put their life in danger to protect me; it is what Guardians do for their mates. I don't want them to die or get hurt because of me, but I know deep down inside that whatever Zayden has planned, someone is going to get hurt at the end of it.

"I know," I say back. I know he wants more from me; I can feel it. But I can't, not right now.

"Do you trust us, sweetness?" He asks.

"Yes," I confess without needing to think.

"We will burn it all down for you if we have to," Loyal whispers.

I sit up and slightly turn around in his arms. He allows me, and our eyes lock. I can't help but search his eyes, even though he won't let me see more than he wants me to. I can feel it, his emotions radiating off of him in waves.

He lifts his hand and gently brushes my face with the back of it, a gesture he has never done before, but I can't help but lean into his touch.

"We love you, Nellie," he says with so much confidence it takes my breath away.

"I love you guys, too," I say, looking into his eyes.

Loyal leans in and connects his lips to mine, and just like that, all the anxiety, fear, and racing thoughts inside my head are gone and replaced with him, all of them. All of their love and need for me hit straight into my heart.

19

Ashton

Day 6

I enter the loud and busy club and through the crowd. Argento has been managing things for the past few days, and even though my cousins and the others haven't come out of the pool house, they have been texting me, asking me to check on everything.

Even though they should focus on their mate, they can't completely step back. They need to know what is going on, so the only way I can find out how things are going is to go to the source, and right now, that is my uncle.

There is nothing I wouldn't do for my family, including dealing with my uncle. He and I haven't seen eye to eye on everything, but he is fair and loyal and does what he needs to do to keep his people in order. He is the one Guardian we can trust to keep things going in the right direction.

Argento has stepped down, but I know it was hard for him to do so. He has been King for so fucking long that I think it would be hard for any of us to pass over our power and take a step back from being the King. He is now seen as what humans call an adviser. He will give advice when needed, but will not be in the loop with everything once my cousins leave the pool house.

It is the way of our world, passing down power, each of us doing our jobs to ensure the kingdom doesn't fall.

I push open the office door and walk inside, closing the door behind me. Argento is standing up with his hands behind his back, looking out the window. He is wearing a black button-up shirt, and the sleeves are pulled past his elbows, showing off his tattoos. He is wearing black slacks with black shoes. I don't know what it is about the color black, but almost all of our kind wear it.

I stop at his side and look out the window at the rain. It has been raining and storming for the past two days, making it hard to track, but I will find everyone who has been involved in hurting my family. It might take some time, but before my cousins leave the pool house, I will have names, and Guardians and humans alike will suffer for what they have done.

I have already failed my family once, and I will not let that fucking happen again.

"How are they doing?" Argento asks calmly.

"Fine, I think. They locked themselves in the pool house," I reply amusingly. They were scared that Nellie might run again, so they made sure she couldn't leave again, and neither could they. I understand why they do it, but it still makes me smile. It shows me what I have to look forward to once I am mated. Being overly possessive, obsessed, and jealous. All the things we already are only a million times worse.

Argento smiles and shakes his head. "I knew one day my sons would be mated, but I didn't think it would include another family. This is good for all of us," he says more to himself than to me, but it makes me curious. Argento is always talking in riddles and seems to see things the rest of us do not, which is why he has been King for so fucking long.

"Why do you say that?" I ask, looking at him.

Argento turns and looks at me. "Because it means my sons will have a family when I am gone," he says calmly.

If I had a beating heart, this is when I know it would have sunk with his words. His thinking about his death after being alive for centuries concerns me. Guardians and humans have risen against us before, but we have always won at the end. He is thinking about his death, but I will not let that happen. It will not get that fucking far. We will find Zayden and whoever else is fucking helping him, and we will put a stop to their plan. We have always won against those who thought they could take what doesn't belong to them, and this time will be no different; it is just going to take a little more time.

"What do you mean?" I ask, watching him closely

"One day, it will be my time to die, just like one day it will be yours. The human, Zayden, has been making a lot of noise, but my people can't seem to find him. This human makes me nervous, Ash, very fucking nervous," he says in a low concerned voice. I watch him closely as he searches my eyes.

Zayden is making noise, we have all heard it, but that is all it is right now fucking noise. He is a little bitch that runs away and talks a big game, but in the end, he will fail. He will not get Nellie or anything else he believes belongs to him. We should have killed him when we killed his father. We should have fucking known he would grow up to be a fucking problem; that is a mistake we will not make again. We have learned from Zayden, and we will make sure that his memory, or whatever the fuck you want to call it, dies with him, and he will die; I don't fucking know when, but he will.

"I have been searching for him, so far, no luck," I confess.

"Luck has nothing to do with it, Ashton. Someone is helping him, and we need to find out who," Argento says, turning back and looking out the window.

He is right; if we find out who the fuck is feeding him information, we will find him, and he will not be able to escape our fucking wrath.

"I have a good idea of who is helping him, Sir," I confess, turning and looking out the window. The wind and rain are picking up as the night takes over everything.

"Good, find proof of who the fuck is going against us, Ash," he says through gritted teeth.

"Yes, Sir, I will," I confirm confidently.

I turn and make my way over to the door.

"Protect their mate, Ash. She is more important than you realize," he says darkly.

I think there is more to her than any of us fucking knows, but I will not let anything happen to her that I can promise.

"I will, I promise," I say with as much confidence now.

I open the door and walk out, closing it behind me. The smell of sex and booze takes over my nose, and the music takes over my hearing. I make my way down the hallway and back through the crowd. I walk to the front, and the Guardians open the door for me and nod.

I walk out into the rain and stop momentarily, and my hands form into fists as I look out at the forest. There have been eyes on me for the past few days.

My hands release the fists as I keep my eyes on a tree.

Ace.

I watch him walk out from behind a tree.

I quickly make my way over to him, stopping in front of him. "What are you doing here?" I ask, keeping my eyes on him.

"Watching your back like always, my friend," he says with a smile.

Ace has always had my back, even when I didn't know I needed it, but he needs to remember I can't fucking die, at least not yet, but he can. And most of my kind don't fucking like him or his kind. I really don't want to have to fuck up more Guardians for them trying to harm my friend. The best thing for him is to keep his distance.

"Have you heard anything?" I ask him. He has been searching and listening around town, trying to find Zayden and the others who have been helping him.

He takes a deep breath and shakes his head as my eyes go to the dagger tattoo underneath his left eye, reminding me that he hasn't found his mate yet.

"We will find him. It will just take time," I say, trying to reassure the both of us.

We both nod and turn and walk into the forest. I need to go back to the pool house and make sure that everything is going smoothly there, but I am not yet ready to go back just yet. I want to check a few places first, and maybe tonight we will get lucky and find that little motherfucker.

There are only so many places he can hide in this city, which belongs to us. Eventually, he is going to fuck up, and I am going to make sure I am right there when he fucking does.

20

Zayden

Day 7

I pull up to Nellie's old house, where I forced her to hear me. I know she knows about her father and sister; that fucking Guardian made that clear meeting me in the woods. I hate how they fucking think they are so smart or how they believe we need to fear them for what they are. They might have been immortals, but they no longer are once they mated with Nellie and fell to their knees for her. Which means they are weaker now than they ever have been before. Nellie's Guardians can fucking die now, and I know the consequences for her if they do, but she will have me. I will be able to mend her hollow heart, I fucking know it. She just needs to give me a fucking chance to do so.

I thought I would need to find a way to break the connection, and I thought that there had to be a fucking way to do so. Thanks to the Falco brothers, I now know that is not true; it can't be broken, but it can be disconnected if I kill her Guardians. Her heart will turn hollow, and once again, she will be changed, but at least she will be my fucking Nellie again. So now, with my new fucking information, I just have to wait for the right time to get to her and them and fucking end this once and for all.

I know that once she is pregnant, they will all be vulnerable because the connection is complete. So I just need to be fucking patient for four more weeks, and then she will be mine, and they will fear a human before they die. I need to fucking see the fear in their eyes as they realize that they have lost everything they care about.

The thought of her fucking being pregnant with one of their children makes me fucking sick to my stomach.

I take a deep breath as I look out the windshield at the house. I can't tell you how often I have been here watching Nellie, watching everything she was doing. I have had so many dreams of watching her sleep and shower. She is fucking intoxicating and has completely taken over my entire life since the moment I laid eyes on her.

When she ran into me, she changed my life; all I wanted was her. I wanted to love her, please her, and pleasure her. Those fuckers think they can love her better than I can. They think they can please and satisfy her better than I can, but they fucking cant. No one can love her, please her, pleasure her the way I can. She will see and see she doesn't need them; all she needs is me.

Nellie has no idea what I have given up for her or what I have done for her to keep her safe, but soon her eyes will be opened to every fucking thing I have done for her, and maybe just fucking maybe, she will finally see things my way. She fucking has to. She doesn't know what I have done or how far I have gone to ensure she remains mine. She will soon realize that no one, and I mean fucking no one, can love her or worship her the way I can, the way I fucking have.

I open the car door and get out. The rain and wind have taken everything over, and another storm is coming into our world again. Maybe it is for the best, the storm that is coming is the same storm I feel inside myself, and soon I am going to fucking lose my shit. The Falco brothers have kept their word so far, and they have been feeding me more and more information. But I won't know if they are going to keep their end until the day comes and we are face to face with Nellie and her fucking Guardians.

I know the Falco brothers want them to die, but I also know I don't fucking trust them, and I know they don't trust me either. This will end in one of two ways: either we all get what we want, or we will die. It will be interesting to see what way things turn. All I know is I am willing to die and take them all down with me without a second thought. I want to have a life with Nellie, and I want to live with her, but if it comes down to either we all die, or I lose her, I will gladly fucking take my life and hers.

As long as they don't have her, honestly, I don't fucking care anymore. It is about revenge, but it is about so much more than that now. I want those fucker to suffer for taking her away from me, for turning her against me.

I should have fucking driven away with her as soon as she got into my car outside of their fucking house. I should have driven away and taken her as far away from this place as possible. But I didn't, and now I am again paying for my mistake. Whatever is happening to her inside those fucking walls, it should be me doing it. I should be the one causing her to scream and moan, and it should be my fucking kid inside her belly.

Fuck me.

If my father were still alive, he would be beating the shit out of me for letting it all happen this way. He would be fucking ashamed of me. I can't fucking disappoint my father's memory. I will make sure to avenge him, and I will make sure the Guardians fall one way or another. I will fuck their shit up.

I should have done so many fucking things differently, and now she is inside that fucking pool mansion with them, behind locked doors and windows, and they even fucking put shades up so no one can fucking see what is happening inside. They think by doing that, they are keeping her safe from me. It is not me that she needs to be safe from it is them; it has always been them. I don't know why she can't fucking see them for what they are. The connection has to be fucking with her.

It is the only thing that makes any logical sense of why she is acting like this towards me.

She is not listening to my warnings, and she doesn't fucking trust me anymore, but all of this is her fucking fault. If she did go with me outside the club, the connection might be broken, and none of this would be happening. She has no idea what she has done by falling in love with those fucking fuck boys, but I will make her see, she will feel my pain, and she will see what I see when I look at them soon enough.

I walk up the steps and into the broken door. I cross through the living room and into her room. Everything is the same as it was the last time I was here. Her smell still fills my nose; I fucking miss her smell so fucking much. I miss her touch and seeing her smile and say my name.

I unbutton my pants as I make my way to her bed. I can't tell you how often I stood outside her window and watched her sleep. She is fucking gorgeous in every sense of the word.

I lay on her bed, pull out my dick, and lay face first into her pillow, wrapping myself into her sheets; this will do for now.

My heart starts to race as I start to stroke my cock from base to tip, taking a deep breath of her scent from her pillow. The memories begin to flood my mind and will keep my cravings at bay for her for now.

5 Years Ago

I watched Nellie leave this morning. I fucking hate it when she decides to leave her house and go out into public. I hate knowing that there are so many fucking eyes on her. They are looking at what is mine; she is fucking mine.

She doesn't know it yet, but she is and will always be mine. As soon as I made her run into me, I had fucking claimed her.

I want to fuck her, hear her scream my name. I need to fucking claim her before she is mated; if I fuck her first, they will throw her away. They don't want a woman that is not pure.

If I make her unpure, they will never fucking take her from me. I have had so many women, but none of them made me feel the way she did when she looked at me. We haven't even fucking done anything yet, and she has already taken over my life.

I continue to follow her through the crowd of people. She always goes to the same fucking coffee shop and finds the same seat in the French Quarter. She likes to people-watch. I wonder if it is because she wishes that she was normal.

Just a normal girl, but she isn't, and she never will be. The moment she was born, the Guardians had already claimed her, those greedy motherfuckers. They take all the good fucking women. They say it is for our own good that they need to continue to their bloodlines.

But I can give two fucks about their damn bloodlines, and this time I will keep this girl. This girl doesn't even know how people look at her.

She is already getting attention from human men and Guardians as she walks through the crowd toward the coffee shop. She pays them no mind, which makes me happy and also pisses me off. If she doesn't see them, does that mean she doesn't see me?

I have tried reaching out to her, but she has never responded. I got her number from a friend of hers, but she hasn't gotten back to me. Is that because she is getting ready to dance?

That fucking slutty dance that will make it to where she gets mated. I want her to dance for me and only for me, but the only way that can happen is by convincing her that she loves me as much as I have already fallen in love with her.

Don't fucking judge me; our world doesn't follow the normal rules of the human world. In the human world, people keep sex behind closed doors, but in our world, the humans and Guardians fuck wherever the fuck they want to.

That is the only good thing about our world with the Guardians is that sexual desires and fantasies are welcomed, and no one is ashamed or tries to hide them.

I want to do so many fucking things to Nellie, things that the Guardians could or would never do to her.

She will scream my name.

I stop at the building and watch her go into the coffee shop. I lean against the building as I watch the normal people walking by. They have no fucking idea about our world, which honestly is insane, but they are blinded.

I take a deep breath as Nellie returns from the coffee shop and finds a seat on a chair facing the street.

I take out my phone and send her a quick text.

My heart stops as she picks up her phone, shakes her head, and puts it back down. I lift my phone and turn on my camera, taking as many pictures as I can of her. One day she will see what she means to me; I will fucking make sure of that shit.

She might be able to ignore me right now, but soon I will make it impossible for her to fucking ignore me. She will fall in love with me, and she will fuck me, and I will fuck her. That will be a beautiful, breathtaking day.

I feel my balls tighten as I stroke my cock faster, screaming out my release into the pillow as I cum all over her sheets and my hand. There is nothing I can do; my mind, body, and heart belong to Nellie, the thoughts of her and how she has made me feel.

My body sinks back into the bed, and the sheets are completely wrapped around my naked body as I release my dick. I grab onto the blanket, lift my head, and take a deep breath. I can't fucking wait to have her pussy wrapped tightly around my dick. Thoughts of her turn me on and get me off, but it is nothing to the real thing. The real thing will be mine soon. I close my eyes and take another deep breath.

Images of Nellie flood into my mind even more. She has no fucking idea just how much I love her, and she has no idea just how fucking far I am willing to go to make her mine, but she fucking will. They all will.

When her fuck boys are dead and their secrets are brought to light, she will have no choice but to fucking give in to me because I will be the only thing she has left. I will fucking make sure of that.

21

Darius

4 Years Ago

I enter the club, and before I can do anything, Christos has his hand on my chest, getting my attention. My brother only touches me when he is trying to make a point or give me a warning. Usually, either way, I don't like what he has to tell me; that much I have fucking learned. Lately, everything he says is about my woman, and it is never fucking good. Never fucking good.

"I think it is best you leave, brother," Christos warns me in a low, dark voice.

For fuck sake, what the fuck did she do now.

"What? Why?" I ask, even though I already fucking know. I know she is doing something Christos is trying to protect me from. But honestly, nothing will protect me from what she is doing.

I don't know what has happened to Taylor lately, but she loves to push me over the fucking edge, and I know she is doing it on fucking purpose. There is no way in fuck she can think I would be okay with her fucking others. What is even worse is she doesn't even try to fucking hide it. She usually does it in front of humans and other Guardians, so it always gets back to me one way or another.

"You know why. Your whore is at it again, and you don't need to watch that shit," Christos says. My brother has always watched out for me, even when I don't watch out for myself, and with Taylor, I seem to lose all sense of what is best for me, and she fucking knows it too. She keeps doing fucked up shit; she knows I will take her back. I always fucking take her back.

I push past him and go through the crowd towards the stage. It is empty, and all the dancers are on the floor entertaining the Guardians and humans. For fuck sake.

I stop dead when I see Taylor grinding on some human guy. That is not what pisses me off, though. What pisses me off is this time, it is a fucking human. A human that can get her fucking pregnant. Does it hurt when she fucks other Guardians? Yes, it fucking hurts, but at least I know she can't have their fucking children, but with her fucking humans, I am not so sure?

Taylor is different from the other Chosen Women waiting to be mated. She isn't pure, not at all. I know that for a fact because I am the one that made her unpure, and since then, she has been fucking so many other Guardians I lost count a long ass time ago. It is like we bring out the worst in each other, and neither of us can walk away. What a fucked up situation all the fuck around.

Taylor is known as the Guardian and human whore, which drives me fucking bat shit crazy, but she has done it to herself, and what is even worse is when she is proud of her fucking nickname.

I clench my hands into fists as I storm through the crowd and grab the man by the back of the neck, pulling him away from her. The human quickly turns around. He is about my height, smaller, but can hold his own if he was dealing with a human, but he isn't.

I felt my brother come up behind me, even though he asked me to leave, and I refused; he will always have my back. Even if it means I am causing trouble with the humans.

Christos is not a fan of Taylor, and things between her and me have been rocky. She has been playing games and fucking whoever she wants. What I thought we were before is not anymore. But for the life of me, I can't fucking walk away, and she knows that I can't. She knows how I feel about her, or at least, what I try to feel without a beating heart or a soul.

She has been playing me from the beginning. She was just some unknown Chosen until I fucked her, and now everyone knows her name and wants her. She is using me, and I know it, but I can't break the chains she has on me. I don't need her; I want her. But that want is so fucking strong it takes over any reason I would typically have.

Christos says it is because she is playing games, but he doesn't know her like I do or understand. I might not be mated to her, and I might not even be able to love her truly, but I know what I do feel for her is as close to love as I am going to get without her being my mate. I am a prisoner to her, for her. I thought she was the same to me, but I was wrong, so fucking wrong.

She got what she wanted from me; now, she is famous and known because of who I am. Maybe that is what she always wanted, and I just couldn't fucking see it until she was openly fucking others in front of me.

I can't truly feel pain or betrayal, but I know I would be feeling it right now if I could. I can't fucking let her go, and even though we both know one day I will be forced to, until that day comes when I am mated, or she is, she is fucking mine, even if she fucks with my head, which I didn't even know was possible for a Guardian like me. She has opened my eyes to a lot of things, and she is teaching me what happens when you give yourself to another. She is teaching me that love is nothing but a lie, and thinking someone else can care about someone like me, I am just fucking kidding myself.

She surprises me with what she does and puts me through, and I am even more surprised I am putting up with this shit, but I would die for her if I could. I don't understand why I can't be enough for her. She is always looking elsewhere, and then she says she is sorry, and then it happens again. But I always fall for her sorries because I want to fucking believe her. I want to see the light in her eyes she had for me at the beginning, but slowly, that light has been fading.

I watched it start to fade and was kidding myself when I thought I could fucking bring it back. She isn't the type that wants one Guardian or man. Nope, she fucking wants more and more, and she is fine with being called a whore. She is okay with the way our people see her. I wish she cared, I wish she cared about the way I can fucking care for her, but I am kidding myself.

She is causing me to fucking cross over the lines I should never cross for her, but I can't fucking help it. I am not just going to sit back and let some other human fucking playboy fuck my woman because that is exactly what she is, mine.

"What the fuck!" The human says, actually looking me in the fucking eyes.

I have to say one thing, she does have a fucking type. She finds the alphas in both Guardians and humans.

"Don't touch what doesn't belong to you, human," I say through gritted teeth.

"She doesn't belong to anyone yet. She can fuck whoever she wants," the human snaps back.

Another thing she is drawn to is confidence, and she has a type, a type that turns her on, if only I were enough. If only she would fully give me herself, I could be what she needs. I know I fucking can, but she keeps doing shit like this.

Does she want me to walk away?

Is she trying to piss me the fuck off?

If she is, she is doing it fucking well, because one of these times I will fucking walk away.

One of these times, I will fucking kill every lover she has, just to make sure she fucking suffers.

I release the back of his neck and grab him by the throat, pulling him into me. "She fucking belongs to me," I yell in his face. I hate that I am losing control, but I can't fucking help it. She makes me come completely unhinged.

"Dude, she doesn't. She is not mated to you or anyone else. Let the whore be a fucking whore," the human says in an amused voice. He is right, and it fucking pisses me off. My claim on her doesn't mean shit. I am not her mate, but that doesn't matter. None of it matters; I just want her.

"Darius walk away. She isn't fucking worth it," he says in a low tone.

I release my grip on his throat and push him back, grabbing her by the arm and pulling her against me.

"Whatever, you want the bitch, fucking take her," he says disgustingly.

The man quickly turns around and disappears into the crowd of Guardians and humans. I tighten my grip on her arm and turn around, forcing her to come with me to the back of the club. I walk down the hallway and out of the back door. I don't need to turn around to know my brother is behind me.

I push the door open and take a few steps outside. I release my grip on her arm, take a few more steps into the rain, and run my hand through my hair.

"Why the fuck do you do this, Taylor?" I ask, trying to keep my cool.

"Baby, I am sorry," she pleads with me in the same voice she has used so many times.

I quickly turn around, walk into her, and grab her by the throat, making damn fucking sure she can't get away from me. "If you were sorry, you wouldn't fucking keep doing it." I snap at her as I walk into her, forcing her to step back into the building.

Her breathing is rapid as I reach down and pull up her dress. I reach in and cup her pussy. "You are mine."

"I am yours," she whispers.

I grab onto her leg, pinning it against my hip as I reach between us and grab my hard cock. She wants to be fucked like a whore. I can do that, and I can do that for her.

I push my dick into her already wet pussy. I tighten my grip on her throat and grab onto her leg as I slam into her, making her scream my name. I keep my eyes on her as I fuck her hard and violently. If this is how she wants to be treated, if this is what I need to do to fucking make her mine, then I will fucking do it.

22

Neo

Present Day

WEEK 2 – DAY 8

Giving Nellie a few days off was more challenging than I ever thought it would be because I could feel all of our need for her and feel her need for us. It made it fucking harder, but we kept our distance, at least sexually. I had to be close even if it wasn't in the way I wanted it to be.

I watched her sleep, dream, sit by the fire, and have conversations with Loyal. Her defenses are coming down more and more. We even heard her laughing a few times; it was good to hear that sound. She has been so overwhelmed with being mated to all of us and, of course, Zayden and what he has done.

I really thought we were going to lose her, not physically but mentally and emotionally, and in my opinion is way worse. Luckily, we were able to bring her back to us. I think the sex distracts her just enough so her grief doesn't drown her. We will continue to distract her as much as she needs us to.

I could be balls fucking deep into her for the rest of my life, and I would be a happy fucking Guardian. I will never get enough of her. We are all going to want her more and more, like a drug. She is our fucking drug.

Today is the day that I get to show her my world. It is my turn to watch the others make her submit, it will be fucking glorious. All of our kinks speak to us in different ways, and we all have used them on other women, but it feels different with Nellie; it is different with her.

She has been different for all of us since the moment we saw her in the club. Our relationship with her has moved quickly and has given us all whiplash, but I wouldn't fucking change a thing. She is ours, and we are hers. At the end of this, she will have experienced all of our kinks, and hopefully, it will have opened up a few new ones that she wants to explore with us. She will take off whatever masks she feels that she wears, and she will bear her body and soul to us, just like we have.

All of this is so fucking easy with her, which is why sometimes I need to look around and blink a few times to make sure that it is fucking real and not just inside my head. I have waited for fucking ever to find my mate, and none of what has happened is what I thought it would be; it is so much fucking better. She is amazing, caring, and beautiful, and I have a feeling that we will not be the only ones to teach her things. She will also teach us as well.

She will help us understand our humanity and our emotions. We are getting a better handle on all of it, but we are still a work in progress. At the end of this, she will be our wife, she will be carrying one of our children, and she will leave this pool house a fucking Queen.

Zayden thinks he deserves her and that he can do whatever the fuck he wants. He actually fucking thinks that there are no repercussions for what he has done to our mate, but he is wrong so fucking wrong. Once we complete the connection, he will see how fucking dangerous we can be.

I tighten my grip on Nellie's hand and lead her down the hallway toward my room. It is important that she experiences each of us, which is why she needs to visit and understand how each of our sex rooms reveals a deeper piece of ourselves to her. Once we enter this room, I know that everything I need will be in there to show her who I am without all my masks.

We all wear different masks outside this pool house and have to act a certain way because of who we are. But within the many walls of the pool house, we will show her that regardless of things outside of here, we are nothing more than her mates. Mates that will open her eyes to a new world where sex and kinks are able to come to life without feeling shame for what turns us on and gets us off.

"Where are we going?" She asks as I open the door and walk inside, bringing her with me. I let go of her hand and turned to face her and the others. They come in, closing and locking the door behind them.

"This is my room, baby girl. We all have a sex kink room, including one for you to set up however you desire. This week, we will be spending time in this room. It is my turn to take off my masks for you," I whisper, watching her look around the room in wonder.

She gasps in surprise when I grab her hand, guide her to the bed, and force her to sit down. Christos, Darius, and Loyal sit in one of the chairs situated along the walls and watch me as I go to the drawers built into the wall. This room is perfect; everything I would ever need is in this room. Nellie will understand after this what submission is and how much power and control she will gain by doing it.

It is hard to explain, but when someone thoroughly fucking submits, it allows them to let go and trust that no matter what happens, I will be there to take care of all her needs and desires. She can let go of all her worries and know that she is safe, but it also lets her know that while I may be controlling the scene, she has the ultimate control and power behind what happens. I hope by teaching her the art of submission, she will build her trust in all of us and show her a different side of power and control that she holds over us. I will show her what it means to be my mate, what it means to be our Queen.

Submission can be intimidating for some, which is why her safe words will be vital while we explore this room. I will not force her to do anything she doesn't want to do. She has complete control here, but I will teach her to give in to me and all of us. By the end of this week, I will make sure that she understands that she is the only one who has the right to see us this vulnerable. Even after we leave this house to resume our everyday activities, all she will have to do is ask, and we will give her anything and everything we can within our power. It will be that simple for us, she asks, and we will provide without question.

My kink is simple yet fucking intoxicating.

Do you know what it feels like to have someone completely fucking submit to your will?

Do you know what it feels like to have someone moan your name while knowing that they trust you enough to push you to your limits by doing whatever the fuck you want to them?

There is nothing like having someone submit to you. I have had many women submit to me, even Darius has, but Nellie is the one I need to submit to me. She is the one I need to hear scream my name and beg as I fuck her. This week she will see how deep inside I need, fucking need to see it in her eyes, her touch, her voice, the submission that only she can give me.

I open a few different drawers and grab a few things. Turning around, I walk across the room and kneel down in front of her with a choker and chain in my hand. Her eyes followed me, and she was staring into my eyes. I can feel her desire and excitement, but I also catch tendrils of fear and confusion.

"Do you remember your safety words, baby girl?" I ask as my dick hardens in my sweatpants.

She nods, her eyes locked with mine.

I smile and shake my head. "You have to use your words for me. I need to hear you say it," I whisper.

"Yes, I remember my safe words," she replies.

"In this room, you will refer to me as *'My King.'* When you are asked a question, your response should always be either, *'Yes, My King,'* or *'No, My King,'* understand?" I ask, tilting my head to the side.

She smiles. "Yes, My King," she replies without question.

Fuck me. Fuck me. Hearing those three little words roll off her tongue makes me want to bend her over and fuck her right now, but I can't. I have to stick to what I really need from her right now. There will be plenty of time for plain fucking later.

My heart pounds against my chest as I stand and look down at her. She is wearing one of my T-shirts. I have noticed that she has been switching between all of our clothes, and fuck, seeing her in it makes my mouth water.

I lift my hand and gently brush my fingers down the side of her face, making her breathing come out in short breaths. I leave her sitting on the bed, and I turn around, walk across the room, and sit in one of the chairs facing the bed, holding the leather choker and chain tightly in my hand.

I feel everyone's eyes on me as I sit back and look over Nellie.

"Take off my shirt, baby girl," I say through gritted teeth.

I don't know how the fuck Loyal keeps such a fucking balance between being dominant and gentle. I am fucking trying, but I can feel myself battling the urge to let go. Fuck, this is going to be harder than I thought.

"Yes, My King," she answers as she stands up from the bed, removes the t-shirt, and throws it onto the ground.

I reach down and squeeze my dick, trying to ease the tension while she stands perfectly still, awaiting my next command. A smile forms across my lips; our little mate is learning quickly.

"Crawl to me, Nellie," I say darkly.

"Yes, my King," she whispers as she lowers herself to the ground and begins to crawl across the floor towards me. Her round tits and ass move with each movement of her arms and legs. Her ass has a little more swing in it the closer she gets.

I hear Christos, Loyal, and Darius growl, widening my smile.

She stops between my legs and sits back on her ankles with her hands on her knees. Her eyes searched mine. I lean forward and press a gentle kiss to her forehead before I wrap the choker around her throat and secure the buckle, testing to make sure it isn't too tight. I clip the leash to the ring, lean back in the chair, and admire how she looks.

My cock is so fucking hard, my sweats are tented, and I know if I were to look, there would be a wet spot where my precum has soaked through the material. Seeing the fucking choker around her neck makes my heart stop. She is so fucking gorgeous like this, naked on her knees before me with a fucking choker on. Oh yeah, she will be wearing this for as long as I can get her to. Fuck!

I gently pull on the chain, instructing her to move forward without having to say a word. I gather the chain around my hand as she continues to move and crawl up into my lap. The heat from her naked pussy sits on my hard, throbbing cock. I pull the chain until her face is in front of mine, and I smash my lips to hers, just needing to taste her, just one fucking taste.

I pull back, breaking the kiss, even though it is the last thing I want. "Have you ever sucked dick, baby girl?" I ask curiously. I know everything she has done with us, but I must know if Zayden forced her to suck his dick. I need to fucking know if he forced her on her knees for him.

"No, My King," she answers. She knows what I am asking; she has to know.

Holy fucking shit.

I take a calming breath as she presses her hands against my chest and leans in; her breath but a whisper across my lips. "I never did this for him, Neo," she confesses.

"I love you," I profess to her, needing her to hear me.

"I love you, too, My King," she whispers.

"Get back on your knees, my Queen," I demand.

She smiles and nods. "Yes, My King."

I watch her closely as she eases her way off my lap, sliding her pussy against me before she positions herself back on the floor in front of me. I slowly stand up, and she follows my movements with her eyes as I move to stand in front of her. I watch as she slowly licks her bottom lip. Fuck, she is fucking beautiful on her knees, looking up at me with nothing but adoration and desire in her eyes.

"Pull down my sweatpants," I command through gritted teeth.

"Yes, My King," she says sweetly. She is going to make me fucking cum before she does anything.

She reaches up, sliding her fingers under the waistband, and pulls them down, freeing my cock. She watches as it smacks against my stomach and bobs in front of her face before she pushes my pants down until they pool at my feet.

I pull on the chain, bringing her up to her knees. My heart is racing so fucking fast as she looks at my dick then looks back up at me. "White, My King," she whispers.

I pull on the chain again, bringing her face closer to my erection.

"Grab it," I growl under my breath.

She does as I ask without a second thought. Her petite hand is barely big enough to wrap around me. She slides her hand across the smooth skin, bringing the tip directly in front of her face, precum leaking from the tip.

I pull on the chain, forcing her face to get closer. "Open your mouth, my Queen." The name leaves my lips and makes my heart stop for a moment. We have all been waiting so fucking long, not just for a mate, but for a fucking queen. And now we have her, we fucking have her, and we are never going to fucking let her go.

"Yes, My King," she says softly.

She licks her lips before she complies and opens her mouth wide. I pull on the chain harder, forcing her to take the tip into her mouth. Her tongue swipes the moisture before I grab the back of her head and close my eyes as she wraps her lips around me and presses her hands against my thighs. Her mouth is wet and warm, and she takes me all the way down her throat, gagging and coughing as I hit the back. The sound of her gagging almost has me spilling my seed down her throat.

I pull out, giving her a chance to catch her breath, but she sucks me back in, hollowing out her cheeks. She moans against my dick, making my balls tighten as I fuck her mouth harder. Tears fall from her eyes, and spit drips from her mouth as she continues to suck and press her tongue against me while I take what I need from her mouth.

Oh fuck!

I feel a set of lips press against the back of my neck, and I let my head fall back. Darius.

He leans to the side and bites down on my neck, forcing me to growl as my balls tighten further, and before I can stop, I shoot ropes of cum into Nellie's mouth. Between her warm mouth locked around my cock, and Darius sucking my blood down his throat, there was no fucking way I could hold back any longer.

Darius pulls his teeth from my neck, licking the tender spot as I look down at Nellie. She looks up at me, tears stain her cheeks, and I slowly pull my dick from her mouth. She smiles up at me before she swallows my cum. Fucking hell.

I pull on the chain hard enough to force her to her feet and smash my lips to her. She opens her mouth, our tongues twisting together as I deepen the kiss. I can taste myself on her tongue, making me groan as I fuck her mouth with my tongue.

She is going to be the fucking death of me.

23

Loyal

Day 9

I lean against the wall and watch my brother remove the choker from Nellie's neck and back up into Darius. This whole experience, this whole fucking thing, is just nuts. We have been waiting for this moment, these next few weeks, for centuries, and now that it is actually happening, sometimes I don't know what to do or say. This is odd for me, very odd. I always know what to say and fucking do, but with Nellie, a lot of the time, I am at a loss for words, and I just react in the moment.

Things may not have gone how we wanted, but it appears it has worked out how it was supposed to. Ashton has stayed in contact with us, making sure that we are all safe. This is the time when we are the most vulnerable with her, so we need to have Guardians and humans we can trust to watch over this pool house to ensure nothing happens or goes wrong. Trust is a word I don't use much, but in this world, you need someone that you can fucking trust. And Ashton is one of them. He would die for us if he could, and I know I can trust that he will keep things in line on the outside as we give ourselves to Nellie inside these walls.

It makes me smile knowing that all the Guardians standing guard can hear us and her. Some would be jealous that others can hear, but I don't give two fucks. They can listen all they want; they can even fucking look and watch if they want. But touching her, now that is something I will not fucking allow. There is something about knowing that others want her, knowing that others want what we fucking have, that turns me on for a whole new fucking reason.

There is something about their desire, their want for her, and what we have that makes me proud and makes me want her even more. Nellie is one of a kind, that is for sure. She is like no other woman I have ever met or been with. There are many surprises that will come forth, and I am ready for each and every one of them. As long as we have her, the world can burn to the ground, and we will be okay because of her.

Ashton has been searching for Zayden, his little pussy friends, and the other Guardians that didn't do their job of watching over Nellie before she was mated. Father is keeping everything in order on the streets, which isn't surprising since he was King for such a long fucking time. He built what our kingdom is now, and he is a Guardian you can't help but love and want approval from.

He is proud of us, and I know he is happy that two families that used to be at war are now on the same side. We have many enemies, but now we are stronger and will not be beaten. Whoever stands against our family will fucking fall to their knees and will suffer for their betrayal. Betrayal happens more often than I would like to admit. Everyone wants more power and control, and it is a never-ending fucking dangerous cycle that we all play a hand in. Father is tired, but he will never turn down taking back his power and control, even if it's for a short amount of time.

We can all feel Neo doesn't want to back away from her. He wants more and craves more of her. My brother is addicted, fuck who am I kidding, we are all fucking addicted. We all crave her. The word *crave* doesn't seem to do justice to what we feel for Nellie. Being able to feel at all is an amazing thing, but being able to feel her love and being able to actually fucking love her back, man, there are no fucking words invented yet. We will find a way to tell her; we have to.

This is what we need to do, and we need to learn how to share and experience her together. It is the only way the connection will be completed. It is the only way that we will be able to come together and fucking destroy Zayden and the others. If they see that we are separated at all, that we are not on the same side, things can go from fucking bad to fucking worse, and we don't need worse.

It was evident in the club that none of us were happy about all of us being mated to her, but she has somehow brought us all together. We have all come to an understanding when it comes to her and being a family.

From what I have heard, the Delucas and the Rosettis have hated each other since the beginning of time, and now, for the first time in our history, we are not killing each other. Instead, we have not only fallen for Nellie, but we have fallen for each other. What a crazy ass concept. I see it when I look at my brother and Darius, and I can feel it when Christos is by me, the way he laughs, the way he walks slowly by me, and the way he looks at me.

I never saw any of this fucking coming, but I am grateful for it. We are stronger together. Plus, we have always loved bending and breaking, and our relationship does just that.

We are naturally selfish, cruel, distant, violent, and extremely fucking possessive, and that will not change. If anything, it is just going to get fucking worse.

I watch Darius rest his hands on my brother's shoulders, and it is a fucking sight to see them together. It was hot as fuck watching Darius bite my brother as Nellie was giving Neo head. I thought we all had intense sexual experiences before, but now I realize how wrong we were. There is nothing that can compare to what we are experiencing with our mate. Our beautiful, curious, and loving mate.

She has no idea how we see her or how we feel when we are with her. I mean, she has an idea since she can feel our emotions, but it doesn't even compare to what is happening inside me right now. We are all learning how to control what Nellie feels from us and what we feel from each other. We are not perfect, but it is progress compared to how it was when we first fell to our knees.

Neo has always been into submission. I have watched him bring other women to kneel for him, and other women have tried to pleasure him, but I have never seen him act like this before. He is more vulnerable than I have ever seen, but we all are. It amazes me how far we have come with her in such a short amount of time.

Our father was not lying when he said that we would do anything for our mate and that she would be the most important thing to us. He was right about everything. But how he tried to explain it is entirely different from experiencing it firsthand. Not to mention everything about her is completely fucking different.

It is fucking scary to be with Nellie like this. The worry and fear of her turning us away at the start of this almost drove me insane. Now, I can tell she is not only curious about who we are but also in love with who we are. She doesn't know everything yet, but she knows enough that I can feel her heart beats for us, just like our hearts beat for her.

I walk up behind Nellie, and she is standing there, breathing rapidly. I grasp her arm and turn her around to face me, Neo's cum all over her face. Fuck! What a fucking turn-on. I lean in and run my tongue across her lips. I groan as I taste her and my brother.

I grab her throat and pull her into me. I am usually the one that finds balance and can control myself, but this fucking time, I won't be able to control myself; I know that. I force us both to back up, and she lets me guide her, stopping us next to the bench.

I look down and see the handcuffs meant to keep her hands in place, and my dick hardens in my sweats as I look back at Nellie.

"We love you and need you, but those words don't mean shit if we can't back it up, sweetness. It is time I show you just how real those fucking words are," I whisper, releasing her throat.

"Stand in front of the bench and spread your legs, my Queen," I demand. I can't fucking wait anymore, I just fucking can't. Experiencing all of our sexual desires is bringing out a side of me that I didn't even know was fucking there.

She nods and smiles; what a beautiful sight to see. "Yes, My King."

I back up and give her room to do what I asked. I watch her walk around the bench. She places her hands in the right spots and then bends over for me, giving me a perfect fucking view of her ass. When she spreads her legs open for me, giving me a view of her dripping wet pussy. She is needy and waiting for me, waiting for the pleasure that only I can fucking give her.

Do you know what it feels to truly need someone, not fucking want them, but need them?

I thought I knew; I thought I fucking had an understanding, but once again, Nellie has proven me wrong. She is teaching me so much about myself, and she isn't even fucking trying; it is just who she is. She is the type of woman you will do anything for without question, but she also makes you question everything you think you know. She is dangerous, dangerous in the most seductive and desirable way.

I walk in front of her, bend down, and place the handcuffs around her wrists, ensuring that she can't fucking get away. Part of me wishes she would fight back and run away from us, forcing us to chase her, but we will have plenty of time for that little game, which I am looking forward to.

I stand back up, walk behind her while removing my sweatpants, and kneel down in front of her ass. Fuck me. I lean in and lick around her tight hole, the hole only Darius has claimed. I have never been much for anal sex, but I like playing with it. I am down for anything that has to do with Nellie and giving her pleasure. I will claim her ass. Eventually, we all will, but I want to lick and taste her right now. I want to hear her moan and struggle against her restraints.

I run my tongue from her ass to her cunt, closing my eyes; I groan as her sweet pussy juices coat my tongue. I repeat the process a few times, listening to her sweet moans until I can't wait any longer. I stand and grab my dick by the base and give it a few hard long strokes before I slide it through her folds, lubing it in her juices. I press the tip into her entrance as I lean over her back, press a kiss between her shoulder blades, and push into her wet pussy. She stretches around me, gripping me tightly as I slowly move in and out of her wet heat.

I push a finger in beside my dick, coating it with her essence, and I bring it to her puckered hole and smear her wetness around her. She whimpers as I slowly breach her tight ring in slow movements. I spit and watch as it slides down her crack and adds lubrication as I push through until I am able to slowly fuck her ass as my cock fills her pussy. I push in with my cock and pull out with my finger and repeat the process as she moans and wiggles beneath me. I know what she needs. I release her hip and slide my hand around to her clit, and rub circles around her engorged clit. She is panting, and I can tell she is close by the way her pussy is clenching around my hardness.

"You will cum as I fuck you, my Queen," I growl as I increase the pressure on her clit and the pace of my thrusts into her body.

"Yes, my King," she screams as both of her holes wrap tightly around my cock and finger. As she starts to come undone around me, I push a second finger into her ass and continue to pound into her sweet cunt and ass.

I see Christos move and feel him come behind me. He presses his hand in the center of my back, forcing me to pull my fingers from Nellie's ass and clit. I lean over her back and place my hands on top of hers. My heart races from the emotions I feel coming from Christos. We have been laughing and flirting back and forth, but we have never done anything past that.

But I know, I fucking know that is about to change. I have always been the alpha, but with all of us being alphas, we each need power and control and crave submission. Maybe not as much as Neo, but it turns us all on differently.

"She is not the only one that will cum," Christos says from behind me.

My dick pulses inside Nellie as I feel Christos behind me, spreading my ass cheeks and rubbing his tip against my hole. I try to relax by taking a deep, unsteady breath because I can feel his intentions. He isn't going to prep me, and before I can release my breath, he pushes his dick through my tight rings, causing me to scream out in pain and pleasure.

My entire body shakes against Nellie's, her breaths and mine filling the room as Christos fucks me into Nellie, and I fuck myself on his dick when I pull out of Nellie. We all move together, matching thrust for thrust.

Holy fucking shit.

"You're such a good girl, Nellie. Cum for me again, sweetness," I moan out the words.

Her pussy wraps my cock in a death grip, ripping my orgasm from me. We both scream out our releases, our bodies shaking as one.

What the fuck? How the fuck can it feel this fucking good?

"You're such a good boy, Loyal," Christos whispers from behind me as he pulls out.

My body sinks down on top of Nellie, my fingers intertwined with hers.

I have experienced many things in my centuries, but I have never fucking experienced anything like that before.

24

Christos

Day 10

I watch Nellie as she sits on the bed. She is completely naked and waiting for me. I lean against the St. Andrews Cross with my arms across my bare chest. This whole experience is opening our eyes to other sexual desires that we never thought we would like. Each of us brings our own brand of kink within each room. Typically, we would stick with what we know and love. But within these walls, we are exploring other forms of kinks and desires that we never knew we had or wanted.

Nellie's eyes are not the only ones that are being opened to new things. So far, we have all been able to come together and enjoy what has been happening. I can feel the connection getting stronger and stronger with every sexual act that takes place and becoming more complete.

Something is changing in all of us, something I can't put my finger on just yet, but soon we will all understand what is happening. We have all prepared for this to happen our entire lives, and now that it is happening, it has taken us all by surprise. Sex was just sex before; kinks were just kinks before, but now they both mean so much more.

It is one thing fucking a woman, it is another thing fucking her while also making love to her, and that is the balance we are figuring out, how to fuck and love at the same time. We have to be able to keep the balance because Nellie is not just some whore, just some random woman we are using to get off. She will be the mother of our children, and she is our Queen, which means she needs to be treated differently while still being able to show her the real us.

What a crazy ass concept, but I love the fucking challenge of it.

I thought we were all so fucking different, but with Nellie, I see how much we are all the same, but only with her, only for her.

Seeing her bend over like she did, taking whatever Loyal wanted to give her, is the most beautiful thing I have ever seen. His giving in to me while also giving in to her was a feeling I had never felt before. I was prepared for a mate, but I was not prepared for a lover. Loyal is my lover, Nellie is my mate, and I am completely in love with both of them.

I have heard over the centuries people's point of view on the relationship we have with Nellie and each other. What the outsiders don't understand is that in our world, this is normal. In our world, we accept each other without judgment, regardless of sex, kinks, or desires.

It is wild how people try to hide sex away, how they try to make an outline of what is right and wrong for someone. There are no lines we won't cross sexually. To us, sex is our way of showing our love and claim. There is no shame in wanting and needing someone sexually. But I know not everyone sees it that way. It's a good thing we have never given a fuck what others think anyways.

With Nellie, that is just going to get even worse, us not giving a fuck. If it makes her happy, then we will do it without question. I can tell she is tired, sore, and overwhelmed by everything happening between us, but that is what it is supposed to be like. Nothing about us is soft, sweet, and slow. Even with us trying to make love to her, our primal side always seems to come out at the end.

As long as she continues to say the word, we will continue; that is how this works. She has more control than what she realizes over us. Her words are now our laws, and we will not go against them.

I approach Nellie, grab her arm, and turn her around, and her eyes meet mine. Fuck she is gorgeous. Her emotions are chaotic and wild. She is still uncertain of herself. I can feel it; she doesn't know how to feel, and she doesn't know how to act. But she doesn't understand that she is perfect just the way she is. She doesn't need to know how to act with us. She doesn't need to know what to do. We like her naive and inexperienced.

I love seeing the surprise, excitement and desire in her eyes as she experiences the kinks, as she experiences the pleasure we are giving her. As she shares the pleasure that only we can give her. We are getting just as much pleasure as she is; watching her open up, allowing us to teach her, and being the first to help her experience any of this is a turn-on. Plus, knowing that Zayden has not had her like this is just a cherry on top of the fucking cake.

Of course, this is about all of us, but this is mainly about her. This is all about her, for her. She will get used to being the center of our attention because that will never change; if anything, it will get more intense. The thought of her being anywhere without us makes me see fucking red.

I guess her thoughts and emotions are not the only ones that are jumbled. I am a fucking mess, I might act like I am good, but on the inside, there is a storm of my own I am fighting. It is hard being gentle, and it is hard holding back what I really want to do to her. It is about finding a balance between pleasure and pain, but for so long, I just gave the pain to get off, and with her, I am trying to be different; I fucking have to be different.

I turn her and force her to start backing up until her back hits the St. Andrews Cross and her breathing increases. Zayden seems to be on her mind a lot. She doesn't have to tell us, we know. He is taking up space in all of our minds, which pisses me off. This is the only way I know how to bring her back to me, to us. She will scream and moan, and I need to feel her release on my cock and her warmth against my icy skin. I need to fucking feel her pussy wrap tightly around my dick as she allows herself to let go.

I just fucking need her.

I lean in and gently kiss her lips before I grab her wrists, pull them above her head, and strap each one into the leather restraints fastened to the wooden cross. She holds her arms up for me, making it easier for me to secure her. I step back and admire her naked body. Her arms are strapped tightly so she can't move, and her feet are on the soft pad beneath her, helping to take the pressure off her shoulders. I think about chaining her ankles and spreading her out for me, but I think I'll wait. I want to fuck her, control her legs, control her.

I push my sleep pants down my legs and kick them off to the side before bending down to grab her legs off the ground to position myself between them. Fuck me. This is not what I had planned. I planned on using the flogger and a vibrator to make her scream and beg to cum, but now that I am near her, all of my plans went out the fucking window, and the only thing I can think about is feeling her warm, wet pussy wrapped around me.

Fuck. I don't have control anymore, and I don't know if I ever will with her.

At this moment, she has all the control. She has all of it and doesn't even know it. I am craving her, needing her, desiring her more than I have ever needed, wanted, or craved anything in my entire life.

We all fucking feel the pull of the connection. The beautifully complicated connection that will forever intertwine all of us together. It is alive, strong, and pulling us together in a perfect, imperfect puzzle.

She keeps her eyes on me as she wraps her legs around my waist, digging her feet into my ass. I lean in, placing my hands against the cross. "You belong to us," I say softly.

She smiles. "Yes, My King."

"He doesn't get to take you from us, Nellie. Do you understand me?" I ask and demand.

She hasn't said much about Zayden, but I know, we all fucking know he is taking her away from us inside her head. We can feel it from her emotions. She is improving at controlling her emotions but can't hide from us; we feel it and need her back. I am jealous and selfish and want all of her fucking attention at this moment; in every fucking moment, we want her.

He doesn't fucking deserve to be inside her head, and I will fuck him away. I will.

She doesn't respond at first; she only nods slowly.

I lean in closer, my lips almost touching hers. "Say...the...words."

"Yes, My King, I understand," she replies softly.

I smile at her and press my lips against hers, pressing gentle kisses before I press my tongue between them to deepen the kiss. She opens for me without needing further prompts. I slide my hand between us, grab my dick, and press it against her soaked core. I consume her mouth, making me groan as the taste of her blinds me to reason, and I slam into her. She cries out, and I swallow her sounds as I continue to explore her mouth with my tongue. Her body slams against the cross as I fuck her roughly, needing the fucking friction between us. I hold her hips in a punishing grip while working my cock into her wet hole.

Fuck, she is already submitting to me without needing to say a fucking word. She is our good girl.

I reach up and grip her throat in my hand, and she closes her eyes. I tighten my grip, cutting off more of her air supply, making sure she remembers who the fuck she belongs to, and her pussy tightens around my cock.

"Open your eyes, Nellie. I want you to look at me while I fuck you," I say through gritted teeth.

She does as I ask and opens her eyes. Her eyes tell me she is turned on and needs more.

Our needy little slut.

She moans out as I slam into her, tilting her hips so I can sink deeper into her. I tighten my grip on her throat even more. Her face starts to turn red, and her eyes begin to close. I loosen my grip, she sucks in a deep breath, and her pussy clenches my cock, and my balls tighten. At this point, I am primal, and there is no stopping the release that is building, and when her pussy starts to pulse around me, we both shout out as our orgasms rip through us like a tsunami. Leaving us both breathing heavily, shaking, and covered in sweat.

The sex doesn't last long, but it doesn't fucking need to. We will be able to have her like this for the rest of our lives. It isn't about the length of time right now. It is about experiencing every single fucking pleasure with her, no matter how long or short it is.

I press my mouth to her ear. Our hearts are pounding against each other's chests. "We love you, Nellie. Give yourself to us."

I pull back and look at her beautiful, sweat-covered face, her eyes searching mine as I continue to push my hard cock in and out of her at a slower, more gentle pace.

Her pussy starts to flutter around me again. "You are more than just a breeder. You are our entire world, love."

I lean back in and connect my lips to hers, and she opens her mouth, moaning as I begin to make love to her. I can do this; I can do this for her.

25

Darius

Day 11

I walk into the bathroom and see Nellie lying in the bathtub. Her head is resting against the back of the tub, her eyes are closed, and the bubbles have hidden her gorgeous body from my sight.

I remove my sweatpants and approach her, gently touching the side of her face as I make my way into the tub and lower myself into the hot, steamy water. She opens her eyes and lowers her head, her eyes locked onto me. Since the first moment we locked eyes, I have always felt like when she looks at me, she can see deep inside, the side that no one else has seen. The side of me that others would shy away from, but not her. Even after how I treated her, she has always looked at me the way she is right now.

Her eyes slowly look over my chest, making my heart race. Even though I am covered in tattoos, the scars from Taylor are bright and shine through. I tried to cover them and forget about them, but every time I look into the mirror, I see them, reminding me of what she did to me, the games she played, and the games that I fell for. It reminds me of how toxic we were and how we brought out the worst in one another.

Nellie does the very opposite for me. There are no games, and there are no hidden agendas with her. She is kind and sweet and brings out the best in me. A part of myself that I never knew existed but a side I never want to go away.

Nellie slowly slides over to me and sits on my lap, her pussy pressed against my cock. She looks down at my chest and then back up at my eyes as she rests her hands on my chest. There was a time I would not have allowed her to touch me like this, but now, now I fucking crave her warmth and touch. I don't feel like a monster when she touches me. A monster that I know I am, but with her, I feel human, just a human man who is completely fucking in love with a woman.

How crazy is that?

"I'm sorry, Darius," she whispers painedly.

"What are you sorry for?" I ask, watching her closely. She is filled with sadness, anxiety, and desire. What an odd combination. I never want her to feel sorry for me. I want to show her that I am okay; I am okay because of her. But honestly, I don't know how to replace the emotions she is feeling right now. I have never had someone feel sorry for me. What happened between Taylor and me changed me for the worst and took over my life, but because of Nellie, I have been able to start to heal, whatever the fuck that means, but I feel different.

Taylor does not surround my thoughts and dreams anymore; they have been replaced with Nellie.

She leans in and gently starts to kiss the scars on my chest. My heart plummets into my stomach as my eyes fall closed, and I let my head fall back. I am completely uncomfortable with what she is doing, but I can't bring myself to make her stop.

She pulls back, and I can feel her stare, but I can feel her love for me radiating off her in waves. I open my eyes and look at her. "I will kiss away all your pain. I will replace her, like how you have replaced Zayden. I will take away your pain and help you heal," she vows.

I sit in silence as she reaches between us and grabs my dick. She sits up enough to slide me into her wet pussy and sits down on me, sinking on me until her pelvis meets mine. Her pussy stretched around me and gripped my cock in a vice grip. Her breath hitches as she sinks down, and I moan when her pussy spasms around me, making my balls tighten. Her gentle touch and kind words already had me on edge, but feeling her heat wrap around me was taking everything I had to keep from painting her insides with my sperm.

Where the fuck did she come from?

"Let me love you, Darius," she begs me, tears building in my eyes with her words.

"I'm trying," I say softly as she rocks her hips against me.

"Give yourself to me. Let me be your safe place, baby." She leans in and starts to lick and nip at my neck, and my head falls back again. This was the time that I was supposed to make her submit to me, but I was submitting to her.

I need her, and I need what she is promising me.

So, for the first time, I give everything I am to her, everything I have left, all my broken pieces, all of me is hers.

I sit up quickly and wrap my arms around her, and help lift her up and down my throbbing cock. I thrust up into her as I bring her down on me, sloshing water over the edge of the tub. We continue to give and take from each other, getting lost in the feeling of our bodies coming together as one. When her pussy starts to pulse around me, I bury my face into her neck and growl out my release as she moans out my name as she milks my cock with her own orgasm.

I need to replace Zayden for her, and she will replace Taylor for me. After this, I will never be the same.

26

Nellie

Day 12

I wrap the towel around my naked body as I make my way down the small hallway towards the pool and hot tub. I have spent some time in the living room by the fire, but I need to find something to help my tired and sore muscles. Soaking in the hot tub sounds fucking incredible right now. I think I am becoming addicted to sex, which I know is a thing. It has to be a thing, and there is no way I am going to be able to stop. Even though I am fucking tired, the only thing I can think about is fucking my guys.

I can feel their emotions, and they feel the same. They want the same thing I want– to get lost in each other. When they are fucking me, showing me who they really are deep down inside, it makes me want them even more, knowing that I am the only woman they have been like this with. I feel honored to be their first for all of this, just like they are my first for everything.

With Zayden, I questioned if I should do things with him. I was on guard, even though I desired him in that way. But with Loyal, Christos, Darius, and Neo, I don't question, and I am not on guard. Being able to say one word to give them permission makes me feel powerful, beautiful, and strong.

I know when I get pregnant, I will not want to go into the hot tub or do a lot of things I want to do right now. When that happens, my entire life is going to change. My body is going to change, and my guys are going to change, too. That is, after all, what we have all been preparing for, for me to continue their bloodlines for them. I want to do my duty for them, and I want to become their wife and the mother to their children. I would be lying if I said I wasn't scared. But the fear doesn't last long and is not that loud. My desire to make them happy, to pleasure them, and to complete them the way they have for me has taken over everything else.

I am not scared of my guys, not at all. I am scared of what will happen once we leave the safety of these walls. This place has become my safe haven, and it is the one place I know for a fucking fact Zayden can't touch me or my guys. But once we leave here, they will have things they need to do as the Kings, and I will have things to do as their wife, their mate. I am ready to do whatever it is I need to do, but I would feel better knowing Zayden wasn't out there just waiting for me.

I would feel better if I knew that Ashton had found him and he couldn't hurt my Guardians. They act as if they are fine, but I can feel it; they are nervous. Zayden is testing them in ways a human never has before, and he is proving to be more dangerous than any of us knew. I thought once I was mated, he would move on, but he hasn't. My being mated has changed him and made him more violent, reckless, and unhinged.

One thing I can say about Zayden is he is patient when he really wants something, and he has made it clear that I am the center of his obsession. I can't fucking believe I didn't see this in him before. I was so stupid. I would do things differently if I had the chance, or at least I think I would.

Loyal, Darius, Neo, and Christos have been doing their best to try and distract me from my drowning and unhinged thoughts and emotions. For the most part, they have been able to, but in times like this, the thoughts of my sister and father bury me under heavy emotions, making it hard to breathe.

My entire body is fucking sore, but at the same time, I have never felt more alive than I do right now. How is that even possible to be so fucking sore and tired and still feel alive and full of energy?

These Guardians have awakened something inside me that I don't understand, but I know I want more of all of them. I never want to leave this pool house. I wish we could just stay here forever, just me and them. But we can't; there is too much being asked of us, and we have obligations to our people.

Obligations we will never be able to escape. My insecurities make me feel like they are only with me because of the obligation to their people, but then my heart and body remind me that is the furthest thing from the truth. I would be able to feel it if it were, but it doesn't stop my thoughts from trying to convince me.

My Guardians are rough but at the same time gentle. They are taking off their masks for me, or at least that is what they call them. I don't fully understand what they mean, but I think I am starting to. They are trying to be different for me. I can see it, feel it. They are trying to show me that they do love me, and I know that I love them. What we have together has to be love. You can't feel like this and not be in love.

I wish my mother was here; she would know just the right thing to say to calm down my anxiety and my irrational thoughts. But she is gone, my sister is gone, and so is my father. The only people I have left are my Guardians, and I will do whatever I can to keep them. I don't think I would survive it if I lost them. I know my heart would turn hollow, and I would not be the same person I am right now, and the thought of Zayden hurting them or taking them away from me makes me sick to my stomach.

I can only trust and hope that everything works out in our favor, not Zayden's. So far, he has been steps ahead of us and winning, but he can't win; I won't let him. He will fucking let me go one way or another.

When Loyal, Darius, Neo, and Christos are out on the streets, at the clubs, or selling drugs, they have to be a certain way. Their people expect them to be a certain way, and they need respect and fear to rule and keep the power and control they have. But inside these walls, they are just my guys, my lovers, my Kings. Inside these walls, they have power and control in a different way, and so do I.

It is crazy to think back before I was mated to them. It seems like such a long time ago. I remember who I was before them, but now I want to be the woman they are helping me become in these walls. They keep calling me their Queen, but I still don't see it. I see strength, courage, violence, and madness in each of them, and sometimes, I still feel out of place, like I don't belong.

But as soon as the thought enters my mind, they find a way to make it disappear and replace it with what they see when they look at me–their Queen.

A smile spreads across my face when I think about everything that we have done together this far. They are showing me that my body enjoys everything they have to offer. I crave what only they can give me, and I can tell I am doing the same for them.

I entered the indoor pool area, but it was empty. The steam hovers around the hot tub, and my heart races as I look around the beautiful room. Besides a six-person hot tub, there is an Olympic-sized heated pool with lounge chairs positioned around it. Everything is done in either red or black marble throughout the whole pool house. They sure do like their dark marble theme.

I have never been in a hot tub before. I was always so busy dancing and preparing to be mated to my Guardians that I really didn't live much of a life, but I have a feeling that is going to change. They are not at all what I thought they were. And now that we all have been giving in to each other, things continue to change rapidly, which is hard to keep up with sometimes.

I drape my towel over the back of a chair before I step into the hot tub and lower myself into the hot, steamy water. I press the button on the panel, and the jets turn on. I rest my head back as the jets massage my sore muscles. My pussy is so sore right now, and I have a feeling that isn't going to change any time soon. But the pain from being sore enhances the pleasure I get when they claim me over and over again.

They are right. Exploring all these different sexual kinks is helping me to discover what I like. I think I might be a kink whore, if there is such a thing, because so far, I have enjoyed everything we have done, and it gets me off. There is nothing they have done that has turned me off. If anything, it has sent me over the edge time and time again.

I take a deep breath and sink deeper into the hot water. I hear someone enter the room, and when I open my eyes, I see Loyal and Christos walking towards me. They are both naked, giving me a clear view of their muscular bodies that are covered in tattoos, as well as their massive dicks. My mouth waters at the sight of them, and I can't help but squeeze my thighs together as I watch them step into the hot tub and lower themselves into the water. They glide through the water and sit on either side of me.

"Hey, sweetness," Loyal whispers as he grabs onto my throat and pulls me against him.

"Hey," I whisper back.

"We missed you, love," Christos says from behind me. He presses his chest against my back as Loyal lifts me onto his lap. I place my hands on his muscular shoulders.

Loyal tightens his grip on my throat as I gaze at his chest and back to his eyes; a gorgeous smile lights up his face. "You are beautiful," I whisper.

He pulls me into him, and I can feel his dick between us. I start to grind against him, rubbing my clit against his hardening dick.

"I have been called many things, Nellie, but beautiful is not one of them," Loyal says amusingly.

I smile as he pulls me closer to him, our lips almost touching. I continue to grind against his dick, needing him inside me but also wanting to play a little.

"Maybe that is because they weren't actually seeing you, sweetheart," I whisper, boldly using my nickname for him.

"I love you calling me that," Loyal confesses to me.

I feel Christos come up behind me. He rests his hands on my legs as I continue to grind against Loyal. Christos bites down on my shoulder, his teeth cutting through my skin, and a moan escapes me as Loyal smashes his lips to mine. I feel Loyal reach over, grab something, and move between us. I don't know what it was, though.

My brain always gets fuzzy when they bite me, the sexual sensation and tension building inside me like a hot fucking flame. Christos licks and sucks on my neck as Loyal pulls back and searches my eyes.

I look down into the water and see a gun in his hand. The barrel is positioned at my pussy's entrance forcing me to stop grinding. My heart is racing so fucking fast as I look back up at Loyal. A smile forms across his lips. "White," I whisper.

He leans back in and smashes his lips to mine as he tightens his grip on my throat, and Christos bites down fucking harder onto my shoulder, causing me to open my mouth and moan into Loyal's. His tongue enters my mouth as I feel him push the barrel of the gun into my pussy. I whimper into his mouth as my pussy stretches to try and fit the object inside me.

He begins to push the gun in and out of my pussy, and I can feel myself wrapping tighter and tighter around the gun as Christos continues to bite down on my shoulder.

Loyal pulls back as I let out a moan, my nails digging into his strong chest.

"Look at me, Nellie," Loyal says through gritted teeth.

I do as he demands. How can I not?

I lock eyes with him as my hips rock back and forth with the gun.

"We love you, we will die for you, and we will burn the whole fucking kingdom down for you. Do you understand?"

I lean in, keeping my eyes on him. "I love you all. I will die for you all, and I will burn the whole fucking kingdom down for all of you. Do you understand?" I say in a low, dark tone

"You were made for us," he confesses and demands.

"Yes, I was," I scream out as I orgasm on the gun and Loyal's hand underneath the water. My heart is racing so fucking fast, I can hear it in my ears.

Loyal chuckles as I pull back, and he pulls the gun out of my really sore pussy.

Christos pulls back and wraps his arm around my stomach, pulling me off of Loyal. He turns me around to face him. He smiles as he turns me back around to face Loyal. He is fucking gorgeous, and I can see his dick is still hard underneath the water. Christos grabs my wrists and pulls them behind my back as Loyal grabs his dick underneath the water and points it up toward me.

Christos leans in, resting his lips against my ear, and before he can say anything, I say, "White."

Christos bends me over at the waist, my face right above the water. As he tightens his grip on my wrists, he pushes into my already wet pussy without warning. He grabs my hair and pushes my head underneath the water. I open my mouth, and Loyal shoves his dick into it. I gag, I can't fucking breathe, but holy fuck, this is hot.

My pussy wraps tightly around Christos's dick as he starts to push in and out of me, and Loyal starts to fuck my face. I slam my eyes shut as I try and calm down my racing heart, but I have a feeling I won't be able to, not as Christos is fucking me from behind and Loyal is fucking my mouth under the water.

What the fuck is happening, I don't know, but I do know I don't want it to fucking stop.

27

Ashton

Day 13

The last few days have been very fucking interesting. I don't know when we started to lose control over our Chosen Humans, but something has changed between us and them. We thought everything was good between us, but the more I dig, the more I realize that the humans are not happy, and they have been getting louder and louder about it since Zayden has been starting shit.

Not only are some of the humans not happy with how we are running things, but there are Guardians are fucking people that are taking Zaydens side. I don't fucking understand, I don't understand any of it. But I will fucking find the Guardians that have decided to turn their backs on their own kind. Some I will be able to kill, and others I will make fucking sure they suffer for the rest of their lives, and for our kind, that can be fucking forever.

We need to stop this before it fucking spreads because once it does, there is no way to fucking contain it. Revenge can spread faster than a fucking virus, and it is the fucking virus. If you give Guardians and humans hope that they don't need to fucking listen to the rules, and that they don't have to follow the laws before we know it, everything we have built will be destroyed. Cracks in a foundation can spread and eventually, the whole fucking thing will fall.

Rules and laws keep order. Without them, people will do whatever the fuck they want, and that can't fucking happen. I will find the source of all of this fucking chaos. Zayden, that fucking man, if you even want to call him that, will pay for what he is doing. Luckily, nothing has spread too far, not yet. The sooner I find Zayden, the sooner this bullshit ends.

I should have killed him in the fucking woods, but not knowing who was watching made me stop from snapping his neck. There are consequences to every fucking behavior, so I need to be careful. I need to watch what I do and how I do it so it doesn't come back and destroy my fucking family.

I will do my best to stop this before it gets that far, but I can't promise shit, which pisses me off. I want to be able to tell the others that everything is going to be okay, but I can't, not yet, anyway.

There is now a bridge between us and certain humans and Guardians, and we plan on burning that fucking bridge. We plan to make every single human and Guardian suffer that has been going against us, and the list is getting fucking longer and longer. I don't know who exactly is on our side and who the fuck is on Zayden's, but sooner than later, I will fucking get ahead of him. His luck will fucking run out. If you want to call it that.

What happened with the uprising will never fucking happen again. We need to be smart with how we react to what we now know they have been up to. But they will all suffer, they will feel the wrath of our kind, and they will learn to never ever fucking try and go against us again.

I make my way across the yard towards the main house. My cousins and the others are still locked away in the pool house, and from what I have heard, they are all doing what they need to do. When they come out of that mansion, things will be different for all of us, and we need to be prepared. I need to fucking make sure I have something good to tell them.

Nellie deserves to get revenge for her father and sister, and Zayden deserves to be punished for the rest of his life for what he has done and for what he plans on doing to our family and to Nellie.

It took a lot longer than I wanted it to, but with the help of Ajax and Ace, we have been able to track down Zayden's friends. The men that left their friend behind when Christos and Loyal were teaching Zayden a little lesson, a lesson that he didn't fucking learn.

How the fuck can you call someone a friend when they fucking leave you to save their own asses?

Humans don't know what it means to be loyal, to put your life on the line for another. Over the centuries, I have seen what humans do when they are afraid when they allow fear to take them over. Honestly, I don't understand it. Guardians will do anything to protect those that they call family, but Zayden's friends and even Zayden himself aren't like that; they will do anything to fucking save themselves. It is fucking disgusting. Do they have no fucking honor at all?

Zayden did not choose wisely with his fucking friends, but I can say that he choose wisely with whoever the fuck is helping him. I will give him credit for that. This little fucker has become a fucking pain in my side.

Zayden's friends were hiding in some abandoned house in the middle of the bayou. Fucking cowards, they didn't put up a fight as we took them back here. Now, from what I can hear, they are crying like some little bitches. It amazes me how a human will crack if you apply the right amount of pressure. They can act tough all they fucking want to, but in the end, they will never be the same. After we are done with them, they will wish for death.

I have learned over the centuries that it is not death men fear the most, fuck no, it is being powerless and out of control. Death is too easy, too fucking quick.

I look ahead and see Ace and Ajax leaning against the house, waiting for me to let them in and go in the back way. We have kept the two fuckers in the basement for the last few days, and they have given up a lot of information about the humans. Apparently, there are a lot more against us than we ever thought, but they have not given up where Zayden is or who is helping him.

With what we have put them through, their screams filling the house, their bodies bleeding, they can't give up something they don't know. Zayden is smarter than I thought he was. He made sure not to tell them the really important shit. But still, they will have to be the ones to pay for what Zayden has done.

They could have warned us, or they could have talked some reason into their crazy-ass friend, but they didn't. They just stood back and let things unfold. They were the ones who started the fight at the club because Zayden told them to. These fuckers have no fucking backbone, and they do whatever the person in charge says.

We follow rules and laws, but we always do whatever the fuck we want; we have backbones. Try telling a Guardian they can't do something and see what happens.

One thing I know these fuckers do know is the Guardians that were watching over Nellie turned the other cheek. I need to know their fucking names, and if I can't fucking torture Zayden, then our fucking people that betrayed us will have to do for now.

I stop a foot away from Ajax and Ace; they are covered in blood. They have been torturing the poor fuckers while I have been out searching for Zayden.

I never thought I would work beside a Shadow, but Ajax is different. All three of us have something in common. I am the enforcer for the Guardians, Ace is the enforcer for his pack of Night Walkers, and Ajax is the enforcer for the Shadows. He is one of the only ones that I have met that have met the Queen—the Queen of the Shadows.

All three of us are outsiders; we still haven't found our mates, and we will do whatever it takes to protect our family.

So far, I trust Ajax and know I can trust Ace.

"You ready for this?" I ask, looking at Ace and then at Ajax

They both nod. I walk between them and open the door, walking inside and down the stairs to the basement.

We haven't had to use the basement much, but since this whole Zayden thing started, I have a feeling we will be using it a lot more.

I open the door and walk into the room, and it smells like blood and piss. These fuckers didn't last long before they pissed themselves. They thought they were tough, tough enough to go against us. Man, they didn't last long at all; it was disappointing. Actually, it is more fun when they try to fight back, but these fuckers gave in as soon as we started to cut.

I have given Ace and Ajax free rain to beat the fuck out of these two the last few days. It gave me time to try and track down Zayden, I thought I had him once but he is quick, and I keep losing the fucking trail. It is annoying, and he is testing me in ways I haven't been tested in a long time.

He thinks this is a game, and he thinks that this is a game he will win. He hasn't met anyone like me. He will regret the day he set his eyes on Nellie.

I stop in front of the two men who are hanging from the chains that are attached to the ceiling. Their shirts have been removed, and the only thing they are wearing is their jeans which are soaked in their piss and blood.

Their chests and stomachs are covered in fresh cuts. From what I can tell, they have lost a lot of blood, and I know from experience that if they lose much more, they will not survive.

I slowly look up their chests and stop on the one that calls himself Wes. He has been the toughest to break out of the two, and I have respect for him, at least a little bit. Mal, on the other hand, broke after a few cuts. If only they actually had the information I needed, but I know they don't. If they did, they would have said it already, but now I am after something else, something that I fucking know they know. And they are going to fucking give it to me.

"I have a very simple question to ask. Answer my question, and the cutting stops. Lie to me and you will wish the cutting was the only thing we were doing to you, understand?" I say through gritted teeth.

I am not in the mood for any more games. They tell me what I want. I might spare them; we will see. I can't make any promises.

They both nod, their eyes filled with fear and rage. The rage won't help them, though. They have no power or control over what happens to them. They can only pray and hope that they survive, and I haven't figured out if I am in the mood for mercy today or not; it will depend on their answer.

I turn and walk to the window that looks over the pool and towards the pool mansion. "I know you both know which Guardians were supposed to be watching over Nellie before she was mated. I need to know who the Guardians were."

"Shouldn't you know?" Wes asks curiously.

"If I knew, I wouldn't be asking, you ass fuck. Things are more blurred than I thought, and the information has been erased. Give me their fucking names," I say, turning around and looking back at the hanging men.

They look at each other and then over at Ajax and Ace. Their eyes stay on them as my two friends stalk behind them, knives in their hands. Ajax and Ace stop behind each man and place the knife against their throats.

"Give me their fucking names," I scream as I close the distance between me and Wes. His eyes stay locked on me as his breathing starts to increase.

"Zion, Stetson, and Baylor," Wes whispers in a defeated and pained voice.

I stumble back, no fucking shit.

I look at Ace and Ajax and nod. I watch them pull both men's heads back and slice their fucking throats.

Ace and Ajax do it without a second thought. Their screams fill the room but quickly die off as their bodies go limp, hanging from the fucking chains.

I run my hands down my face.

"Who are Zion, Stetson, and Baylor?" Ace asks, making his way over to me. He stops in front of me as Ajax stops at my side, both of them waiting for me to answer.

"They are the trusted Guardians of Argento," I say as calmly as possible.

What the fuck is going on?

"What?" Ace asks, but I know he fucking heard me.

I look at Ace and lower my hands from my face. "They are his fucking Guardians," I yell.

"Is he in on this?" Ajax asks in a concerned voice. This is the first time I have heard any kind of fucking concern in his voice, which honestly makes me fucking nervous.

"I don't know, Ajax. I fucking don't know, but you better believe we are about to go fucking find out." I seeth.

I quickly turn around and run up the stairs and out of the back door. I can feel Ajax and Ace right on my heels as I run past the pool house. "Stay fucking here," I say to one of the Guardians. They nod as I take off into the forest.

If Argento is a part of this, then nothing we know and believe in is fucking true or real. This can't fucking be. I refuse to believe my uncle is on this shit, and if he doesn't know about his Guardians, he needs to fucking know. Those are the same Guardians that watch over him and his wife.

Fuck me, man, how deep does the betrayal go?

28

Zayden

Day 14

I continue to sit on the step looking out at the bayou I can't say how many times I have been here remembering the moments I spent with Nellie. We use to escape in the bayou, a place where her mother use to go before she was taken by the Guardians, or mated, or whatever the fuck you want to call it. Nellie has always been humble and understanding of what was going to be asked of her, but at the same time, I saw the anxiety and fear in her, the anxiety and fear that caused her to talk about running away with me.

At times though, I know for a fucking fact she did wish she was someone else, but in the end, like with so many others, she fell for the Guardians and what they asked of her, and now she is falling in love with those fuckers, and letting them do whatever they want to her. I have been told what will go on for the next five weeks, I want to attack, I want to rip her from their arms, but it wouldn't be smart. I have to be the smart one in this fucking equation, or everything I have done this far would be for fucking nothing.

Those memories of her and I laughing, kissing, her allowing me to touch her, hold her, and look into her eyes now seem so fucking far away. Things have gotten so fucking crazy and out of control. Even if I wanted to take back what has happened, I can't, there is no fucking taking it back. There is no saying I am sorry because I know even if I told her I was sorry, she wouldn't fucking believe me. Not now. She doesn't trust me anymore.

Nellie doesn't look at me like she once did, if she was still the Nellie, I knew she would have left with me at the club. She would fucking be with me right now, but they have bent her, twisted her, and molded her into what they want her to fucking be, and she doesn't see it. She is just allowing this shit to happen. She said she loved me, and she wanted a life with me first, way before these fuckers came into the picture. But now that they are in the picture, she pushed me aside.

She pushed me away when I tried to claim her, and since that day, she has never looked at me the same, she changed that day, which I know is my fault, but it is also her fucking fault. if she just let things happen between us both of us would not be in the fucking situation we are in now.

She trusts those fucking Guardians. I took it too far with her, I went too fast, I should have had the ability to hold back and keep control of her, but I couldn't, I just fucking couldn't, and now I am paying the price for it. She will soon pay the price as well. She wants to be fucked like an animal, she wants to be treated like a fucking whore, I can do that for her, I would do anything for her. Even though she isn't asking for me, I know deep down inside she wants me, I will be able to awaken the feelings she once felt for me. I fucking know it.

I just need the fucking chance to show her, I need to fucking open her eyes to the reality of the Guardians. She has fallen in love with them I know she has, I can tell without even being around her that they are claiming her, and she is fucking letting them.

I will show her I am not the monster she thinks I am, once she is back in my arms again everything will fucking be okay, it has to be fucking okay.

The Guardians have normalized stealing our women, they have normalized forcing our women to dance like sluts, and be raised believing that being mated or chosen or whatever the fuck it is. That it is the best thing for them and their families. It is not what is best for them, or anyone else. The only ones it fucking benefits and is good for is the fucking Guardians.

If they can't continue their bloodlines they lose their fucking power and control over us, so in reality all we have to do is take all of our fucking women away and leave, go to a place that they cant follow and that would solve that shit. but it isn't that fucking simple, this town belongs to us and not them, and I will not be the one to leave, and I know they won't just fucking pack their shit and leave, so it will end in blood. I think it was always going to end in war, we were just kidding ourselves that it wouldn't.

Before I had a reason for revenge and to get back at them, but now my reason has changed and my obsession has only grown, and Nellie is the fucking center of all of it. she is the reason I am doing any of this shit, she is what is driving me to continue to make sure that they pay for what they have done. I never thought I would fall for her, I never thought that my obsession would turn into love for her, but it has, it fucking has and I can't just walk away because she wants me to, I can't.

My father told me once that if you love something you have to do whatever you have to do to fucking keep it, and that is exactly what I am going to do.

I can't fucking believe how blind everyone is to the real facts. I think they know, they have to fucking know that none of this is fucking right for our people, but they choose to fucking ignore it, they choose to just fall in line like good little fucking bitches. it makes me sick how almost everyone is just doing as they are told without question. It makes me sick that my people think that this is okay. None of this is fucking okay.

The facts are: One we are not fucking free, we work and severe the Guardians. We work and serve them how they want us to, and they expect us to just do it without question or protest. Two whenever we try to gain back any kind of control or power we are killed or punished. They have no lines they will not cross to punish us and make sure that we fall back into line. Three they choose what we do for a living, how we live, who we get to fuck, and who we have to let go.

They get to choose everything for us, and we are supposed to kneel down and say thank you. Thank you for fucking what being at their fucking beck and call whenever they want.

Are we supposed to be thankful that we are in prison without fucking bars?

Does that at all seem like a good fucking life to you?

My people are so fucking used to the Guardians and what they think they provide them, that most are too scared to stand up with me, and the others believe that the Guardians know best. There are more willing to stand up with me than not, but the ones that aren't risk telling them what I am up to, so the best thing is to keep everything to my fucking self and tell the others only what they need to know.

They don't need to know everything, they just need to know that at the end of this, they will be fucking free, that should be fucking good enough for them.

How the flying fuck has this turned into me being the bad guy?

I am now being haunted by Ashton and his men, or whatever the fuck they are. they killed my men, my fucking friends, and Ashton just won't let things fucking fall where they may. I know he has been searching for me, and asking fucking questions, and the funny thing is I have been right underneath his fucking nose this entire time.

I have been ten steps ahead of him this entire fucking time, and I am hoping my luck doesn't run out. I need to stay ahead of all of them until it is the right time to come out and show everyone that they are fucked and going to lose. this is going to end with their deaths, not mine, I will make sure of that. I am smarter than what Ashton and the others know.

They have no idea the madness inside my head, but they will soon enough, I can be patient for a little while longer. I gave Ashton a time limit, a time limit I know for a fact he won't follow, but I didn't think he would, he would be stupid to hand Nellie over to me, and I know her Guardians won't just let her go, the only way to force them to let her go with me is if I make them all suffer and make sure they do not have a fucking choice.

I have continued to come back here and spend time here, and for the life of me, I don't know why Ashton hasn't thought of coming back here.

His pride and ego are stopping him, he and I are a lot alike. I would never tell him that but we are.

I shake my head as I stand up and make my way up the steps and into the house. the house that holds a lot of memories of me and Nellie.

sometimes I wish we could just go back and do things over again. if I could I would change a lot of things, but wishing for things to change will not make them change, you have to force them to change.

I make my way down the hallway into her room, I make my way over to her dresser and pick up the perfume, the smell I have missed so fucking much. I close my eyes as I pick up the perfume and bring it up to my nose, I take in a deep shaky breath as I allow the memories of smelling her skin rushes into my head.

I open my eyes and turn and make my way over to her clothes, I lift up the perfume and begin spraying over her clothes, I might not be able to jack off to the real thing at this moment, but I will fucking get off on my memories of her, the smell of her. one day it will not be her clothes I am cuming on but her face, her entire body will be covered in my cum.

I unzip my pants and pull out my already hard dick. I open my eyes and lean in taking in a deep breath, Nellies perfume fills my nose, making me moan as I start to move up and down my dick, I can't fucking wait until her wet, warm tight pussy is around my dick. I want to hear her scream my name, and moan my name.

I grab onto her jacket and shove my face into it, making it hard for me to breathe, I feel my balls tightening as I continue to move my hand up and down my dick.

She will scream my name if it is the last thing she ever fucking does.

I pull back and rip down her jacket, I watch it fall to the ground as I continue to work my dick.

My heart continues to race as my head falls back, a moan leaves my mouth as I allow my release to go over her jacket.

I can't fucking claim her right now, so I will claim every single thing in this room. one way or another she will know, she will fucking know who she fucking belongs to.

29

Darius

3 Years Ago

My eyes fly open, and as soon as they do, I see Taylor on top of me. Riding me, my dick buried deep in her wet pussy. Fuck how much dope did I do?

I try and move my hands, but I can't. She has wrapped chains around my wrists, and I can feel other hands holding me down. I look up and see two Guardians I have never met on either side of me, holding me down with my hands above my head.

"Taylor, what the fuck do you think you are doing?" I say through gritted teeth.

She smiles down at me as she digs her fingers into my chest. "It is your turn to submit to me, baby," she says in a low, desired voice.

The fuck?

"What the fuck are you talking about?" I ask, hearing the rage in my tone.

If she is trying to make me lose control and punish her, she is doing a very good fucking job.

"You mark me. Now, it is time I mark you," she says, smirking.

She knows what I want from her. I want her to be my whore, a whore who fucking listens. She is not listening, and she is breaking my rules. For some reason, she loves it when I hurt her when I punish her. She is not going to like the punishment I give her when I get my fucking hands on her. I have never met a human woman who likes pain the way she does. Her monster matches my own, which I used to think was a good thing, but now I am not so sure.

"Taylor, get the fuck off of me now," I say, looking her in the fucking eyes. She knows I am not playing. She wants to get a rise out of me by pushing me, but if she keeps pushing, she will be the one bleeding on the fucking floor.

She laughs and shakes her head. If I had a beating heart, this is when it would be racing and sinking at the same time. I try to pull up on the chains and hands holding me, but I can't shake them off. I took way too much fucking dope last night.

Humans don't know it, but booze and dope affect us the same way it affects humans. Maybe not as bad, but it can still put us on our asses.

My tolerance for dope has increased to the point where I have to take a lot to feel it, and now I regret using any last night.

I knew it was fucking weird that she was feeding me more and more and being sweet and kind to me. I should have fucking known right then that something was wrong. We are not sweet and kind to each other; the very opposite. We are cruel and mean and are toxic as fuck. We have always been that way, which is what made me addicted to Taylor. She can dish it back out, and it seemed the worse I treated her, the more she wanted me, so I did just that.

"Taylor, if you don't get the fuck off of me and undo these chains, you will fucking regret it. I promise you," I warn her.

She leans in, her lips almost touching mine. "I don't think so."

She sits up and stops riding my dick for a moment. She reaches over and grabs a blade from the table next to the bed.

"Where the fuck did you get that?" I ask.

"I found it in your things," she says softly with a smile.

This fucking bitch has been looking through my shit.

"You went through my things?" I ask, but I already know the fucking answer. I should have fucking known, of course, she would go through my shit.

"Of course I did." She whispers.

She smiles as she places the blade on my chest. She has no idea what the fuck the blade is, but I do. Me and my brother hid it away for a fucking reason. A reason that Taylor doesn't need to know about. No fucking human needs to know that fucking secret, but I have a feeling she will figure it out shortly.

"I will hurt you," I warn her, but it is more of a fucking promise.

'I know, but I will hurt you first, baby," she taunts me. She has no fear, no fucking fear. I will need to make sure to change that.

Fuck me.

She leans in, kisses my neck, and then starts to slowly slice my chest, over and over and over again.

I try to keep the screams in, but I can't. That knife, the fucking blade burns like acid against my skin.

"Taylor!" I scream as I start to struggle against the chains and the Guardians, but it is no use. I am still sluggish from the dope that is still in my system. And the poison that is in the blade is making me even weaker.

The poison won't kill me, but it will weaken me, and it will leave fucking scars. I squeeze my eyes shut as the pain burns through my body, making me scream out uncontrollably.

I feel Taylor starting to ride my dick again as she makes cuts all over my chest and then moves down to my stomach. She wants to leave her mark and make me suffer, and she found the one way to do it without me having a beating heart or soul.

This fucking bitch will pay for this.

30

Christos

Present Day

Week 3 – Day 15

I place my hands against the shower wall. This week was supposed to be my week to take off my mask and give myself entirely to Nellie, but the truth is my kink; my desire has changed. I have already given her myself and no longer want to harm her.

That is what my kink was; the humans call it impact play, but I do not want to hurt her or cause her pain. She has already been through enough with Zayden. One day, she will be ready for my kink, but right now is not the time, so I want it done to me instead. I can handle the pain, I need the fucking pain.

Now that I have a beating heart and a soul, the pain will feel different, just like everything else fucking feels different and more intense.

Nellie will understand this is about us giving ourselves to her, of her giving herself to us, and I know if I asked her to let me hurt her, she would. She would say the word *white* without thinking, but she doesn't understand what kind of pain I want to inflict. She doesn't understand what it does to me when I cause a woman to scream out in pain.

Honestly, I don't want to be that way anymore. I don't want to punish her. I want to be punished; I need to be punished. It is a fire, a desire inside me right now that is taking over everything else.

I feel lips against my skin, and I know that it is Loyal. My breath hitches when he steps back and slowly runs the knotted leather strips from my flagellation whip down my naked back. He knows what I need because I can't hide my emotions right now. I am naked and vulnerable in more ways than one.

He presses his mouth against my ear. "Is it the pain you inflict that turns you on or the pain you feel by inflicting pain?"

"Both," I whisper as the water rains down on the both of us.

"Let me help you," he says in a low, dark voice. Fuck his voice, his dominance at this moment, all of it turns me the fuck on.

I have whipped myself many times, but the body's reaction is not the same. It is different when you do it to yourself because you know when it's coming and can estimate the pain, but when someone else does it, you give up the power and control, intensifying the experience with so many unknowns.

"Please," I beg as I press my forehead against the shower wall.

I can't explain why I desire and need pain, but I know I need it done to me right now, not the other way around. I need to feel the punishment that I would have given Nellie. Maybe it is because of everything I have done before Nellie or because I believe I should be punished for being a monster. I am unsure, and I really don't care right now. As long as Loyal can give me what I fucking need, that is all that matters to me.

Loyal pulls back and runs the whip down my back again. The knotted leather is wet from the shower now, and it is going to make each strike hurt that much more. It will also leave welts, but that is the point, isn't it? Cause pain without blood.

Make the body hurt so good it gets you off?

I feel the material leave my skin and close my eyes as I anticipate the first strike. I try to control my breathing, but it is nearly impossible, with my heart racing like it is. I feel the air shift behind me and hear the strips fly through the air and water, and seconds later, an aching pain slashes across my back as the knots and leather slash across my skin.

A moan escapes me as he pulls back and hits me repeatedly, each strike harder than the last, causing pain to radiate throughout my body and blood to rush to my now hard cock. I reach down and grab myself and start to slowly run my hand from base to tip of my throbbing cock. The harder Loyal strikes me, the more my dick leaks cum, and the faster I stroke myself.

I feel each hit, feeling the pain and the release I need right now. Not many people understand, but Loyal does, which is another reason why I know I am in love with him.

He knows what I need without words and helps me with the release I need—a release I desire above all else right now.

31

Nellie

Day 16

I hear Neo, Loyal, and Darius laughing and messing around in the kitchen. It is nice hearing them letting go and relaxing around each other. I never thought it would be like this. I know I keep telling myself this, but it is true. I honestly don't know what I thought it would be like. A part of me was scared that they would just fuck me and lock me away until I had their children. But now I see that they are not at all what others think they are or what I thought they would be. People fear what they don't understand. They fear because they haven't experienced what I have experienced with my Guardians. I know not every Guardian-mate relationship is like ours, but I am incredibly grateful my relationship with my mates is evolving the way that it is.

Loyal, Neo, Christos, and Darius have changed my life in every way. Even though I had to leave everything behind for them, it is worth it, and they are worth it. Zayden has complicated things and has put us all on edge, but I will not let him win. I will not let my fear of what he might do next stop me from fully giving myself to my guys.

It makes me smile to hear them laughing and joking with each other. What we have is different and, at times, downright confusing, but each minute we spend in this pool house, the stronger the connection becomes between all of us. I can feel it, and they can, as well. The connection will be complete soon. I don't exactly know what that means, but I know that whatever it is, it is meant to happen, and I am ready for it.

Christos has kept his distance from me since yesterday, and it is throwing me off if I am being honest. He has never been distant from me before, but I did hear him and Loyal in the shower last night: his screams and moans. I wanted to watch and see what he was so afraid to let me see, but I didn't want to impose on their moment and stop what they were doing.

Apparently, Christos needed the release he got from Loyal, but I don't understand what is going on with him. I want to understand, no, I fucking need to understand. I have let them in more than I have ever let anyone else, and now it is Christos' turn to take off his fucking mask and let me see him.

I don't know when I became so bold, but there is a fire inside me that I don't understand, but I want him to help me understand. I know Christos feels conflicted, which makes me nervous and a little uneasy.

The others have shared their kinks and desires with me and have experienced it all with me, but Christos chose to opt out of his week for some reason. It has left me confused and a little jealous that he opened himself up to Loyal but not me. I am jealous that we didn't experience it together.

I know they have a connection between them and that I am the center of their attention, but I don't feel that way right now. I am jealous because I want to experience his sexual needs and desires with him. I want him to allow me to experience pleasure from what pleasures him.

I open his bedroom door and walk in, closing it behind me. I find Christos with his hands resting on the wall on either side of the window, staring at the trees. He is only wearing grey sweatpants; I don't know what it is about my guys and their grey sweatpants, but fuck, they are sexy as hell.

Christos' muscles ripple under his tattoo-covered back as I come up behind him and wrap my arms around his stomach. I gently press my lips against his back and kiss him.

"Hey, love," he whispers.

I love each of their voices; they make me feel safe and grounded, and it turns me on. "Hey, you," I whisper against his skin.

"What are you doing?" He asks curiously, but he knows what I am doing. They started this and opened my eyes to a different side of myself. He shouldn't be surprised that I desire him. He can feel it in me, and I know he can.

"I want you," I say against his cold skin.

He drops his hands from the wall and turns around in my arms, resting his back against the window. I gaze up at him, fuck, he is absolutely fucking gorgeous in the moonlight.

"Nellie, I think it is best we let you rest," he confesses, looking into my eyes.

I shake my head. "I don't want to rest," I say softly.

He takes a deep breath. "Nellie, please," he begs me.

I step back, release my arms from around him, and look into his eyes. I am confused by the conflict I find in his eyes. He confuses me because this is not like him. I don't like this distance or how his emotions become unstable the longer I look into his eyes.

"Please let me in, Christos," I beg back.

He shakes his head. "I can't."

"You can't, or you won't?" I snap back. I know I am not being fair to him and that I am being selfish, but I need him. I want him.

"Is there a difference?" He asks through gritted teeth.

"There is to me," I confess to him, wrapping my arms around myself. I don't understand the emotions that are hitting me on all sides from him.

"You don't want to experience what I want from you, Nellie," he warns me. A sane person would walk away and let him be, but apparently, I am not sane.

"What do you want?" I ask, looking over his gorgeous face.

"Please stop," he begs me again.

My heart is thumping against my chest. "What do you want, Christos?" I ask again as I drop my arms and step toward him.

"Your pain, Nellie. I want your fucking pain," he yells at me.

My heart skips a beat with his confession. It should scare me, he should scare me, but he doesn't. He would never hurt me, not in the way people think. There is a difference between hurting someone and hurting them for pleasure; I have learned that much since being mated to them. They have proven to me time and time again that they love me, and now it is my turn to show Christos that I love him, truly love him, which means I want all of him, damn it.

"Then have it," I say back.

"Love, please stop," he begs me again.

I know I am pushing him, but isn't that what this is all about, pushing each other and making the final connection complete so we can be together?

They have pushed me out of my comfort zone, and they call me their Queen. Well, this is me pushing him out of his comfort zone and being his Queen.

"Do you want to hurt me?" I ask, searching his eyes.

"Yes," he says through gritted teeth.

"Then hurt me," I say simply.

"Nellie," he warns.

"Christos, I am not afraid of you," I confess.

At first, I was afraid of all of them, but that fear is gone, long gone, and has been replaced with nothing but love and desire for them, burning fucking desire.

"Maybe you should be," he says in a pained voice.

"No, I should not. Let me in," I say, pushing myself against him.

"You don't know what you are asking," he says with more pain in his voice.

"Then show me," I plead with him.

"Nellie," he snaps again.

I pull back from him, and there is pain in his eyes. I feel the pain radiating from him. I take a deep breath and slowly turn to walk away, but he grabs my arm and forces me to face him. He's breathing fast as his eyes rapidly search mine. "I don't want to hurt you, love," he confesses.

"What if I want you to hurt me?" I ask.

"Please," he pleads with me.

I turn him back, lift my hands, and cup his face, forcing him to look at me. "Let...me...in!"

He inhales deeply and nods as he slides his hands down my arms and grabs my wrists, lifting them over my head. I look up and watch him put my wrists in cuffs that are attached to a chain bolted to the ceiling. I was so focused on him when I walked in I didn't notice the different contraptions attached to the ceiling throughout his room. With my arms cuffed above my head, he presses his hand on my stomach as he moves around me. I turn my head and watch him walk over to the table and grab what looks like a cluster of leather strips bound together with a handle.

"This is a leather flogger," he whispers as he turns around and looks at me. My heart is racing so fucking fast, but not because I am afraid of him or what he has in his hand. It's racing because I want to experience this with him.

"White," I say softly.

No matter what he is trying to hide from me, it will not change the fact that I love him or that I want him. He has nothing to fear.

I turn back toward the window and close my eyes as he drags the soft strips down my back. The entire room is silent, but in the next breath I take, the strands leave my back until the whip makes contact with my back and immediately returns with a sharp sting across my shoulder blades. It startled me, and I couldn't stop the scream that tore from my throat but quickly turned into a moan as he brushed the strands across the area he had just hit.

"Give me your pain, love," he begs me but in a completely different, low, dark, desired tone.

"Give me you," I say back.

"Done," he whispers as he flicks the flogger in a figure-eight motion across my back over and over again.

Each time he slashes across my back, my pussy pulses, and I can feel my arousal between my thighs every time I squeeze my legs together.

I might not understand the pain and pleasure thing, but I do want to understand him, so if this is what I have to do, then so fucking be it.

32

Ashton

Day 17

Without laws and rules, we lose control; when we lose control, we lose power over those who help keep our world in order and safe. Guardians are supposed to be on my family's side. When our world was created, they all took vows to protect and serve The Born Kingdom, which meant following the King's or Kings' rules and laws. We thought that after the first human uprising, we had figured everything out and found an understanding with them. But Zayden has shown us that what we thought was true was a lie. Not all of the human families forgave our kind, and they have been waiting for another human to stand up against us. Then Zayden happened, and since he has been breaking the laws and rules, others have been breaking them as well, humans and even some Guardians.

I thought that Zayden was just another unstable human wanting something that he would never be able to have. But I realize that what he started goes much deeper than that, at least for the others. Okay, maybe not him; it is clear he wants Nellie. He has been able to get not only humans to turn on us, which is understandable, but also our own kind.

Each Chosen Family is given Guardians to watch over their women and ensure they stay pure and are not harmed while waiting for their mate or mates. We thought the Guardians assigned to the different families were doing as they were told, but that was not the case with Nellie. Zayden somehow got the three Guardians that were watching over Nellie to turn on my family, and in return, he was able to not only get to her but also fall in love with her and get her to fall in love with him. That should have never ever fucking happened. If the Guardians were doing what they were supposed to, he would have never been able to get that close to her.

Zayden is still in the wind, but we are slowly finding the humans and Guardians who have been helping him. We already killed his two fucking friends that helped him with making the distraction at the club so he could try and take Nellie. Now we have found the Guardians that were assigned to protect her, the Guardians that not only failed us but failed her.

They are part of the reason why Zayden's obsession has gotten as bad as it is now. It is time for them to see what happens when you choose the wrong side to fight for. I walk down the steps into the basement and hear my men talking, but there are no screams. I am not surprised; these fucking Guardians are tough, and only one of them is mated, which makes things complicated but also makes it more fun.

It took me a few hours, but I found Zion's mate. He tried to hide her, but he was dumb. Nothing happens that I don't know about, and it was easy to get the humans to flip on Zion. They are not loyal; I don't think they even know what the word fucking means. All you have to do is find their weakness, and you will get what you want from them.

Humans are easy to break; you can make threats you can follow through with. Guardians are a little trickier, but I know how to cause pain in those who are not mated, and I know what will break the one that is. Either way, I will get what I want. For the ones that don't give it, they will spend the rest of their fucking lives chained and disconnected from the world they promised to protect.

By siding with Zayden, they went against their vows. They went against their promise to protect our kind, so, to me, they are nothing. But I know my cousins want things done a certain way, and I will do as I am told. This is not my kingdom to rule, and I serve my cousins until I am mated, and then everything will change for me. I swear our lives are good at giving each of us whiplash, and it is sometimes hard to keep up with.

I open the basement door and walk inside; Ace follows behind me, tightly gripping Zion's mate. The room goes silent as Ace closes the door and stops at my side, holding onto Zion's mate's throat tightly. She has been sobbing since we found her, and from the bruises on her skin and the black eye, I am guessing he likes it rough; good thing.

"Where is Zayden?" I ask calmly.

"We don't fucking know," Zion snaps back.

"I don't believe you, Zion," I growl. There is no way in fuck no one knows where the fuck he is. Someone has to fucking know.

"I don't give two shits what you believe," Zion says through gritted teeth.

He acts all tough, but he forgets he can die. He feels emotions and has a fucking soul. He can act tough all he wants, but I know the truth. He is fucking scared, terrified even. He will never admit it, but he doesn't have to. I can hear it in his voice; he can't hide it from me.

"You will," I reply.

"What do you want from us?" Baylor asks.

"What did he give you to look the other way with Nellie?" I ask, watching him closely.

He shakes his head. "Nothing."

"You're a bad liar, Baylor," I snap at him.

I am sick and tired of Zayden being ten steps ahead of me, and I am sick and tired of these fucking games.

"He promised we would rule, okay," Baylor screams at me.

"Is that all?" I ask, laughing. What the fuck were these fuckers thinking? Zayden can't offer them shit.

"You were all played," I say with amusement.

"We are sick of following the rules. We were meant to live however we fucking want," Zion snaps at me.

"You are dumber than I thought," I say, smiling at him.

We don't care if they are sick of following the rules. There will always be fucking rules and laws to follow; it is just how it works. It doesn't matter if they agree; they are not the ones in charge.

"Tell me where Zayden is," I demand.

"We told you, we don't fucking know," Zion screams again.

I take a deep breath and slowly nod. Ace forces Zion's mate to her knees in front of him and places a knife against her throat. I look at Zion, and his eyes are locked on his mate.

"Answer me this, Zion. Was it worth it?" I ask, tilting my head to the side.

He doesn't answer as Ace slices across the woman's throat. Zion's screams fill the room as he struggles against the chains keeping him hanging. This was his doing. This is all of their doing. I turn and look at Baylor and Stetson.

"You two will never know what the connection feels like for the rest of your lives. You will be locked away from our world and your mates," I say darkly.

For what they have done to my family, to Nellie, they will never feel the connection that I know they crave, the connection that I know they need. I might not be able to kill them, but I can make them suffer in the worst possible way by making damn sure they will never fucking be able to continue their bloodline.

"You can't fucking do this," Stetson snaps back.

I laugh. "I can do whatever the fuck I want. Do you forget who I am?" I ask, looking at him.

"Please don't do this," Baylor begs me.

"Begging will not help you. You chose the wrong side. Remember, there are consequences to every behavior." I say simply.

Before they can respond, I turn and walk out of the basement, slamming the door behind me. I walk up the steps and through the side door leading back outside.

As soon as I walk outside, the wind hits my already cold skin. This is not how I wanted it to be. I never want one of my kind to suffer the way I am forced to make them suffer, but they chose, and they chose wrong.

There is nothing I won't do for my family.

The rumors of what I have done will spread. Everyone needs to know we will not sit back and let this happen. They all need to know that the Kings have spoken, and their words are laws. If you break them, you will suffer in the worst possible ways.

33

Zayden

DAY 18

I make my way up the weather's worn-down steps. The weather has been getting worse, and with no one living here, the house that used to be Nellie's is starting to fall apart. It saddens me a little. Soon, everything will be broken and worn down. Worn down by time and worn down by things that never should have happened.

This house looks like the way I feel inside. I am getting worn down, and I think that is what they want. They want to see if I will give up and walk away, letting them be. I will never stop, and I will never walk away from Nellie. She is rightfully mine, and whether they believe it or not, it doesn't fucking matter. What they are trying to do to her right now will not fucking matter. They will soon see how they have already lost. They are playing into the game that I have started, so, of course, I have to fucking see it through now.

I keep coming back here, trying to remind myself what I am fighting for and why I am doing all of this. Being here is the only time I feel sane. When I am out in the community, I feel unstable and unhinged. It calms me down when I am surrounded by Nellie, her smell, her clothes, where she slept and took a shower, where we used to make food and spend time together.

So many things have changed, which has turned into an all-out war between me and them. They will lose, even though they have done low blows and keep fighting for her; they will lose her in the end. The day I see it in their eyes, the day I get to see the defeat, that will be the day I know I have won. They think they can make me suffer; they have no idea what suffering is, but they will. I will make sure of it.

Before, I just wanted to kill them. I wanted to get it over with and move on with Nellie, but now after everything, death would be too fucking easy, and they don't deserve easy. They deserve to watch me claim her, change her. They deserve to watch me punish her for what they have done.

Nellie will learn to crave what only I can give her, and every single time, I will look into their eyes as I take her and watch them break, scream, and fight, but nothing will change the ending results. They started this, and I will fucking end it.

They are claiming her every single fucking day they are claiming her, showing her their kinks, making her experience them. The Falco brothers have held nothing back, explaining what is happening inside that fucking pool house. When things finally work in my favor, the first fucking thing I am burning down is that damn pool house.

Their house will become mine, and I will force Nellie to live there and move on from her fucking Guardians; her behaviors will not go unpunished. She is to blame as much as they are now. She is giving in to them, allowing them to do things that only I should be allowed to do to her.

She will pay for that, and she will pay for my pain and suffering of watching her fall in love with them.

I still can't fucking see her, but when I am watching the pool house, I can fucking hear her, and I can hear them. All I have to do is close my eyes and imagine that I am making her scream and moan. And one day soon, it will fucking be me.

I make my way into the house and down the same hallway I have walked down a million times. I walk into Nellie's room and begin stripping off my clothes. I have claimed her bed, the clothes in her closet, and now it is time I fucking claim her shower.

I will claim every single room and thing that once belonged to her.

I take off my shirt and walk into the bathroom, stopping and looking up at the light. A smile forms across my lips as I remember putting the camera in the light. I needed to make sure I could keep tabs on her and see what she did when I wasn't around. I had to make sure she was staying pure for me, not for the fucking Guardians.

I open my eyes and walk into the shower, turning on the hot water. I grab her soap and pour some into my hand as I rest my free hand on the shower wall. I grab my dick as the water gets warmer, and I close my eyes and start stroking my dick, letting the memories take me away.

4 Years Ago

I hold onto the camera as I place it into the light. I saw Nellie and her family leave a few hours ago, which means they will be back soon.

I put the light back as it was and looked at it one last time before I turned around and made my way out of her bathroom and room and quickly made my way down the hallway and out of the door, making sure to close and lock it behind me.

The last thing I fucking need is for her or her father or for a fucking Guardian to know what I have done. It is none of their damn business. I have every fucking right to watch over my girl, and she is mine. All fucking mine.

I make my way into the bayou and stop at a tree. I slide down the tree, pull out my phone, and push on the camera app.

I can hear talking and laughing, just in fucking time.

My heart races as I continue to look down at my phone. Nellie walks into the bathroom, removes her clothes, and turns on the shower. I watch her closely as she looks at herself in the mirror, and I quickly take some screenshots for later as I watch her get into the water and grab the soap.

My dick pulses in my jeans. I shove my free hand into my jeans and underneath my boxers to grab my dick. I watch as Nellie washes her body with soap. She is all fucking mine.

A moan escapes me as I continue to work my dick. My forehead rests against the shower wall as I remember watching Nellie soap her perfect, untouched body with her hands.

I have never seen anyone as beautiful as her, and she doesn't even know it. I could tell her a million fucking times, and she would just laugh and shake it off. she doesn't see what I see when I look at her.

I open my eyes and look down and watch my soap-covered hand pump my cock faster until I growl out my release. I watch my cum paint the shower walls and the ground, the water quickly washing it away.

Soon my cum will be so deep inside her that she will be pregnant with my child, not theirs. She will continue my fucking bloodline, not theirs.

She has no idea just how obsessed I am, but I will open her eyes soon enough, and once she finally sees me, she will understand why I had to do all of this.

34

Darius

2 Years Ago

The rain has finally stopped, giving my clothes and cold skin a break. I walk out of the forest and onto the pavement of the parking lot of the fucking club. The club where the girl I thought loved me went to dance to find her mate. I should have fucking listened to my brother, but I didn't, and now here I am, going back in there when I know she is dancing for another Guardian, or she is already fucking them. We will see which one it is this time.

I enter the club and push through the crowd of Guardians and humans; all of them are high or drunk or both. The music is blaring as

I stop in front of the stage where Taylor is dancing like a slut, and her eyes are set on a Guardian to the right of me.

She doesn't see that I am here or that I am watching her; I turn left, make my way to the wall, and lean against it as she continues to dance. Rumors have spread about her and me and why she sought me out. I never thought of it that way until now. Until I see her watching the Guardian, her eyes are not just set on me but on any Guardian that she feels can give her power.

I rest my hand against my chest. The wounds have healed, but the memory and the scars remain. The cuts didn't take long to heal; she didn't know what the blade was, but she also didn't care. Not many things can harm us when we are not mated, but anything made from Starlights has the magic to do so. It fucking feels like acid against our skin, and the scars will forever be on my skin, unable to heal.

The Starlights have a sick sense of humor. They wanted to make sure they held power over us, but when we went to war with them, it was our kind that won. This is why we now run our kingdoms and only go to scheduled meetings with other kinds. None of us want another war; we already have enough issues with the humans, and we don't need a war between us again. I don't think any of us would survive it if we did. Plus, we are stronger together even if we rule apart.

Taylor said she wanted to mark me, but I know what she really wanted. She wanted to make me fall to my knees for her, and she wanted me to submit to her the same way I make her submit to me. She forgets who the fuck I am, and I will never kneel, not until the connection forces me to, and she and I both know she is not my mate, and I am not hers.

But I didn't do it; I screamed. I screamed out in the pain the blade caused me, but I didn't submit, and when I got free, it was a night I knew she would never forget. I don't beat women; it is not my thing, but that night, it was, and you know what she said to me? She asked for more. She is as fucked up as I am, the only difference between her and me is that I don't want power, and that is what she is addicted to.

She is a whore in our world, she is not pure, and she has no lines she won't fucking cross to get what she wants. Even once she is mated, she will not be respected because of how she behaves. Even in our world, we want our women to be pure. I think I always knew what she was and what she wanted from me, but I chose to chase after her anyway. I learned my lesson.

She did one thing, though, that no one else has been able to do; she has broken me.

She has shown me that love is not real.

She has shown me the real monster I am.

She has shown me that I am undeserving of what we all seek.

I am not worthy of a mate because I, too, am fucked up and a true monster.

She showed me that I am not able to change, not in a good way, anyway. I guess I should be grateful to her for opening my eyes, but all I feel is rage.

This is funny because I can't fucking feel anything, but if I could, I imagine that this is what rage feels like, what betrayal feels like.

She will pay; I will make her pay one day.

I will make sure that she has no future, and if she does, it is my face she will remember.

I might bear scars from her that I will never be able to get rid of, but I have marked her in many ways, ways that her mate will not approve of.

I made fucking sure she wasn't pure. She wanted the monster in me; well, she fucking has it. I push off the wall and push through the crowd up onto the stage. I stop in front of Taylor, and her eyes break from the Guardian and land on me. I grab her hair and pull her away from the pole, and she groans as I force her to her knees in front of me.

Because of her, no woman will ever touch me again.

Because of her, no woman will look me in the eyes as I fuck them.

Because of her, I will never allow myself to be put in this situation again.

I unzip my pants and pull out my cock.

"Open your mouth whore," I say through gritted teeth.

She smiles as does as I ask, and I shove my cock into her mouth and force her to suck me off in front of everyone.

I let my head fall back as she gags and chokes while I fuck her face. If she is going to take me down, I will make sure I fucking take her down with me.

35

Darius

Present Day

Day 19

We all enter the room, and Nellie stands beside the window, looking out. It is another stormy day. We usually lead her to the different rooms, but she found her own way this time. She is finding herself more and more each day. She needs us, of course, but she is also able to find balance and be on her own when she needs to.

It drives us all crazy because we always want to be around or inside her, but she needs to rest.

Neo closes the door behind us as I cross the room, stopping behind Nellie. I place my hands on the wall on either side of her as I lean in, placing my lips against her ear. I take a deep breath of her scent; she is fucking intoxicating. I will never get sick of her smell or the feel of her warmth against my ice-cold skin.

She has a way of making all of us feel human, something that I never thought was possible. Something that scares the living fucking shit out of me. But I know with her, everything is going to be okay.

The connection is almost complete; we all can feel it. It is like electricity going through our veins, pulsing. It hurts but in the best possible way.

Last night, I was awakened with a pull on my heart and soul, a pull that was interconnecting all of us to Nellie. I can feel our souls, our hearts beating and exiting as one.

I can still feel the pull, the connection, and the closer I am to Nellie, the stronger it gets.

"Angel," I whisper into her ear.

"Darius," she whispers back.

Her emotions are calmer since she had her interaction with Christos. We all have demons inside us, and we all have something we are trying to fight against. My brother is strong and put together, but he has his own issues that he has to face with a beating heart and a soul.

Having a beating heart and a soul has complicated a lot of things inside us, things that we have to face. Everything has a consequence, and now we are paying for everything we have ever done. We are all overwhelmed with what we have done and who we were before Nellie.

I know we will have to tap back into that part of us to regain control and power. Zayden is not going to give up; I know he wants Nellie. But right now, the only thing that matters is us having her and claiming her.

It is time I introduce her to my kink, and it is time that I take off my final masks and show her the real me, just like how she has shown us the real her.

It will take us all time to get used to all of this, but every day, it is getting better, which I know sounds crazy coming from me. It is odd having my brother be the guarded one, and me be the open one, but I guess anything is possible with Nellie.

She did the one thing he needed at that moment: she pushed him, challenged him, and didn't give up on him, and I think we all need that from her.

I drop my hands from the walls and lean into her, making sure my front is against her back. My dick moves in my sweatpants as I reach into my pocket and pull out the blindfold.

One thing about submission and dominance is giving away control and power to gain it back in a different way.

Nellie will experience the kind of dominance I crave, the type I need.

I lift the blindfold, place it over her eyes, tie it in the back, and place my legs between hers, forcing her to open them for me. Our little slut is ready for us, just wearing my shirt, naughty girl.

I lean in, gently nipping and kissing her neck, and she rests her hands against the window, and her breathing starts to increase. "Give into me angel."

"White," she whispers, making me smile against her skin. I slowly lower myself behind her. I place my hand on her lower stomach, forcing her to move her ass out. I spread her legs a little more, and she rests her head against the window.

"I need to taste you," I say softly as I lean in and lick from her ass down to her pussy. I slowly move my fingers through her wet folds, and a moan escapes her as I push my finger into her tight pussy.

I press a kiss to her inner thigh as I insert two more fingers, stretching her pussy for me. She starts to ride my fingers, and I bite down on her inner thigh. Her blood fills my mouth, and I moan as I swallow down her life force. I lick the spot clean and stand up, positioning myself behind her. I grab her hair, pulling her head back so that I can bite down on her shoulder. She screams out as I suck her blood into my mouth and fuck her with my fingers. Her body starts to shake when I reach around and rub circles around her engorged clit while she rides my hand chasing her release. I double my efforts, pushing her to her limits, and she explodes around my fingers, squirting her release all over my hand and the floor.

Fucking beautiful.

I remove my fingers, pull down my sweats, and turn her around. I press my fingers to her lips, and she opens and sucks my fingers into her mouth, cleaning her pussy juices off. I remove my fingers and replace them with my tongue to taste her while devouring her mouth. I lift her up on the windowsill, and she rests her hands on the wood, keeping herself in place. I pull back from the kiss and reach between us, grabbing my cock and sliding into her pulsing pussy.

"Let us love you, Nellie," I plead with her.

She smiles as I start to push in and out of her. I place my hands on top of hers as she wraps her legs around my waist, pulling me into her deeper. We all remember when we said those words to her before, and her response was love isn't real, and we all promised her that with us it was; it is. This is our way of proving that to her. There is no going back for any of us.

She is our fate, our fucking destiny.

"Let us worship you," I whisper. She lets out a moan as her head falls back against the window.

"Let us be your everything," I whisper.

There is something about her not being able to see me that makes this erotic. Taking away her senses is the best way to show her the dominance I seek, crave, and need.

One day, this will be me, and she will use me in the same way I am using her.

I can't fucking wait.

36
Loyal

Day 20

I lead Nellie into the bedroom, and she allows me to lead her to the bed. The chains are already in place, attached to the headboard.

"Get on the bed, sweetness, face down, stretched out," I whisper into her ear.

Darius took away her sight; tonight, I will be taking away her ability to touch. This is when she will know what it feels like to have no power and control at all, but it is the biggest turn-on for me.

Nellie nods, gets onto the bed face down, and spreads her limbs out for me. She is still wearing my shirt, but I can tell that is the only thing she is wearing. It will be fun cutting it off of her.

I approach the bed, securing her ankles in the chains. I move my way up and do the same with her wrists. Her breathing is already increasing as I lean over and cut my shirt off her perfectly naked body.

I pull the shirt out from underneath her body. I love seeing her this vulnerable; I fucking love having her this vulnerable.

I make my way down to the end of the bed and stare over her. Her face is shoved into the pillow, and she is waiting for me, but she knows I won't do any more until I hear the word.

"Use your words, sweetness," I say softly, hearing the desire and need in my voice.

She lifts her head and turns it to the side. "White," she replies, making my heart skip a beat.

She is curious and beautiful and has never backed down from one of our kinks.

Her eagerness to submit, to try whatever we want to do to her, is a bigger turn-on. The more curious she gets, the more turned on I become.

I make my way onto the bed, and between her legs, I lean down and gently start to kiss up her legs. She pulls down on the chains, making me smile. Our Queen is not going anywhere. She loves to touch us, which is why I chose to be the one to take it away from her.

This time, I will be touching her, and she has to take whatever I want to give her.

I make my way above her, reach down and grab my dick and lower myself on top of her, and I push my dick into her waiting pussy. I release my dick and wrap onto her wrists as I start to move in and out of her at a steady pace; both of our breathing starts to fill the room.

"We love you, Nellie, with everything we are. We love you," I whisper through my own moan. The way my dick fits perfectly into her pussy, the way her walls wrap tightly around me, reminding me that she needs me as much as I need her.

She doesn't respond as I continue to pick up my pace, and the headboard starts to hit the wall. She doesn't need to say a damn word; we can all feel her love for us. The connection strengthens, pulling us all together in an intertwined mess of chaos and pure fucking love.

I can hear groans and moans behind me, making me smile as I lean down and bite onto her shoulder. There is something about her blood that brings me to life. Something in her blood that courses through me like lightning.

My heart beats as fast as hers does, us both needing this, needing each other.

She is our biggest weakness and our biggest strength.

37

Neo

Day 21

I walk into the bathroom, holding the gag and cuffs tightly in my hands. Nellie is in the shower, her head resting against the wall, her hands pressed against the shower wall.

I don't know what it is about us and her and the fucking shower, but it is becoming my new fucking addiction. It just feels different in the shower, more personal, more vulnerable.

Nellie has been acting a little weird since last night, and I can't tell what she is thinking about, but I have a pretty good guess. Zayden always seems to come back into her mind, and the only time she seems free from him is when we are inside her.

It seems that she only feels happy or alive when she is with us, so I am here to remind her that she belongs to us and not him. I am sick and tired of him fucking taking her away from us. He is waiting out there somewhere with some fucking plan, but none of that matters at this moment. The only thing that matters is showing her and proving to her that we love and need her.

I come up behind Nellie and press against her. "Baby girl."

I hear Darius come into the shower and walk over to the bench. We thought it was time to share her and share our connection with her. It is a good idea, a fucking great idea, and I am down to have them both.

"Put your hands behind your back," I whisper. She does as I ask without question.

Such a good fucking girl.

I put the cuffs on her wrists. "Open your mouth," I demand in a low, dark voice.

She does as I ask, and I put the ball gag in her mouth and pull the straps around the back of her head, buckling the straps tightly to make damn sure it stays in fucking place. I press a kiss on her cheek. Her breathing is already rapid as the water falls over us. I grab her wrists and force her to turn, directing her to where Darius is sitting, stroking his hard cock.

He is fucking gorgeous, the scars shining through his tattoos. His six-pack showing through, my mouth begins to water as I shove her onto his lap. Darius presses his cock to her entrance and enters her with one punishing thrust. She moans and whimpers as her wet pussy stretches to accommodate his massive cock. She falls against his chest, and he lifts and lowers her while he thrusts into her sweet cunt. He keeps his eyes locked on mine as I walk behind Nellie; the water cascades down all of us. Bending down, I grab the back of her neck with one hand and my throbbing dick in the other. My heart is pounding in my chest as I nod to Darius. He moves his hands further back on her ass and pulls her cheeks apart, exposing her tight hole to me.

Normally, I would take the time to prepare her better, but not the time. This time, both of us will dominate her, and we will share her, experiencing this with her.

I rub my precum against her ass before I push myself into her tight ass while Darius fucks her through her first orgasm. I groan as her ass clinches my cock tighter as she comes down from her release. Darius and I find a punishing rhythm; I push in as he pulls out. We are slamming into her with a primal need. I can feel Darius' cock through the thin layer that separates us, and it makes this experience so much more intense, feeling him throb against me while her pussy pulses and her ass tightens around me. Nellie presses her face into Darius' neck as she cries out in pleasure and pain.

I lean against her back, lock my eyes on Darius, and smash my lips to his as I release my hold on Nellie and place my hands on either side of

Darius's head. He opens his mouth for me, and our tongues fight for dominance as the sound of skin slapping and Nellie's muffled moans of passion echo off the bathroom walls.

Fuck, they are going to be the death of me.

Before Nellie, I didn't know what love was. And now, with Nellie, I have fallen in love with two people, two that I never thought I would. Nellie completes me in every way I am missing, and Darius, he brings out my darkness in the most beautiful fucking way.

This is just the beginning of our love, of our family. Soon, it will expand, and we will have little ones running around.

Soon, we will have to go to war with a human who thinks this woman, our mate, belongs to him.

Today is never promised, so in this moment, I will give myself to both of them.

No regrets.

No second thoughts.

I pull back just enough so I can see Darius's face. "I love you. I love the both of you," I confess to them.

A smile forms across his face as Nellie bites down on his neck, causing him to moan and scream out in the sexiest way I have ever seen. I smash my mouth back to his, taking in his moan and scream.

38

Christos

Day 22

Nelli stands naked in the middle of the room, holding the feather in my hand as I walk around her, gently brushing the feather against her skin. Loyal is leaning against the wall with his arms crossed over his chest.

I continue to move around Nellie; all their eyes are on us as I stop in front of her. Her eyes slowly open and lock with mine as I release the feather and grab onto her throat, pulling her into me.

"There is nothing we would not do for you, Nellie. Do you understand me?" I ask her as calmly as I can.

"Yes, I understand," she replies confidently.

"You belong to us, and we belong to you, always and forever, our Queen," I confess to her.

A smile spreads across her lips as Loyal pushes off the wall and grabs the ear muffs from the dresser. He stops behind her momentarily, then leans in, resting his lips against her ear. "You walk beside us, not behind us," he whispers as he puts the ear muffs onto her head, removing her hearing.

She keeps her eyes on me as Loyal forces her to her knees in front of me. She looks at the bulge in my sweats, grabs the top of my sweatpants, and pulls them down, freeing my cock from their confines. I hold onto her hair as she looks at my dick, licking her lips.

Loyal comes around Nellie and me and stops behind me. He reaches around me and wraps his hand tightly around my throbbing cock as he grips my throat with his other hand. He nods at Nellie, and I watch her open her mouth willingly.

Loyal shoves my dick into her mouth, and she wraps her lips around me as she runs her tongue along the vein under my cock and sucks me down her throat. Loyal keeps his hand in place as he tightens his grip on my throat and leans down, kissing my shoulder. I growl when he bites down. My cock fucking throbs as Loyal maneuvers my body so my cock slides in and out of Nellie's hot mouth. So much for her being the one to be dominated. I think the positions have been switched.

Loyal licks up my neck and stops at my ear, biting my ear lobe. My heart is racing so fucking fast it is all I can hear. I see Neo kneel behind Nellie Neo stops and kneels down behind Nellie, pulling her ass back as he leans over her kissing her back. He shoves two fingers into her ass, causing her to gag and moan around my cock.

Holy fucking shit.

Loyal continues to push my dick in and out of her mouth as he continues to suck and bite my ear lobe. I glance at Darius, and he is sitting in a chair, rapidly stroking his cock as he watches the show in front of him.

My eyes roll back into the back of my head as my balls begin to tighten. "We love you, Christos. You never have to be ashamed with us," Loyal whispers.

"I love you," is all I can say as another moan leaves my mouth.

Loyal reaches around me and shoves his fingers into my mouth, causing me to gag at the same time that Nellie does against my dick. All this causes me to explode down Nellie's throat as Loyal removes his fingers from my mouth.

"That's our good boy," Loyal says softly into my ear.

No matter what the future brings us, no matter what happens, it doesn't matter because as long as we all have each other, we are home.

39

Ashton

Day 23

I enter the club, which won't open for several hours. Humans and Guardians alike are getting everything ready. I don't trust anyone anymore. That is one thing Zayden has changed for all of us: trust. That word is simple yet powerful. I am keeping my eyes on everyone. We still don't know who else is fucking helping Zayden. We keep finding more and more. It's like he has a never-ending fucking supply of fuckers willing to stand up against us.

I stop for a moment as I watch the Guardians putting up more poles, which means more women can do their dance. This means more Guardians will be able to find their mates. We are always looking for new ways to improve and make the process go faster, but the connection doesn't care about the fucking process. We have no control over the connection and when it happens, we never have.

I used to be obsessed with finding out more about the connection and how it works, and why it happens the way it does, but I consistently hit dead fucking ends. So, I stopped; when it happens, it will happen. It is something I have had to accept.

I take a deep breath as I watch them put up the poles. I don't know how or when the dancing started, but I do know it has been happening since before I was born. So far, it is the only way that the connection is activated. Once things calm down and we deal with Zayden, my cousins want to find a different way. Loyal has spoken about it before; we just haven't had time to look into it. We have a group of new Chosen Women who will be dancing tonight. At the beginning of each month, they always bring new women to dance, putting everyone on edge.

I have never noticed how on edge our kind gets with thinking they might find their mate. I have been thinking about it a lot lately, but I haven't been here to try and see if my mate is dancing. My mind has been so wrapped up in what is happening with my family and trying to find Zayden that I guess it has overtaken everything, including me finding my mate. I have put it on the back burner for now.

They say every single Guardian has a mate, but it can take some centuries to find their mate. I don't know when we got so obsessed with continuing our bloodlines, but it is all our kind thinks and talks about.

I am not obsessed with the bloodline part. I am obsessed with the loving part; it makes me curious, very fucking curious. Watching my cousins and Nellie has just increased my obsession and desire to know what it feels like to be loved, feel love, or feel anything at all.

The only good thing about not being mated is that I can't die. Sometimes we feel hollow, like there is nothing but darkness inside without a beating heart and a soul. I have felt hollow for so long and surrounded by darkness; I honestly don't know what I will do when I can truly feel something else.

The connection changes the Guardian and changes the mate. I have seen it firsthand with Nellie and my cousins, and it makes me very curious about how it will change me and how it will change my mate.

"Lost in your head again, Ashton?" I hear my uncle ask.

I turn and look at him. He is leaning against the wall, looking me over. "Yes, I guess," I reply. My head has always been a dangerous place for me, and lately, it has only gotten worse. I guess Zayden is fucking with us without even needing to be here. Maybe that has been his plan all along to fuck with our minds. It is smart if that is what his plans have been.

It is not good for us, though. Once we become unraveled and unhinged, sometimes it is almost impossible for us to hold back. Maybe that is what he also hopes for, that he won't even have to touch us. He just has to fuck with us enough that we end up destroying everything ourselves.

Argento turns and looks at the poles, standing tall on the dance floor. "Are my sons doing okay?" He asks in a curious and concerned voice. Argento is not big on the whole emotion thing, but he does love his family. That is the only time I see any emotions coming from him.

"Yes, Sir. They are safe, and so is Nellie," I confirm. There is no way in hell Zayden or anyone else will get into that pool house. Not until my cousins open the doors.

"Good, very good." He says, nodding to himself.

"Can I ask you a question, Uncle?" I ask, watching him take a deep breath.

He nods. "Yes,"

"What makes Nellie so special?" I ask calmly.

"Hmmmm, the Shadow say something to you?" He asks curiously. I stand still, watching him closely.

"All the mates are special, but she is our future," he confesses.

"That's all I get?" I ask with a smile. My uncle is good at keeping secrets, sometimes a little too fucking good.

"For now," he says in an amused voice.

I turn back and look at the stage, and it won't be long before the women arrive and will be getting ready. Soon, this place will be filled with humans and Guardians wanting to escape.

It is time I get back to my family and make sure that everything is secure there, and maybe, just maybe, I will come back tonight and see if it is my turn to have my life change.

40

Zayden

Day 24

I sit on the edge of Nellie's bed and take a deep breath as I lift my head and look at her wall with all the memories of her and me. All the times I have watched her, loved her, and protected her.

She doesn't understand what I have done. She doesn't fucking understand.

I rub my hands together as I get up and stand in front of the wall with all the pictures I have taken over the years. Even when she thought

I wasn't watching, I was. I was always watching. The cameras were for her protection. Everything I have done is for her, for her own good.

I tried to protect her from the Guardians and claim her so that they wouldn't want her, but she wouldn't let me. I scared her, and now she is in the arms of my enemy. I frightened her, and now she is allowing them to love her, touch her, fuck her, and whisper things into her ear to turn her against me.

How can she be so fucking blind to what they are doing?

How can she not see they are just using her for her body? They don't care about her. How can they? They are monsters. They say I have no right to her, and they are spreading rumors about me in the community.

They have already tortured Guardians who have helped me and killed some of my trusted friends trying to get to me, and still, they are no closer to finding me.

They will see me soon enough, but not until I am ready to come out of the shadows, and when I do, they will be praying to a God I know they don't believe in. When I do, Nellie will get on her knees, beg me to forgive her, and make her mine.

All I have to do is turn her against them and get her away from them.

It has been made clear to me that there is no way to break the fucking connection, but if I kill them, when I kill them, the connection will no longer matter.

The Falco brothers have tried to warn me of what it will do to her, but it is the only way. She will get over it, and I will help her heal. She doesn't need them; she needs me.

I lift my hand and rest it against the picture I took of her in the shower. She never knew there were cameras, but why would she think there were? She trusted me until recently. I will regain her trust once I let her see that the Guardians she has given herself to are just using her. They don't love her, not like I love her. No one can love her the way I do.

I unzip my pants, sit back on the chair, and pull out my dick. I gaze over my collage of Nellie. Every single place she went, I was there. Whenever she was in her room, outside, running errands, or at the club, I watched, waiting for her.

I close my eyes and fall into one of my favorite memories of her.

3 Years Ago

I sneak out of her closet and into her room. She has been asleep for the last few hours. She is tired and a heavy sleeper, too. Both things work in my favor.

I creep over to her bed and kneel down beside her. Her breathing is steady, and the blanket is wrapped tightly around her. She is so beautiful like this. I love her so much. So much that I would and will kill anyone who tries to take her from me. We have not been in the best place lately, but that won't matter once I claim her; she will belong to me.

She has always belonged to me. My father told me when I was young never to let go of the things you love, no matter what stands in your way. There is always a way to keep what is yours if you are willing to do whatever it takes, and I am willing to do anything to keep her, even if it means she hates me for a little while.

I lean in and gently kiss her forehead. "Soon, my love. We will be together, I promise," I whisper as I stand up and look down at her. She doesn't move as I gently brush the side of her face with the back of my hand.

My heart races as I back up to the window I left open in the bathroom. She never checks things like that; that is how I know she needs me. She will always need me, even if she does not know it. But I will remind her every day for the rest of her life that she needs me just as much as I need her.

I feel my cum shoot all over my hand as I open my eyes and look at the pictures again. All she needs is for me to remind her, and I fucking will because I will not fail her.

I will have her, and everything else will fucking burn.

41

Darius

1 Year Ago

I sit back in the chair as I hold tightly onto the beer in my hand. The music is playing as more humans and Guardians come into my house.

I feel the dope finally kicking in; it took fucking long enough. Dope and booze is the only thing that is going to help me get through this fucking party, a party I didn't want, but one thing my kind does well is throw fucking parties. We all get together and fuck, get high and drunk, and let off steam.

All of us have obligations, and we all have to follow the rules and laws, so the parties are away for us to get away. For us to remove some of the masks we have to wear on the streets and just have fun, if you want to call it that. I wouldn't, but that is because nothing is fun to me, the only time I feel free is when I am either dealing, using, or fucking anyone other than Taylor.

I look over in the corner; my brother is already making out with some human. He needs to feel as wanted as I did until Taylor put her fucking claws in me. Now, the thought of a woman touching me makes my skin crawl. My brother is free, free to fuck, and escape however he wants until he is mated. When that happens, I know my brother, he will change, and he will allow his mate to change him. Me, I am only doing this because of my family, because of my brother.

I used to want a mate, and I used to go to the club and watch the women and hope that that night would be the night that I fell to my knees and my life would change. But now, the thought of falling to my knees for any woman makes me want to run away from everything and everyone. The only reason I haven't is that Christos is my brother, and I would never leave him. I can't. He has dealt with me after what happened with Taylor.

He is the only one that can put up with me. The only one I can trust.

I don't know when it happened, when I got like this, but the last year has been hell. Every time I run into Taylor, she is fucking someone or doing something, so my brother has me running more deals, which means I have been using more trying to find a fucking balance inside my head.

I don't know if finding balance is possible, but it hasn't stopped me from trying. The booze and dope don't work like they did before; my tolerance is too fucking high which is fucking annoying. But I will continue to try and drown out myself. How am I this fucked up without a beating heart and a soul? I have no fucking idea, but Taylor has found a way to do so, good for fucking her.

Things have gone to shit since I forced Taylor to give me head at the club, it didn't do what I thought it, and now I don't even remember what I thought it would do, but now she doesn't try and hide shit, and the sight of her makes me want to throw up and fucking kill her all at the same time.

She doesn't seem to care that I fucking hate her, that I can't fucking stand her, it seems just to turn her on and make her want me more, but it's not me that she wants; it is my money, my status, my power. All things that she will never have because she is not my mate, and now I am glad for that. If she were, I would have locked her up, used her to breed, and then thrown away the fucking keys.

I don't know what happened to her to make her the way she is, but I am guessing I had a significant fucking role in making her the whore she is today.

I turn and watch the front door as it opens, and in walks my worst fucking nightmare.

Taylor is walking in with a Guardian on her arm. She is always trying to get a rise out of me, but I haven't given her one for a while anyway. Tonight will be no different. I don't give a fuck what she does anymore or who she fucks.

I gulp my beer as Taylor makes her way into the living room, making her way to the middle of the dance floor. She turns around and starts to grind her ass against the Guardian's dick.

My eyes narrow on the hickeys on her neck that lead down to her breasts; I am not the Guardian that gave her that. I see the bite marks down her neck and arms, and I am not the Guardian that gave her that either.

Fucking bitch.

She turns and locks eyes with me, and a smile forms across her lips as I stand up from the chair. She stops in front of me, and her eyes go to my bare chest. She lifts her hand and gently outlines one of the scars she made. Her eyes go from the scar to my eyes.

"Do you think your mate will be able to overlook your imperfections, Darius?" She asks in an amused voice.

I lean in, my lips almost touching hers; I hate that her smell of cherries makes my dick pulse.

"Do you think your mate will be able to overlook that you are not pure Taylor?" I ask in a low, dark voice.

The smile disappears from her face and forms across my lips.

She rests her hand against my dick, and I stand up straight, keeping my eyes on her.

"You can act as if you hate me, baby, but you know I am the only one who can love a monster like you," she snaps at me.

I grab onto her throat and pull her against me; I tighten my grip on her throat, making sure to cut off her air as I lean in and rest my lips against her ear. "You do not know how to love Taylor. The only one you love is yourself."

I pull back and look at her, her eyes rapidly searching mine for a moment before I release my grip and push her back, falling back onto the chair.

Her breathing is rapid as her hands form into fists. "One day, you will regret not wanting me back, Darius," she warns me.

"I doubt that," I reply.

"We will see, my love," she whispers as she quickly turns around and leaves the room.

Everyone starts to dance again. Christos comes to my side and kneels down next to my chair. "I'm fine, Christos," I say, trying to reassure him, even though we both know I am not.

"I don't believe you, brother," he says calmly.

"I will be fine," I confess.

"One day, one day you will be," he says softly as he stands up and walks back over to the corner with the two women.

I take a big gulp of the beer, lay my head against the chair, and close my eyes as the dope comes in full swing.

Maybe I will be okay one day, but tonight is not that night. So I will let the dope drown out Taylor and all the madness inside me because if it doesn't, I will fucking break.

42

Nellie

Present Day

Day 25

The last few days, I have not been feeling too well. My guys have backed off a little, and I have a feeling they are as confused as I am. They are trying to keep their distance and the emotions in check around me, but I can feel it. We can't hide anything from each other. Even if we wanted to, we can't. The connection is just too strong now, which is a good thing and always an annoying thing.

I know if they knew what was wrong with me, they would tell me, or at least I hope they would. There are still secrets they are hiding from me, that much I do know. I want to be stronger and show them that I can handle anything with them, but that would be a lie. I am still afraid, afraid of the future, afraid of myself. My Guardians have woken up something inside me, something that is uncontrolled and that is dangerous.

I have spent my whole life trying to be the perfect woman, daughter, and future mate, and now, being here with them, I see that I am not perfect, that they don't want me to be, which scares me. I know this doesn't make sense; it isn't very clear to me as much as it is to them.

They are always trying to protect me, even when I don't know it. They have made that very clear since we have been all mated. My thoughts have been becoming more unhinged, and my emotions have been going all over the place. It is annoying that I can't seem to control myself, but at the same time, they aren't asking me to. They have completely stripped naked for me and have shown me their true selves, and I know they want the same from me, and I am trying, I really am trying.

I don't know who I am since everything that has happened with Zayden. I know I am good at running and shutting people out when I want to, but I don't know what my guys want from me. I don't know how to be naked like they are being, and the silly thing is they do not know how to do it either. They are just doing it.

I am letting them in, I am really, I fucking am, and at the same time, my guard is still up, I am afraid, afraid that Zayden will eventually get what he wants from me, and maybe I am trying to protect myself from the pain I will feel when I am taken from them. I know they will do anything to protect me, but I will also do the same for them. I don't know how all of this is going to end, but I do know that someone is going to get fucking hurt.

Loyal, Darius, Neo, and Christos have been able to control their emotions a lot better than I have been the last few days, all I want to do is cry and laugh, and I feel pissed. I am confused and overwhelmed by what I don't fucking know. I hate being a woman sometimes, I fucking confuse myself, and in return they become confused. I can feel they want to help me feel better, but honestly, I don't know what will make me feel better.

So I will do the only thing I can at this moment. I will take a shower and maybe wash away this sick feeling in my stomach. They haven't done anything wrong. This is all me, not them at all, which pisses me off. This week, it was my turn to share my desired kink with them, but all I wanted to do was shower and lay down next to the fire. My desire for sex has declined over the last few days.

I know it affects them, my behaviors, and my emotions. If I could control them, I would, but I feel completely out of control once again.

I hate not making sense and not knowing what is wrong with me.

My Guardians being patient with me makes me feel even more ashamed of how I am acting. I want to be okay. I was just fine a few days ago. I remember Darius giving himself to all of us, trusting us to take away his senses, and finally showing us his inner desired kink, submission. I shouldn't be surprised, but a part of me is and was.

At the same time, I am honored and filled with love that he opened up the way he has with all of us. The walls he had up before are gone, and I now know he was telling the truth. He is all in with me, with all of us.

I have to say seeing him submit the way he did to me and the others was one of the biggest turn-ons I have experienced. There has been something about Darius that has drowned me in and has scared the fuck out of me, but now I feel nothing but pure fucking love for him.

Maybe because we are coming to the end and will be leaving the pool house and entering our world again, maybe that is what is throwing me off. Maybe my own deep darkest fears are starting to fucking take me over.

My Guardians need a fucking Queen, and that is exactly what I plan on giving them, but I have to figure out what the fuck is going on with me first. When I am ready, I will let them help me process whatever the fuck this is. They think my father and sister are affecting me; maybe they are right. I didn't process or deal with it in a healthy way, and perhaps now everything is starting to catch up to me.

I go into the bathroom and turn on the shower. The water falls, and my head rests against the black and red marble as the water runs down my back.

I feel a set of hands wrap around my stomach. I pull back, but before I can do anything, there is a hand over my mouth, and my body is pinned between the marble shower wall and a strong body. I know it is not one of my guys.

No, it is Zayden. I can never fucking forget what it feels like to have him against me; believe me, I have fucking tried to forget, and I fucking can't.

My heart races as I feel his lips against my ear.

"I have been waiting to fucking touch you again, Nellie. I tried to stay away, but I couldn't. I can't stay away from you," he whispers, kissing down my jawline and neck. Tears form in my eyes; I want to scream and push him off of me, but just like before, I feel frozen.

Once again, he is going to take a piece of me, a piece that doesn't fucking belong to him.

He removes his hand from my mouth, and I feel him feeling down the side of my body, leaving goosebumps behind. When he touches me, it feels different than when my guys touch me. When Zayden touches me, it feels like acid against my skin, but when my guys touch me, it is like a drug I can't fucking get enough of.

His touch makes my stomach twist and turn.

This is not real.

This can't be fucking real.

"How did you get in here?" I ask in a shaky voice. I hate that the fear is overtaking my tone. He knows what he is doing is fucking affecting me in the worst possible way, and I hate it. I hate him.

"Does it matter, my love? All that matters is that I am here with you like this, and fuck Nellie, you are so fucking gorgeous," he says in a dark, desired voice that makes my body shake against his.

He presses his body against mine, and I feel like I might throw up.

"You are going to be a good girl, and you are going to leave with me, Nellie," Zayden demands.

"No," I say back. I wish my voice had more confidence, but there is barely any.

"Yes, you are. You are going to leave them behind. You are mine, fucking mine," he says as he pushes me firmly against the shower wall.

"I can't," I say back. It is the truth. I know what will happen if I try, and so does he, but I am guessing he doesn't fucking care. The only thing he cares about is himself. He doesn't care about me; he loves the idea of me, he loves the idea of taking me away from the Guardians, but he doesn't actually love me for me, but they do, they fucking do.

"What the fuck do you see in them?" He asks, unable to hold back his rage; there is the Zayden I know. The real Zayden, the man he was trying to hide, but now he can't. He can't put the monster back into the cage.

"They are not you," I say as my heart stops.

He pulls back and forces me to turn around. He grabs me by the throat, and before I can do anything, he slaps me hard enough across the face; my head snaps to the side. The tears escape my eyes and roll down my face as he pins me against the wall with his body. He leans in and rests his lips against my ear. "You are mine, Nellie," he says through gritted teeth.

I feel his hand start to move down my body towards my pussy. I know what he wants, and I know what he is going to do. I am not going to let him; I can't.

"Darius!" I scream at the top of my lungs. I know they can feel my emotions.

"Hmmm, one day it will be my name you are screaming," Zayden says so softly I can barely hear him over the water.

"Loyal, Christos, please," I scream as more tears escape my eyes and roll down my face.

"Nellie!" I hear Darius scream. I can hear footsteps running down the hallway.

"Neo, please help me," I say instead of screaming. The shock of what is going to happen is hitting me hard.

Zayden cups my pussy for a moment and licks down the side of my face, causing my stomach to twist more. "I will see you soon, my love," he whispers as he lets me go.

I slide down the wall, the water still washing over me, and when I look up, Zayden is gone.

Darius and the others come rushing into the bathroom.

Without saying a word to them, Christos and Loyal turn back around and run out of the bathroom. They know; they fucking know.

The tears continue rolling down my face as I lean over and throw up. I feel sets of hands on my body and pull back my hair as I place my hand on the wall and continue to throw up.

I have always feared Zayden taking this place from me, and he has. He fucking has just like he has taken so many other things. I can't escape him, he is smart, and he will never fucking stop.

"What the fuck are you doing here?" I hear Darius ask, forcing me to lift my head.

I see a man kneel down beside me. But he is like no man I have ever seen. He is different; his eyes tell me he is different.

I lean against the wall as Darius kneels beside me. His arm is now wrapped around me. Neo kneels in front of me as the man leans in and rests his hand against my naked stomach.

"She is pregnant," the man says calmly.

"What?" Neo asks, looking from the man to me. I turn my head and look at him, then look down at the hand on my stomach.

He removes his hand and stands up. I look up at him; my heart is racing so fast, my head is fuzzy, and my stomach is twisting and turning from what just happened between me and Zayden.

"Ajax, get the fuck out of here," Ashton says from behind him.

The man or thing nods and disappears into the shadows. Fuck, I have to be losing my mind.

Ashton comes to my side and kneels down. "I'm sorry, Nellie. That was Ajax; he is a Shadow," Ashton confesses calmly.

"A what?" I ask.

"Ummmm, in the human world, they are known as a Fae," Ashton says softly.

"Oh," I say because I don't know what else to fucking say. Between Zayden finding a way into the pool house and then disappearing, me being pregnant, and that man or thing just disappearing into the shadows, I feel like I am losing my fucking mind.

Ashton and Neo both stand up at the same time. Darius pulls me into his arms and stands, and I rest my head against his chest as his skin's coldness mixes with my own warmth.

I close my eyes and let the darkness take me away, take me away from this fucking nightmare I am living inside my head.

Zayden once again has shown me that I am not free, that he can do whatever the fuck he wants to me.

But now my Guardians and others are looking for him, and I hope, I fucking hope they find him.

I can't do this anymore and can't keep living like this, not now that I am pregnant.

43

Loyal

Day 26

We thought everything else would fall into place once we got into the pool house and gave ourselves to Nellie. We all thought that after the connection was complete, our issues would die down, and we would be able to handle Zayden and what he was trying to do to us, to Nellie. But we were wrong.

He has been watching this whole fucking time, and he has been waiting for the right moment to come into the pool house and violate her, claim her. Luckily he fucking failed. We all know what he wanted to do to her, but luckily, she screamed. She screamed for us.

If she stayed quiet, if he planned it better, he would have raped her, claimed her, took her away from us, and just the thought of that makes me want to fucking destroy everything and everyone. It makes me want to rip this fucking city apart until my hands are around his throat, and he is begging for fucking mercy.

Us leaving right now is not the best idea, not for us and not for Nellie. We need to stay close to her, we need to make sure that she is taken care of, we need to fucking make this right, and honestly, I have no fucking idea how to do that.

But we need to fucking figure something out and fucking fast because all of our emotions right now are creating a very dangerous storm within all of us, and soon we are all going to fucking break and go over the edge.

I feel the rain coming down on me as I stand still. My heart is still racing in my chest; Nellie cried herself to sleep last night. That fucker found a way in. He found a way to scare her, to try once again and claim her. Her emotions hit all of us like a sack of rocks against our hearts, and we knew something was wrong.

I will never forget what it sounded like to hear her scream our names, and it will be a sound I will never be able to forget. It is imprinted into my mind like a nightmare on a never-ending loop. I love hearing our names come from her mouth, but not like that, never fucking like that, and never for that fucking reason.

Christos and I ran out of the pool house, hoping to catch Zayden in time, but he was gone by the time we got into the forest. His scent was faint; someone was fucking helping him. Someone has to be fucking helping him. It is the only thing that makes fucking sense, the only way he could break through the fucking door.

Why the fuck did we not hear it?

Why the fuck were we not alerted?

So many fucking questions and not enough fucking answers. This is not right none of this fucking feels right.

Pregnant. Our mate is pregnant.

The end goal has always been to continue our bloodlines, but Nellie, fuck man, she is different. Yes, I want her to have our children, we all fucking do, but now, fucking now, I feel like every place she is, is unsafe. I feel like we need to do more, we need to fucking do more to ensure that she is fucking safe, that the baby is fucking safe.

This is not how it was supposed to happen. I thought honestly that Zayden would give up. I thought he would fucking move on eventually, but now I see; my eyes are finally fucking open. He is never going to stop. He has it in his mind that we took Nellie from him. He has it in his mind that she belongs to him.

I have tried to show mercy. I even fucking let him live, now after this, after what he was about to do to her in our fucking house, no more fucking mercy, after this I know Nellie will give us permission to end him, and when she officially does, Zayden will have no place to hide, we will destroy everything to find him, and when we do, when we get our fucking hands on him, he will regret the day he tried to stake a claim to what never belonged to him.

Why the fuck didn't we sense it?

Her pregnancy explains why she has been acting the way she has for the past few days. We should have fucking known. Everything we have been preparing for, wishing for, and hoping for has already happened, and we didn't even know it.

I stand still in the yard, looking at the broken back door of the pool house. The door was not only locked from the outside but was also locked from the fucking inside. At first, we locked everything to keep her inside, and we didn't want her to run; we wanted her to feel whatever she needed to feel with us beside her. It was never meant to keep others out; it was more like keeping us in.

But either way, Zayden did not break that door alone; there is no fucking way. I have seen Zayden he is a big strong man, but not that fucking strong.

I don't know what is motivating him to be so bold and so fucking stupid. His obsession with our mate has gone to a completely different dangerous fucking level. Over the centuries, I have witnessed the obsession and violence that can come from human men to their human women, it is sickening, and they call us the fucking monsters, and maybe we are, but at least there are some lines we won't fucking cross. At least we won't. There are those of our kind that don't have any fucking lines, but we do, we fucking do.

Zayden knows that; he fucking has to. For the first time in my life, I have a reason to break every fucking rule and law our kind has created. I have always prided myself in my ability to have self-control, finding a balance between the monster inside me and the mercy, but now there will be no fucking control, there will be no fucking mercy. As soon as I know that Nellie is okay, I will leave just for a little while and take my anger and fear out on those who have been helping Zayden, helping a man who doesn't deserve a good life.

The only thing he genuinely fucking deserves is to suffer, and he will, he fucking will.

I cross my arms over my chest and watch Ace, Ashton, and Ajax walk around the yard, pointing at different places on the pool house. I don't know how the fuck he broke open the door and got inside, but I have once again underestimated this human motherfucker, not anymore. I'm done fucking playing his games; fucking done.

I feel a set of hands wrap around my stomach, pulling me back. Christos rests his chin on my shoulder as the wind and rain start to pick up. My heart stops and beats faster at the same time. The way I feel when Christos touches me, even a gesture like this, is something I have never experienced before. He awakens something different in me, just like we awaken something in Nellie.

We used to be enemies, and now we are a family; we are lovers. If you told me that I would fall for a Rosetti, I would think that you were high as fuck, and now it is just becoming normal. I care about Christos and our family, which is why what is happening with Zayden is very unsettling. If anything happens to any of us or Nellie because of Zayden because I couldn't protect them, I will never fucking forgive myself.

"She is okay, Loyal," he whispers. I can tell he is trying to convince both of us of his words.

But they are words we both need to hear because they are true. I know she is safe inside the pool house with my brother and Darius, but I don't know if she is doing okay emotionally and mentally. Zayden once again has touched her, has whispered shit into her ear, and once again, we need to fucking replace him. Once again, we need to prove to her that we can keep her safe. Knowing he was in our house pisses me off and makes me see red, but it also opens my eyes to the fact that he is more unhinged than fucking any of us, and he has nothing to fucking lose, which makes him more dangerous than any of us.

We have something to fucking lose. Zayden doesn't seem to care about his own life because if he did, he would have walked away a long ass time ago. He would have walked away after the encounter at the club. He is dangerous because he is more reckless than us. I fear the only way we will be able to stop him is by becoming who we were before we found Nellie, which scares me the most. It scares me because the pull of being that way is addicting and intoxicating. I just hope we all can get back to who we are right now because if we don't, we will lose the most important person in our lives, Nellie.

She doesn't want who we used to be; she wants and loves who we are now because of her. What a fucked up fucking maze. But we have to do whatever it takes, whatever the fuck it takes to keep her and our unborn child safe and alive, even if that means giving into the part of us we don't want anymore.

"I am not so sure," I whisper back. There is so much more I want to say to Christos. I want to let him in, but I can't, right now, I can't, or I will fucking fall apart, and that can't fucking happen right now.

"She needs us right now. She needs us," he says softly.

"I know," is all I can say to him right now. I know he is just trying to comfort me, and Neo and Darius are trying to comfort our mate, this whole fucking situation is becoming more and more complicated.

The connection is complete. There is no undoing it, which I am grateful for, but knowing the connection is complete will not take away Nellie's fear. The only thing that will do that is if we fucking kill Zayden and kill anyone or anything that is helping him.

Christos releases his hold on me and grabs my hand forcing me to turn around and make my way back into the pool house, the others will fix the door and put up more defenses, but I have a feeling nothing is going to stop this fucker, we are going to have to stop him before he does something that can't be fucking undone.

We all know what he wanted to do to Nellie, what he would have done if she didn't scream, if we didn't feel that she was afraid and overwhelmed and needed us. The connection saved her from a man who says he loves her.

He doesn't love her, and it is time we remind Nellie who the fuck does love her and what we are willing to do for her. Right now, she needs assurance that we are here, that we are not going anywhere, and that is precisely what we are going to do. We will validate her for the rest of our fucking lives.

44

Neo

Day 27

Nellie continues to sit on the floor in front of the fire, rocking back and forth; her emotions are drowning her, taking her far away from us. All we want to do is take her pain away, take away her fear. It pains me, pains all of us to see her like this. Zayden has violated her once more, and I don't know how to make it better; none of us do. I know how she is feeling; it is hitting me hard, all of her emotions twirling inside her.

I sit behind her, wrap my arms around her stomach, and pull her back against me. She rests her head against my chest as I rest my chin on her shoulder, my hands resting against her stomach. Knowing that one of our children is growing inside her turns me on and scares the living shit out of me. Darius is sitting next to us with his hand on her leg. We have all been sitting in silence for hours.

I don't know what to fucking say right now. We can't just fucking sit here in silence, correction; I can't just fucking sit here in silence anymore.

"We are right here, baby girl. We are right here," I whisper as I continue to rest my hands against her stomach.

She lifts her hands and rests them on top of mine, making my heart race in my chest. Her small gestures mean the world to all of us. I don't know if she knows what she does. I think it is just a normal reaction for her. It is usual for her to be kind and try to comfort us when it is our job to comfort her. She is so sweet it fucking hurts. She should be angry, losing control. She should be cold and distant from what has happened with Zayden, but instead, she is doing the very opposite, which makes me want to rip him apart even more.

What he has done, what he plans on doing, all of it is just hurting her more and more. Can't he fucking see what he is doing to her? Maybe he can see it, and he just doesn't care, or maybe he actually fucking believes his behaviors are justified because he genuinely believes she belongs to him.

I don't know what the fuck is going through his head, which scares me even more. He is beyond just our fucking enemy now, the word has not been invented yet for what he is, but soon I will be able to fucking makeup one. He thinks he has seen what we are willing to do to protect our mate, but he hasn't seen anything yet.

"Do you think he will ever stop?" Nellie asks in a low, feared voice, making my heart sink into my already twisted stomach

"I don't know, baby girl, but I do know we will force him to," I confirm and promise. We will not let anything else happen to her. We have failed already so many fucking times before. We have underestimated this fucker, no more, no fucking more.

"Thank you," she says as she sits up, slightly turns around, and locks eyes with me. I lift my hand and brush the side of her face with my hand. She makes me want to be more than what I am. She makes me want to be everything she needs and wants and so much fucking more. She is our biggest weakness and our biggest fucking strength. She is our fucking Queen.

"You never have to thank us, baby girl," I say softly. We will love her, worship her, and protect her for the rest of our lives. It is what you do for someone you love.

"Yes, I do. I'm sorry," she says with guilt and shame laced in her words.

I hate that this is making her feel like she needs to be sorry. I hate that all of this is making her doubt herself and her worth to us. I can't fucking stand seeing her like this.

"What the fuck are you sorry for?" Darius asks in a concerned voice. She turns and looks at him. I watch her closely as she rests her hand against his chest. Before, he would have never let her touch him or look at him like she is right now, but now this is proof that everything has changed between us and her in the best possible fucking way. She has healed us, and it is our turn to fucking heal her.

"I'm sorry for causing all this to happen," she confesses.

"Angel, this is not on you. This is on him, you hear me," he says as he grabs her throat and pulls her to him. I keep my hand on her stomach as I watch her breathing increase.

"I hear you, baby," she whispers back.

Darius leans in and gently connects his lips to hers. This is how he has been with her lately: gentle. He is trying, and we are all trying to be more for her because she deserves more. We don't want to be monsters in her eyes, but we will be monsters to everyone else because that is what we need to be to keep her safe. But in these walls, we will be as gentle, loving, and kind as we can be, and at the same time, we will make her scream, moan and forget about that fucker.

I can feel it radiating from my brother; he is afraid, and we are all afraid of losing ourselves in trying to fight against Zayden. We are all afraid of losing ourselves in the worst way. I never thought we would fear what we were before Nellie, but we are, we all fucking are. But we have to do it, and we have to send a very loud and chilling message to Zayden, to fucking all of them. We will, very fucking soon.

But we have something to fight for and a reason not to let our evil ways consume us. Nellie needs us, our unborn child needs us, and they both need us this way, not the way we were before.

Darius pulls back and releases his hold on Nellie. She turns around in my arms, forcing me to pull back a little. She moves onto my lap, her legs on either side of me, her pussy now directly on top of my dick.

"What do you want Nellie?" I ask, looking at her.

"I want you, I want all of you," she confesses.

"We can do that," I say softly.

We will do whatever we can to help her through this–no second thoughts or questions asked.

"I need to forget him," she confesses in a low sad voice.

My heart races with her words. She trusts us, she fucking trusts us, even after us showing her what we are underneath. Instead of turning us away, she embraced us and experienced each of our kinks. She has opened herself up to us like a bleeding wound. We will never take her for granted, and we will never do anything to hurt her, not unless she wants us to.

"We can do that too," Darius and I both answer at the same time, making me smile.

"I need all of you to love me," she says with tears in her eyes.

"We can do that. We promise," All four of us say at the same time. My brother and Christos make their way into the living room. We all need this right now. We all need to fucking escape together.

She leans in and connects her lips to mine, and she starts to grind on my dick, causing me to open my mouth and moan. She pushes her tongue into my mouth and wraps her arms around my neck, pulling me into her more. I like her taking control. I need to be the dominant one, but I can feel she needs the power and control. I can give it to her, and she can do whatever the fuck she wants to me, to us. We are hers to use as she needs.

She pushes me down onto my back, grabs my hands, and forces them above my head. I smile against her lips as she continues to grind against me.

I keep my eyes on her as she deepens the kiss. Christos and Loyal kneel down on either side of her, touching her, licking her, and nipping and kissing her skin.

Darius leans forward and grabs my dick as Nellie moves up. Darius aligns me to her wet pussy, and she slowly sinks down on me. Her pussy wrapped around me so tightly that I groan. She pulls back and starts to ride me, her hands tightening on mine, keeping them pinned down to the floor.

Holy fucking shit.

Darius comes up behind her and pushes her down enough that she is hovering over me. Her eyes are closed as she moans. Darius aligns his dick with her ass and pushes into her without warning. Her body starts to shake a little as he starts to move in and out of her. My balls tighten as my brother and Christos bite down on her shoulders, causing her to scream in pleasure.

We all need this. We all need each other.

Zayden will not win, we won't fucking let him.

45

Christos

Day 28

I tighten my grip on Nellie's hands, and we all lead her toward the front doors of the pool house. We have been able to distract her just enough to where her emotions are finally becoming more stable. We all figured out what her kink was; she wanted all of us at the same time, and that is exactly what she got.

It turns me on knowing that her kink is allowing us to all have her and allowing us to have each other. She amazes me; every fucking day. She takes me off guard in the best way.

While we have been pleasing her, Ashton, Ace, and Ajax have been working hard to find Zayden. They haven't found them yet, but they have found some other fucking humans that have been working with Zayden. Our eyes are opened to the fact that there is more against us than we thought. Zayden's stupidity is spreading to others, and we need to fucking put a stop to it now before it completely gets out of fucking hand.

It is time we send him a little fucking message, and it is time we send all these fuckers a message. For some reason, they are beginning to think they can do whatever they fucking want without consequences, I don't know when it happened, but it appears they have forgotten who the fuck we are, and it is time to fucking remind them.

After everything we have given, after everything we have done to protect these fuckers, they are choosing to stand against us. I am trying to understand their reasoning, but nothing is a good enough reason for them to do what they are doing.

After tonight, Zayden will hear and learn that we are no longer standing for this shit. He needs to see that we will not let this shit fly anymore. When we were in the pool house, there wasn't much we could do, but now it is time we leave the pool house and show our people that we are one, that even though Zayden has tried to fucking destroy us, he has failed, all of his fucking attempts have failed.

The night has taken over the city, and the woods are filling with both Humans and Guardians alike who are loyal to us and our families. Even though some are going against us, plenty are still standing with us. There are still plenty who would give their lives for ours and Nellie's. Zayden will see that we are not alone, and plenty of our kind and humans will stand against him.

I hope he is fucking watching us right now, and this is the one time that I am hoping he is seeing what is about to happen. It is the biggest fuck you we could think of, and it will give him right between the fucking eyeballs. He believes that he has shaken us enough to break us, and he thinks he has broken Nellie, but he fucking hasn't. We will never let that fucking happen.

We will make this quick, but it needs to happen, and Nellie needs to see, she needs to witness what we are willing to do for her, that the rules and laws will not stop us from getting revenge for her. There is nothing that will prevent us from proving to her that we love her and need her.

We fucking need her. There is a big difference between wanting someone and needing someone. Wanting someone is a desire deep down inside, a desire that can change with time. Someone you want, you can live without. Needing someone is a connection to the soul, a connection that can never change, and outside forces can not sway that. You need someone you can not live without, and you need them like you need air to breathe. We need her, for she is the reason our hearts beat; without her, we are nothing but then hollow fucking monsters, but with her, we are fucking Kings.

Neo, Darius, and Loyal open the front door and walk out into the rain and darkness of night. I step out of the pool house but don't get far. Nellie pulls back, forcing me to stop. My heart sinks as the emotions surround us all, crashing into us.

Fuck man, I hate not being able to take this away for her. We fucking hate the fact that Zayden is in her head, he is controlling her. Fuck man, this whole fucking situation is eating away at all of us, slowly chipping away at our ability to fucking keep control.

Soon we will no longer be able to hold back, and we will fucking snap, and when we do, everyone will see a side of us that they have never seen before, and this whole fucking city will run red with blood, screams, and violence. We don't want it to come to that, but if we can't stop Zayden soon, that is exactly what will fucking happen.

We all stop and turn and look at her. Her free hand holds onto the side of the door frame, keeping her inside the pool house. Her breathing is rapid and unsteady, and her emotions smash into all of us: her fear and anxiety.

I take a step into her, releasing her hand, and she immediately puts it against her stomach as she looks from the others to me; her eyes are filled with tears.

"It's okay, love," I say softly as my chest touches her chest. I need to feel her. I need to feel her warmth spreading across my ice-cold skin. She is the only one who can remind us all that now we are alive and we are not who we were before her. Sometimes, I think we forget, but with her like this right now, we are reminded of just how much things have changed over a short amount of time.

She takes a deep breath and shakes her head slowly. "I do not want to go out there," she confesses.

"He will not hurt you, love. We promise," I say calmly as I lift my hand and rest it against the side of her face, trying my best to bring her back to us. We will not lose her to Zayden or her imploding negative thoughts. We are selfish as fuck, and we don't want to share her with anyone or anything else except for each other.

She takes a deep, shaky breath, and I reach out my hand to her and lean in, kissing her forehead. She leans into my affection, making my heart skip a beat. She grabs my hand as I pull back and turn around, pulling on her hand and forcing her to step outside into the rain. I wrap my arm around her, pulling her close to me. Darius comes to her other side, and we begin to lead her toward the woods. Loyal and Neo are behind us, and Ashton, Ace, and Ajax are walking in front of us.

Zayden would be fucking stupid to try anything right now, she is surrounded by all of us, and if he wants to get to her, he would have to get through all of us, which is never going to fucking happen.

We continue to walk into the woods. I can hear the Guardians and people ahead, and I see the flames from the fire rising as we all stop around the fire.

My eyes lock on the four men hanging from the chains.

They thought they could go against us and we wouldn't find out, but we have, and tonight they will learn the most important lesson: that when you go against our family, the only way to make it right is to give your life.

I release my hold on Nellie and lean in, gently kissing her on the side of the head. I begin to make my way around the fire; Loyal, Neo, and Darius do the same. We all make our way around, each of the four men stopping behind them.

We are each handed a knife, and all four of us place them against the human's throats and look out to our people, the humans, and Nellie. Her hands are resting against her stomach as Ace, Ashton, and Ajax all surround her.

"It has been brought to our attention that there are some that think the laws and rules don't apply to them," I say through gritted teeth.

"It has been brought to our attention that these four humans here believe it is okay to stand against us," Neo says calmly.

"It has been brought to our attention that some have forgotten who we are," Loyal says in a low, dark voice.

"It has been brought to our attention that some believe they have a claim on our Queen," Darius says, unable to hold back the rage in his voice.

"Nellie, this is for you, our Queen. There is nothing we will not do for you." We all say at the same time.

We each take a deep breath and slice across the human's throats. Their screams fill the forest but quickly die down as we each step back and drop the knives to the ground.

All four of us step around the dying humans and stop in front of the fire.

"The connection has been completed; from this night on, Nellie Ocean is now our Queen. She is your Queen. She does not stand behind us; she stands beside us." Loyal confesses to everyone that is standing still and staring at each of us.

"If anyone disrespects her or touches her without permission, you will suffer," Darius warns.

"We are always watching," Neo says, looking at the Guardians and humans.

"Now go find that motherfucker that believes our Queen is his," I yell at them.

All the humans and Guardians nod, quickly turn around, and disappear, leaving us, Nellie, Ace, Ashton, and Ajax alone in the woods.

All four of us make our way to Nellie. Ace, Ashton, and Ajax take a few steps back, allowing us to surround and box her in. Darius falls to his knees in front of her and slowly lifts her dress, exposing her naked pussy. Loyal and I lean in, and both bite down on her neck, resting our hands on her stomach. Neo stands behind her, her strong foundation, as we all start to worship and love her.

We are not ashamed of her or us all being together. I hope that fucker is watching right now. I hope he is seeing all of this. He needs to finally realize that Nellie was never fucking his.

She has always been ours, and she will be ours until the end of time.

46

Darius

Day 29

Loyal parks the car in front of Zayden's family house. It didn't take us fucking long to figure out everything about him, where he lived, who the fuck his father was, who his mother was, how he did in training, and when exactly he ran into Nellie. There is a lot about him that she didn't even know. He was stalking her long before he actually got her to fall for him.

I have to say he is one smart mother fucker that is for sure. It is sick how obsessed he has become with Nellie, all the things he has done that she didn't know about. He was possessive and made a claim on her before she was even officially with him. He takes obsession and jealousy to a whole new fucking level, and in some ways, he puts us to fucking shame.

We don't want to be like him, I do not want to fucking be like him, and the more we find out about him, the more I realize that the way I was treating her was like how he was treating her, and it makes me fucking sick to my stomach. I was a fucking fool at the beginning of all of this. I was fucking stupid to even put Nellie and Taylor in the same fucking thought.

I know she has forgiven me for what I was doing and how I acted initially, but I still haven't forgiven myself. She deserves to be treated like a Queen, not a fucking whore, and that is the way I was treating her. I have to make up for it, and I have to continue to prove to her that she is not a whore to me; she is my fucking life.

This is how I show her; this is how we all fucking show her. Zayden thinks he is the only one with a plan, that he is the only one that can surprise and do fucked up shit, he has no idea what we are capable of, but he will get the message soon enough.

I hope he is fucking watching right now, watching what we are about to do.

He has been stalking Nellie, all of us, for I don't even know how long, but it is the only thing that explains how he knows what he knows. He has been watching us, making others watch us, well, I hope they are all fucking watching right now.

I hope he hears her moan and screams our names, and I hope he witnesses how we pleasure her, how she loves us.

It just confirms that she never loved him, not in the way he wanted her to.

It looks like no one has been here for a while. He would be stupid to be holding up here, but part of me hoped he would be. Even if no one is staying here, burning it to the fucking ground will open Zayden's friend's eyes. Maybe it will make them second guess going against us. We will burn this city piece by piece, building by building, if we fucking have to. He will be forced to eventually come out and fucking face us. Then we will see just how fucking tough he really is; making him watch us claim her is the plan.

Nellie has agreed. She has agreed to let us use her to show him just how little power and control he actually has. In his sick mind, he will get her back, but the reality is, in the end, he will fucking die by our hands, and he will never have her, not in the way he craves to have her. The only ones that will have her like this are us, and we will torture and kill anyone who says any different.

I don't like the idea of her being out here in the open, but at the same time, Zayden needs to be shown that we are not afraid of him and that she is not scared of him. The goal is to make him mad, piss him off to the point where he fucks up and makes a mistake. We will not let anything happen to her; none of us will let him fucking touch her.

Loyal and Neo get out first, then I open my door and grab Nellie's hand, forcing her to follow behind me. We both get out of the car, and I slam the door, wrapping my arms tightly around her as we look out at Zayden's house.

I see Ashton, Ace, and Ajax making their way to the house with the lit-up torches. Zayden wants to play fucking games, and we are ready to fucking play. He is not prepared for us. We have been holding back for Nellie's sake, we were trying to be more than what we were before her, but we see now that we all will have to go back in time and be the monsters everyone thinks we are in order to beat him at his own fucking game.

Ashton, Ace, and Ajax all stop and turn around, looking right at Nellie. It makes me proud that they are stopping and asking for her permission; it will show the others that she is in control, and what she says goes. She slowly nods. I know she doesn't want any of this, and neither do we, but it has come down to him or us, and I am not going to lose her or my family because o this jealous motherfucker that can't let go.

They turn back around and start to make their way around the old house, setting piece by piece of it on fire.

The smoke starts to spread as the wind picks up, helping the flames grow and spread. Neo, Christos, and Loyal all come up behind us, ensuring that a part of them touches Nellie as I tighten my grip on her. Part of me still fears that this is all a dream, that she is nothing but a dream.

I wake up in the middle of the night needing to watch her, needing to touch her to make sure that she is fucking real. Our biggest fear is losing her, and Zayden knows that. And he is going to try and use it against us, but if we have any say in it, he won't be able to. We make sure to keep her with us at all times, and we have more and more humans and Guardians standing up with us and protecting Nellie. He will have to find an opening that no longer exists.

He found his way into the pool house, and since then, we have learned our fucking lesson. We will make it fucking impossible for him to get her alone. If he wants her, he will have to come out of the shadows and fucking try and take her. he will have to face us head-on, and he will have to stop his pussy little hiding game he has been playing.

The killings of the humans last night have been spreading. Everyone now knows who Nellie is to us, and they now know what we are not hiding and that there is nothing we will not do for her. She is now their Queen as well, and all of them would give their life for her. It is what happens when you have a kingdom. When you are who we are, our name matters, and now hers also matters.

Zayden will need to be smarter with his attacks. He will need to come up with a bulletproof plan, we still don't know who is helping him, but we have a pretty good fucking idea, and we have been watching them.

They know we are watching, but unlike Zayden and whoever is helping him, we don't hide like fucking cowards.

I release my hold on Nellie and slowly lead her to the front of the car. I force her to lean back against the war as I kneel down in front of her.

Fuck man, I hope Zayden is watching. I hope this pains him, and he breaks and suffers inside, knowing that we get her like this. Knowing that she has willingly given herself to us in ways that she would never give herself to him. I hope this image is forever imprinted inside his mind, and no matter who he fucks, how much he drinks or gets high, he will never fucking forget it.

That, for him, is worse than death. Forcing him to watch us claim her and, on top of it, her wanting and needing us. Revenge is a sweet, sweet fucking thing. Violence is not the only way to get revenge. Sometimes it is just the little things that cut deeper than any fucking knife could.

He never deserved her and has never earned her like we have. Nellie is not someone that can be bought or forced, and she is the type of woman that needs to be earned. He would know that if he actually fucking loved and cared for her, but he doesn't, and he will never get the opportunity to do so.

I lift her shirt, exposing her pussy to me. I look up at Nellie; she is looking down at me, her weight being held up by her elbows, as the others come to her side, leaning in and starting to kiss her neck, touching her perfect fucking breasts.

"White," she whispers as she lies down on the hood of the car. I lift her legs and rest them on my shoulders as I lean in and begin to lick between her folds as we all can hear the flames destroying the house.

We have made our strike; now it is his turn to do the same. We are patient. We will wait to see what he does next.

I lean in, pushing my tongue into her wet pulsing pussy; her walls wrap tightly around my tongue as she starts to ride my face. I close my eyes, allowing myself to taste her sweet taste fully. There is nothing else like it. No drug or booze or pussy that tastes this fucking good.

She screams out as the guys bite down on her neck and breasts. All of them needed to taste her intoxicating, addicting blood.

There is something about her juices, her blood, that makes us crave her, crave it, I have never experienced anything like it before, and I can't believe that for the rest of our lives, we get her in every fucking way.

47

Ashton

Day 30

I lean against the car and cross my arms over my chest as I watch my cousins and the others lead Nellie into the house. She tries to go back into the pool house, but they are leading her to the mansion instead.

She feels safe in the pool house, even though Zayden found a way inside, she has felt safe in that house. That is where after all the connection was completed. I think it will continue to be a special place for all of them. Seeing her like this is hard, it is hard because I know what it is doing to Loyal, Neo, and the others. They want to keep her safe, they want to keep her protected, and they probably feel as if they have failed.

I know that feeling all too fucking well lately. Zayden is testing all of us, but now we are pushing back. It might take us some time, but he will lose at his own fucking game. I will help as much as I can to make sure that we win and Zayden fucking falls straight on his fucking face.

I thought I had seen some fucked up humans in the centuries I have been alive, but once again, I was proven wrong because Zayden has turned out to be one of the worst, the way he thinks, what he is willing to do to get the object of his obsession fucking takes all of us off guard in the worst kind of way.

I want to help her; we all fucking do. Seeing her this unhinged and scared affects me because it affects my cousins. I can see how they are struggling. Burning down Zayden's house and claiming her in his driveway was their way of saying fuck you to Zayden. It was their way of reclaiming their power and control, and I don't fucking blame them.

Zayden has been watching all of us and them the most. If I were in their shoes, I would feel a fucking need to claim my mate back, to claim my power and control back. The thought that Zayden has been watching Nellie makes my own skin crawl, and I am not the one with a beating heart, so that says something about his fucking character.

I have to say I am Impressed. Zayden's attacks are calculated and somewhat thought through. My cousins and the other's way is not as calculated, but fuck man, it sure delivers a fucking punch to Zayden's gut. They want Zayden to witness them loving her, worshiping her. They want him to see what she looks like when she actually fucking gives in. It is a punch to the gut and his fucking face.

If any man or Guardian needs to force themselves onto a woman sexually, they have no right to live. We might be fucking monsters and might even cross over lines that most won't, but there is something about a man or Guardian pushing themselves onto a woman that makes me see fucking red.

We all know that some Guardians do not fall in love with their mates, and they do just treat them like breeders, but for the most part, our goal is not just to continue our bloodlines, but we actually want to be loved and loved by someone, I know that sounds odd, but it is the truth. I know that is what I desire. I want to love and be loved when it is my time.

We all know that he was watching us burn his house, which means he saw them claim her on the hood of the car, and I have to say it was hot as fuck. It turned me the fuck on and made me see why they love her and desire her. It also opened my eyes to what it looks like to love someone to open up and remove all the masks we wear for the outside world.

I have never seen my cousins like this, but then again, they have never had a beating heart or soul to go along with it. It is a beautiful thing to see. Their love has changed all of them, even Darius; I think he has changed the most. I keep my eyes on them as they take her into the house. I watch as Darius comes up behind her and wraps his arms around her, making her laugh. Even from here, I can hear the amusement in her voice.

Fuck me, that is what I hope for. Zayden wants that from her, but he will never get it. Her heart doesn't belong to him; it never did. It always fucking belonged to my cousins to the Rosettis. It was written long ago that they were fated, meant to be mated together.

At first, I was nervous about combining two families that were once enemies, and now, seeing them like this, I can't picture it any other way.

What they have with her is something I have longed for, for as long as I can remember, and one day, one fucking day, I will be able to experience what they have with Nellie, or at least I hope it is like what they have with her. We can only hope that when it is time for the rest of us to find our mates, we have a connection like they have with her.

Even without a beating fucking heart or soul, I know that they love her and that she loves them. They want to protect her, but I have seen it in her eyes. She will do whatever she has to do to make sure she protects them as well, even if that means giving her life for theirs.

Seeing my cousins and the Rosettis change and fall in love is fascinating. It is not something you can miss; it is actually loud and clear, and they are not hiding it. And it is a beautiful fucking thing.

"You envy them," Ajax asks as he leans against the car and looks at Nellie and the guys. They go into the house and close the door, and we don't have to guess; we know what they are about to do.

"Don't you?" I ask, turning and looking at him.

He slowly nods. "I do. I want what they have. I know you do, too, and so does Ace."

"Well, eventually, we will get it," I say, watching him closely. I can tell he has been on his own for a while. He is standoffish, and the scars running down his face tell me that he has seen a lot of violence and has also been a part of it.

I guess we all have in some way; we all have seen violence and have been a part of it.

"I hope so. I have waited centuries to get what they have. Over the years, I have lost hope, but they give me hope," Ajax confesses softly. This is the most he has talked to me, let alone confessed to me.

"You are different than what I thought you would be, you know?" I ask, watching him.

He smiles and locks eyes with me. "What did you think I would be?" He asks in a curious voice.

I have seen many Shadows but have never been this close, this personal with one of them. They are powerful and mostly feared. I think, like our kind, they are misunderstood.

"A monster," I say calmly.

"I am, but aren't we all? In our own ways, we are monsters, Ashton." He says, continuing to look into my eyes. His eyes are a deep blue. He is a mystery to me, but I think he likes it that way. Shadows don't let anyone close except for the Starlights, their mates, and others of their kind.

"Yes, that is true," I reply.

"I am loyal to you, Nellie, and Ace," he says confidently. I believe him. If he wanted to hurt us, he would have already tried. Shadows have powers that we don't even know about. They are the best at keeping fucking secrets.

"I believe you. I just don't understand why," I confess to him. He hasn't said why he is here or why the fuck he is helping us, but I do believe he is loyal to me and my family and to Ace. I can't tell you why I believe him, but there is something about him, about his voice, that lets me know that I can trust him.

"It is because of her. She is more important than any of us realize, and the others fear when she discovers it," Ajax says in a calm yet dark voice.

"What do you mean?" I ask, turning to get a better look at him.

"You know she has a Touches," he says, not asking. He knows that I fucking know. We all know that mates have Tocuhes, that is why the women are protected once mated. They are essential to our kind, to all of us, actually.

I nod.

She has a lot more than that," he says, a smile forming across his scarred lips.

The fuck he mean by that?

"What?" I ask, needing to know more.

"In due time, my friend, more secrets will come out, and no one will be fully ready for them," he says with even more amusement.

Before I can ask more questions, he turns and disappears into the shadows.

I turn back and look at the house, and Ace is making his way over to me

"I hate it when he fucking does that. It is creepy as fuck" Ace says, chuckling. Yeah, no fucking kidding. It's creepy and fucking badass if you think about it.

"I agree, my friend, I agree," I say, nodding. Ajax's words echo inside my head. I don't know what the fuck he meant, but I have a feeling we will find out soon enough.

"Are you okay?" Ace asks me.

"Yeah, but I will be better once we find Zayden," I reply.

"I put more men on the Falco brothers. If they do anything with Zayden, we will know. Should I call Blaze?" He asks, searching my eyes. I don't know what the fuck he is looking for, and I know he wouldn't tell me even if I asked. Ajax is not the only one that is a mystery to me.

I shake my head. "No, not yet. I don't want to call in the pack unless we have to."

"Okay, my friend, the offer is there, you know that," he says, trying to reassure me. I know the pack has our back, but I don't want to use them unless we have to.

"Thank you, Ace," I say softly as I lean against the car.

He leans against the car as the rain continues coming down on us both. I think a lot of secrets will be coming out, and it will change everything; the world as we know it now will be changed forever. Ready or not.

48

Zayden

Day 31

I stand unmoving as the rain comes down, starting to put out the fire that has consumed my home, my childhood home. I clench my hands into fists as I look over everything that is burning. Everything, every fucking thing that I owned that belonged to my family is fucking gone. I was waiting for them to make a move, but I didn't expect them to go after my family home.

These motherfuckers have been silent and backing off, but then they decided to go after my family home, and that is not even the worst fucking part. You would think them burning my home, all my fucking family pictures and memories were the worst part, but it wasn't; it's not.

The worst part was having to watch them pleasure Nellie on the hood of the car, watching them bite her, lick her, go down on her, and finally, each of them fucking her. It was bad enough that they did it all in my driveway, but they did all that in front of humans and Guardians, and she fucking let them do it. She fucking enjoyed it.

She screamed and moaned each of their names, and when they were done with her like some fucking whore, she actually fucking kissed each of them and told them that she fucking loved them.

That should be me.

It should be me that is fucking her.

It should be me who is going down on her.

It should be me marking her body with my mouth, my fucking teeth.

It should be me that she is fucking in love with.

But no, it is not me. She doesn't love me, not like she loves them. They have brainwashed her so fucking much I don't even know if the woman I loved is in there anymore. And if she is, she is fucking buried underneath what they have turned her into.

I fucking had her. I should have fucking taken her from the bathroom, from the pool house, but there just wasn't enough time. I fucked up once again, just like I did outside of the club.

None of this is going how I want it to, and I need the fucking Falco brothers to keep their word. By now, Ashton knows that my threat was fake. It has been over four weeks, and he never delivered her to me. I should have fucking known he wasn't going to, and deep down inside, I think I knew. I just wanted to fucking hope that maybe he would fall for it, but of course, he didn't.

They even took away what I had created for her at her house. They have destroyed fucking everything I have created and done. I have been patient and allowed the Guardians to take things at their pace, but now I am starting to lose my fucking mind.

The Falco brothers watched what they did to Nellie on the hood of the car, and they got off watching her. They have no right watching her, just like the Guardians have no right to fucking have her.

# 49

Nellie

3 Months Later

Loyal and the others led me into the main living room of the mansion. They have been making changes for the past few months. They have been trying to make things more comfortable for me. I appreciate them and love them very much for taking the time to do all of the things they are doing for me. It still surprises me how much we all have changed since being in the pool mansion.

A lot of things happened between me and them inside those walls. They told me some of their secrets, and I opened up to them about Zayden. I saw the rage and pain in their eyes as I sat down and told them how Zayden made me feel and what he did to me. Zayden never was able to get too far, but what he has done will leave lasting scars inside me.

The things I told them I was even running away from and never really faced. My Guardians didn't judge me. They didn't look at me any differently. In fact, they surrounded me and claimed me repeatedly, doing their best to try and replace what had happened to me.

I honestly don't know if I will ever get over what has happened between Zayden and me. I don't know if I can ever heal, but I can try. Today, we will find out who the father of my child is. To me, it really doesn't matter; to me, I am pregnant with all of their child, not just one of them.

They want to know, or it seems they need to know. I am nervous, nervous about what the future holds for all of us. My entire life, I have been preparing to be mated and preparing to have children, and now that it is all coming true, I still wake up, and it feels like a dream sometimes.

I sometimes have to look around and remind myself that I am no longer just Nellie Ocean; I am now a queen. Which is weird to say, but it also makes my stomach fill with butterflies.

We continue to walk through the house, which is fucking big, I still get lost when I try and find my way around, but I think I am getting a better handle on where stuff is, and other days the guys have to come to find me because I get completely fucking lost.

I haven't been outside much, partly because of the weather, and I am always tired. The other part is we don't know where Zayden is. Loyal and Christos went to my house to get some of my things, and what they discovered was fucking disturbing and scary. Zayden was staying in my house, or at least he kept returning there.

I know my guys found more stuff than what they told me about. What they did tell me about made my heart drop. I felt sick for days, knowing that Zayden was in my house doing whatever he was doing. His obsession for me has grown to a dangerous level, and we are all on edge because of it. Now, with me being pregnant, I feel my own fear drowning me. Whenever I hear a noise, I fucking jump, which is not like me, but I can't fucking help it.

Zayden is everywhere, and even though my guys try to replace my thoughts with them, Zayden is always in the back of my head. He has a plan he fucking has to, and I know when he found out that Ash killed his friends, he probably lost his shit, and he plans on getting revenge that much, I do know.

We are trying to prepare for whatever is going to happen, but Zayden has always been ten steps ahead of my guys, which makes me even more nervous. They think they know who is helping him, but we have no proof. Ashton went batshit crazy on the Guardians that were supposed to be watching me before I was mated.

Loyal, Neo, Christos, and Darius have kept all their promises to me, including making those suffer that have played a hand in me being able to build a relationship with Zayden. They don't blame me. I can feel it, but I blame myself. I never should have started anything with him. I should have walked away when I still had the chance before it turned into anything, but I didn't know. I didn't know who he really was, and I still don't.

All I know is that Zayden is not the man I thought he was. He was good at convincing me he was a good man, he was good at convincing me that he loved me, but now we have all seen his true colors, and no matter what he says and does to try and convince me that he loves me and that he is what best for me, I don't believe him and I don't fucking trust him.

My Guardians are willing to die for me, but what they don't understand is that I am also willing to die for them. They won't let anything happen to me, and I will do everything in my power to make sure nothing happens to them, either.

In the pool house, they told me about what Tocuhes is and what I am. I am a Delicate; it is why I went to my father's house and could feel exactly what he went through when Zayden killed him. They tell me that my Tocuhes are very powerful, and we must keep it a secret. I believe them. I will keep what I am a secret for them. We have enough to worry about with Zayden, and we don't need everyone to know what my Touches is. It would just make things more complicated, and right now, with me being pregnant, we need less complicated, not more.

I rest my hand on my stomach as Darius tightens his grip on my other hand. We all walk into the living room.

I see a chair in the middle of the room next to a set of couches, and monitors are everywhere. I stop dead in my tracks as my heart starts to race.

Darius stops and turns, stepping in front of me. He rests his hand over mine on my stomach. I look at him, his eyes searching mine for a moment. He releases his grip on my hand and lifts his hand, resting it gently against the side of my face. A gesture I thought I would never experience with him, but things have changed for all of us, for him.

Darius has let me in, just like the other three have, and I have given each of them all of me. I love them all equally, and now we are a family. Now, the connection is finally completed. I can feel all of them more clearly now and know which emotions belong to which Guardian. We all have grown in the five weeks we were in the pool house.

Things I once was nervous about, I no longer am. They have taken it all away from me and have replaced it with love and acceptance. They don't judge me, and they give into me as much as I give into them. They are my Kings, and I am their Queen. I walk beside them, not behind them.

Christos, Loyal, and Neo stop behind me, all three of them making sure their chests are touching a part of me.

"Everything is okay, angel. The doctor will take a little blood from each of us and run a quick test. We made sure he has everything he needs in this room," Darius confesses and confirms. His voice is soft and gentle.

"Okay," I whisper as I continue to look at Darius.

He leans in, his lips almost touching mine. "We need you, Nellie," Darius whispers.

My heart begins to race for a whole new reason. I thought I knew what love was. I thought that what Zayden and I had was love at one point, but my guys have proven me wrong. This is what love feels like and what it means to be loved by a Guardian. Everything we thought we knew about them has been wrong. We didn't know anything. We feared what we didn't understand, but now I understand, I understand them.

I love them, all of them, everything about them. They opened themselves up to me in that pool house and removed their masks, and I couldn't look away; I wasn't afraid. I want to know them, every single part of them. And now I have, and I have only fallen more in love with who they really are. Nothing they can do or say would make me turn away from them. They have me; they have all of me.

I smile and nod as he leans in, connecting his lips to mine for a moment. I can't help but lean into him, needing more of him.

He pulls back, drops his hands from me, and steps aside. Loyal grabs my hips and forces me to move forward and sit on the chair.

I watch closely as all four of them sit on the couch next to me. I want to reach out to them. I feel my emotions unravel, and Darius leans forward and places his hand on my leg, taking away all the negative feelings and replacing them.

Christos, Loyal, and Neo lean forward, keeping their eyes on me.

I take a deep breath as I turn and look at the doctor. He is watching me, watching us. He looks down at my stomach, forcing me to rest my hand against my stomach. I don't like him looking at me, but he has a job to do, and I know my guys won't let anything happen to me.

The doctor makes his way over to Darius, Neo, Christos, and Loyal. I watch him make a small slice into each of their wrists and remove some of their blood. My stomach twists and turns as the doctor then comes to me. He leans down and grabs my free hand, and I watch him closely.

"Careful," Darius warns the doctor, a small smile forms across my lips.

I love how controlling, possessive, and even jealous they are with me. Zayden turned it into something ugly, but these Guardians have shown me they are this way because they love and desire me.

The doctor nods and makes a small slice into my wrist.

My heart is racing as he moves back and turns around, heading over to a table with different equipment.

I want to ask what it all is, but in the end, it doesn't matter as long as we all find out who the father is of the child that is currently growing inside me.

We all sit in silence, all of us keeping our eyes on the doctor as he moves around the table doing things I don't understand.

Soon, we will know who the father is and whose baby is in my womb. I am scared, happy, and nervous, all wrapped up into one.

My attention is pulled away from the doctor when the side doors open, and Argento and his wife, Loyal's and Neo's mother and father walk in.

They both quickly make their way across the room. The woman sits next to Neo, resting her hand on his leg, and Argento kneels down in front of me and lifts his hand, resting it on top of mine.

He looks up at me and smiles. "Thank you, Nellie."

I don't respond because I don't know what to say right now. Argento stands up and makes his way over, taking a seat next to his wife.

I look at each of them, all of them watching me and watching the doctor. All I wanted was a different life. So many times, I wished I was just normal, but now, I am proud of who I am and what has been asked of me. The dancing, the connection, all of it has brought me to this perfect moment.

The doctor turns around and makes his way back over to me. Darius tightens his hold on my leg, and we all wait for the news that will put together the ripped pieces of our hearts and bring us closer together if that is even possible.

50

Darius

We all continue to watch the doctor as he stands in front of us. I can't fucking tell what the fuck is going on, but all I know is we are dying to know what only he knows now. I don't think I can hold back any longer, and I am going to lose my shit if I have to wait any longer to find out the results.

I hear the back door open and close again, and I don't need to turn around to know that it is Ashton, Ace, and Ajax. Even though we usually don't deal with Night Walkers or Shadows, these two have become a part of our family because of Ashton; as we were in the pool house, they helped Ashton. They are the ones that have had Ashton's back so we could be with our wife. I owe them; we all do.

If Ashton trusts them, then so do we. And we need all the help we can get with bringing down Zayden. He has been too fucking quiet over the last few months. We all know he is planning something, but we still can't fucking get ahead of him. Whatever is going to happen is going to happen. I am fucking terrified now because of Nellie and the baby. I can feel it; we are all afraid. But we will deal with Zayden and whoever is helping him as a family. We will now do everything as a family because that is what we are.

"What does the test say, doc?" Arengto asks calmly. It amazes me that we have made this much progress with the Deluca's, so much so that the Guardian that used to be king is sitting here with us, wanting to know the test results.

There is no longer just the Rosettis and just the Delucas; we are one. The moment we all fell to our knees in front of Nellie, we became one; even though I fought against it at first, I will never fight against it again. I am all in and have been since the moment I took Nellie from Zayden's car. There is no going back to the way things were.

The doctor smiles and looks from Arengto to Nellie. "Congratulations, you are carrying Darius' child," the doc says calmly and with pride. We have trusted this man's family for generations, and now he gets to be part of a new generation.

My heart stops as I turn and look at Nellie; her hands cover her mouth as the tears start to build in her eyes.

I slowly stand up and reach my hand out to our wife. She takes it without needing to think about it. I pull her against me, her hands resting against my cold chest as I lift my hand and brush her cheek with the back of my hand. I watch the tears escape her eyes and roll down her face. She shoves her face into my chest as I wrap my arms tightly around her.

I rest my chin on her head and allow my own tears to escape my eyes and roll down my face. After everything we have all been through, after what we have all survived, I never thought we would get to this moment. I never thought I would get to this moment where I am not only mated but also a father.

Taylor made me feel unworthy, crazy, and unstable, and Nellie does the opposite for me; she makes me feel loved, stable, and needed. All the things that Taylor never could give me. All the things I never thought I deserved because of what I am. We removed all our masks Inside the pool house, and Nellie loved us anyway. Her feelings didn't change.

We were made for her, and she was made for us.

I wanted Taylor, but I fucking need Nellie.

There is a big difference between wanting someone and needing someone. I never knew the difference myself until Nellie came into my life.

I know I can't live without her, and I know that my heart beats for only her, and my soul craves her in a way I never thought was possible.

I used to be a monster, and now I feel more human than I ever thought I could. I feel like a father.

"Oh, how fucking cute," I hear a voice say from across the room.

My heart stops as Nellie pulls back and looks towards the living room entrance. Zayden is leaning against the door frame, his arms crossed over his chest. Standing next to him is Taylor, standing behind her is Salem, and next to her is Nellie's sister Emma, and standing behind her is Gain.

"What the fuck are you doing here?" I ask through gritted teeth. How the fuck did they get in?

My eyes are locked on Taylor, and Nellie grabs onto my shirt.

"Hey lover, it is good to see you too," she says with a smile. The same smile that used to win me over every time, and now it just makes me fucking sick to my stomach.

Christos, Neo, and Loyal stand up as I force Nellie to move behind me. I turn and stand still, looking at Taylor, then at Zayden. My hands form into fists as Nellie grabs onto the back of my shirt, and Christos, Neo, and Loyal all surround her, boxing her in the middle of us.

Fuck, fuck. Of course, it was the Falco brothers. Of course, it was them who were helping Zayden.

"You are a father, Darius; that is such good news," Zayden smiles and pushes off the wall. As soon as he does, Guardians storms into the living room. My heart is racing so fast I can hear it in my ears.

Zayden walks around the room and stops in front of me. I look down and see the knife in his hand.

"You should have never taken what didn't belong to you," Zayden warns me.

I laugh because I can't hold it back. This motherfucker still thinks he is what is best for Nellie. After what we found in her father's house, he should fucking be locked up, he is insane. He will die soon, very fucking soon. If he thinks his showing up here scares us, he is wrong. If he wants her, he is going to have to go through us, through me. I will not submit. I will never submit to him.

"She is ours," I snap back.

Zayden tilts his head to the side and laughs. "You actually fucking believe that."

Nellie tightens her grip on the back of my shirt. Her emotions and the others rush into my body, making my heart stop with fear and rage.

"Nellie, I love you, Angel. Please remember that," I say as calmly as I can. They will not fucking touch her.

"Darius," she whispers through her fear.

I take a deep breath as I walk into Zayden, forcing him to back up and forcing Nellie to let me go.

"No, please," Nellie screams from behind me.

I slightly turn around and lock eyes with our wife. "I love you," I whisper to her.

Loyal has his arms around her, keeping her in place. I watch the tears escape her eyes, roll down her face, and look down at her stomach. Loyal starts to back up with her, forcing her to move back and make more distance. Ashton, Ace, and Ajax are right behind him. Neo and Christos stay at her side as Loyal forces her. The space kills me inside, but she is the most important person in this room.

I never deserved her or to be a father. If this is what needs to happen to keep her safe, then I will give my life for hers.

I look at Ashton, Ace, and Ajax; their eyes are wide, and their hands are in fists as their breathing increases. I nod at Ashton as he pulls out his phone. He knows what he needs to do. We need backup, we need help. I know the Night Walkers will come; they have to come.

I turn back around and look at my ex, Nellie's sister, and the Falco brothers; all of them were in on this from the beginning. I look at Zayden; his eyes are dead-locked onto me.

"It would be wise if you guys leave the way you came," Argento says, standing up from the couch; his wife is right at his side. She is human but powerful; I can feel it.

Zayden laughs, "I am not scared of you. You all deserve to suffer for what you have done, and whoever stands in my way from having Nellie will fucking die."

Argento moves in front of me and stops in front of Zayden. "I am ready to die, kid. Can you say the same?"

Zayden laughs and takes a step back.

"Whatever happens, sons, protect your fucking mate. She is important, so fucking important to our kind," Argento says. Before any of us can respond, Argento rushes towards Salem, and all hell fucking breaks loose.

Guardian fighting Guardian. I can hear Nellie screaming. I turn and watch Loyal and the others backing her up towards the back door.

I turn back around and lock eyes with Zayden.

"Was she worth it, Guardian?" Zayden asks in a low, dark voice

"You have no fucking idea, but you are about to," I say.

Zayden screams and rushes towards me. I punch him in the face, causing him to fall back. His screams fill the room as I hear Guardian fighting against Guardian.

I rush into Zayden and grab him by the throat.

"She doesn't want you," I whisper, looking Zayden in the eyes. He struggles in my grip. I tighten my hold on him, pulling him closer to me.

"You don't know shit, she will," Zayden replies with sickening confidence.

"You will never have her," I say through gritted teeth.

The entire room goes silent as the screams from Argento and his wife fill the room.

I turn my head and see Salem's and Gain's hands in the chest of Argento and his wife, and they pull their hands out, removing their hearts.

My heart stops as they both fall to their knees, then face-first onto the ground. I look at Salem and Gain. They are smiling as they drop their hearts to the ground.

"You're next," Zayden whispers, getting my attention back. I turn and look at him, my hand firmly around his neck. My heart is racing, and my ears fill with Nellie's screams.

Zayden's eyes narrow on me. He lets out a scream as he stabs me right in the heart.

The pain from all of us radiates through my body.

A scream leaves me as Zayden backs up. I fall to my knees, and my hand wraps around the handle of the knife.

I can feel my heart slowing as all of our emotions intertwine into one.

A storm of emotions. I close my eyes and try and take a deep breath. Nellie's screams fill the room as my heart continues to slow. The blade doing what it was intended to do.

You Made It This Far

Do you need more?
 Don't worry, Boo Boo, I got you covered!!!
The story continues in Ripped Destiny Book 3.

About Author

Sasha R.C. is quickly becoming recognized as The Queen of Dark Romance. She overcame her addiction to alcohol and drugs and now lives a life of recovery, all thanks to her higher power and her strong support system of family and friends. She now reaches out to help others overcome that same addiction as an alcohol and drug counselor.

Sasha loves getting lost in a good Dark Romance book. Her favorites include Den of Vipers, Church, The Ritual, The Sinner, The Sacrifice, The Joker, The Psycho, The Reaper, Haunting Adeline, and Hunting Adeline.

Sasha currently resides in Oregon with her husband and two dogs, Smokey and Bandit.

Sasha is currently working on a lot of different dark standalone romances, so stay tuned.

Thank you

THANK YOU FOR TAKING THE TIME TO READ RIPPED HEARTS.

Please consider leaving a review on Amazon.

Come follow me on social media: sasharcauthor

TikTok
Instagram
Twitter
Facebook
www.authorsashachristophersen.org

Other Books by Sasha R.C.

The Born Trilogy – A Dark Why Choose Vampire Romance

Ripped Souls Book 1
Ripped Hearts Book 2
Ripped Destiny Book 3

The Fated Trilogy – A Dark Why Choose Werewolf MC Romance

Blood Beast MC Book 1
Blood Beast MC Book 2
Blood Beast MC Book 3

The Crown Trilogy – A Dark Why Choose Witch Romance

Covenant of the Crown Book 1
Covenant of the Crown Book 2
Covenant of the Crown Book 3

The Shadow Trilogy- A Dark Why Choose FAE Romance

Queen of the Shadows Book 1
Queen of the Shadows Book 2
Queen of the Shadows Book 3

Standalone in Same Universe – The Forgotten Dragon – A Dark Why Choose Dragon Romance

The Secret Praise Series – A Dark Why Choose Bully College Romance

Torn Sunset Book 1
Fractured Sunset Book 2
Shattered Sunset Book 3
Crushed Sunset Book 4

Standalone:

Awakened Craving – A Dark Taboo Forbidden Romance
CrissCrossed – A Dark Why Choose High School Bully Romance
Kiss of Sin – A Dark Love Triangle Romance
Unworthy of Your Love – A Dark Why Choose Romance
Broken Like Me – A Dark Why Choose College Romance

Fatal Vows – A Dark Why Choose DV Romance

Fatal Attraction – A Dark Why Choose Mafia Romance

Our Beautiful Creature – A Dark Why Choose Retelling Romance

Dark Souls – A Dark MC Romance

Silent Tears – A Dark Mafia Romance

Him and I – A Dark Romance

Made in the USA
Columbia, SC
28 January 2024

82cebca4-e62b-4bec-8817-3e17a8ab5a4bR01